Feelings

Don't

Play

Fair

Feelings Don't Play Fair

By Caz May

Book 3 in The Always Only You Series

First Published 2019
ISBN 9780648499855

Published by Caz May

To all my amazing readers who have loved Travis
from when we met him in book one.
This book is for you.
I hope you fall for my broken player
as much as I have.

Table of Contents

Author's Preface

Hello lovely reader! I thank you for purchasing my book.

This story is told in first person alternating point of views. If there is only a chapter title then the chapter is told from the main protagonists' point of view. If another name is underneath the chapter title that chapter is narrated by another character.

Below is the pronunciations for my characters names.

Travis/Travy: Trav-is & Trav-e (main protagonist)

Bella/Bel: Bell-a & Bell

Annika/Anni: Ann-ic-a & An-e

Jairus/Jai: Jye-rus & Jye

Austin/Aust: Aus-tin & Aus-t

Dana/Dan: Day-na & D-an

Elyse/Ely: El-lease & El-e

Kaden/Kad: Kay-den & K-ad-d

At the end of the book you will find a slang glossary which contains most of the Australian slang references you will find in the story.

I truly hope you love Travis as much as I do.

Caz May

xx

Also by Caz May

Always Only You Series

Bk 1-Roommates Don't Kiss & Tell

Bk 2-Friends Don't Say Goodbye

The longer you hide your feelings for someone

The more you fall for them

Unknown

Prologue | Its all New

In Jai's penthouse at their New Year's Eve party, I feel like a fucking intruder, not able to feign happiness that another year has slipped by without having accomplished anything near to what my best mate has. Even though I've downed about five beers and a couple of whiskeys, I'm a sad sack of shit, considering flaking it way too early for New Year's Eve.

I'm listening to snippets of conversations floating, trying not to glance at Bella across the room.

She looks so carefree, her luscious brown hair in curls falling around her shoulders that are exposed in a midriff baring tube top that accentuates her tits into perfect mounds.

Dark denim high waisted shorts graze her belly button and watching her I see the intake of breath when she laughs, tipping her head back when Annika says something that I can't make out. Gulping hard I clutch a hand to the fatty that's risen in the front of my jeans, just fucking looking at her has me so turned on I want to dak myself and wank in the middle of the crowded penthouse.

It's only been a month or so since I'd woken up with her half naked in my bed. Barely even a month since she rushed out of my house without another word and every fucking second she's been on my mind, especially when I'm so painfully hard thinking about her kisses that are a lightning bolt to my cock.

About to confront her, to smash my lips against hers and drag her back to my shitty apartment for the night, to rip the barely there clothes off her lightly tanned skin I'm sidelined by my best mate slapping an arm around my back.

He pulls me to his side in an awkward bro hug and I cringe a little when he slurs his words, "Travv...maate, youu nnneed a driiink."

"Nah, Jai man. I'm good, thinking of heading out. I...can't face her looking so fucking hot and not being able to have her."

He laughs, sobering up with his next words, "Haven't you already fucked her?"

It's my turn to laugh, but my chest constricts when I reply, "Man I wish. If I have and can't remember that's a fucking shame cause I want to fuck her until she can't walk."

"Well, get on it, " Jairus replies jovially and out of character.

He'd always told me to stay away from Bella, even when we'd been partnered up in his wedding. But nothing could stop me from wanting the chestnut-haired beauty who is quite possibly the only sheila who didn't succumb to my kicker melting charm. One look, one kiss from me usually got me a gobby, before I stripped a sheila of clothes and tasted and fucked her until we came apart screaming like banshees.

In the past month, I've fantasised about what Bella would sound like when I make her come. I've thought about how beautiful she'd look when riding my cock, in my T-shirt the morning after. God, I fucking want her bad, more than I've wanted any sheila in my thirty-two years of life; well since I was fifteen and I got my first hard on seeing the hot as hell P.E teacher changing after class one day. That was my wank goto thought for months, before I discovered actresses and the miracle that is porn.

But since meeting Bella a couple of years ago, even though we've barely spoken or touched until recently I've not needed to watch porn to wank. All I need to do is think of is her.

Jairus has left me standing in the middle of the room, and Annika is announcing something that I don't really care about until I see Dana step up to hug her. She holds up her hand and Annika grins from ear to ear.

It makes sense when a guy steps up behind her, kissing her hair. She's obviously engaged to him, Annika's best friend whose name I know also starts with 'a', but I can't for the life of me ever seem to remember it.

My fuck buddy is gone now, and even though it turns my gut I saunter up to congratulate her before making a hasty exit to find a replacement bed buddy for the night.

I can't have Dana anymore, and I can't have Bella.I'm fucked and not in the cream my daks way.

Walking out of the apartment building, I pull my phone from my pocket to call a cab.

It's eleven thirty, practically the new year and I sigh deeply shoving my phone back into my pocket as I head to the tram instead, feeling defeated.

It's the worse New Year's Eve, ever.

I'm not getting a New Years kiss at midnight or fucking a sheila into oblivion for the first day of January.

That is all new to me, and fuck it feels like shit.

One | After Game Mischief

9 months earlier-Late March 2018

The change rooms are quiet, only Jai and I are left as everyone else has cleared out for drinks at the pub. He slaps me on the back, "You good man?"

"Yeah, man, sweet. Just gonna have a shower and deal with this fucking hard on."

Jairus looks at my crotch, laughing, "You need a girlfriend man, you're seriously like the only guy I know who gets a hard-on from looking at a girl in the cheer squad."

"It's not my damn fault she's a goddess who purrs when I fuck her."

"Trav, man, you're fucking disgusting," he jeers at me, slinging his bag over his shoulder as he turns to leave.

"You'd know what I mean if your cock came to the party last year when I told you to fuck her."

"True, but only Anni gets me hard and I keep it in my pants when I need to."

"You're just pussy whipped," I laugh slapping his arm.

"No Trav, I'm in love and engaged," he says grinning, "anyway, I'll leave you to wank and catch ya at training on Monday, captain."

Before he leaves he gives me a salute, laughing with a cocky grin on his face.

I start to strip, pulling my guernsey off and shoving it into my bag in my locker. My cock is aching for release and I fist it as I pull my shorts down. About to kick them off and grab my towel I hear footsteps approaching, making me freeze on the spot.

Usually, the cleaners were pottering around the ground, but they never came up to the change rooms this early.

My hard cock stiffens more when she walks in, wearing only a guernsey and the shortest netball skirt I've ever fucking seen.

I can practically see she's commando underneath, and the small triangle of pubic hair points straight to her honey pot.

"Hey sexy," she says seductively, licking her lips as she walks closer to me.

She grabs my waist, running her fingers along the v of my muscles, before she daks me, jocks and shorts in one swift movement.

I gulp hard. She bites her lip when I speak, "Hey Dan, baby, what are you doing here?"

Her hand finds my cock, grabbing it hard in her grip, "Coming to see if the team captain needs an after game massage."

"Mmm, fuck Dan," I groan, as her hand starts sliding up and down my cock.

Her eyes lock on mine, "Were you thinking about me?"

"You know I was, baby. I'm hard as fuck for you."

Squeezing my balls, she stretches up on her tiptoes to whisper in my ear, "I'm not wearing any underwear."

"Fuck Dan, baby, you tease me," I moan grabbing the front of the guernsey in my fists to pull her closer and smash my lips against hers. She devours my mouth, licking my lips and taking my tongue with hers. My cock has a mind of it's own, lifting up the front of her barely there netball skirt.

When she breaks the kiss she teases, "How about that massage, sexy?"

Pushing my hands up the front of the guernsey I ask, "Will you be naked?"

She nods, blushing, and I lift the guernsey over her head, throwing it on the floor beside us.

"Mmm, Dan, I fucking love your tits," I groan taking one into my mouth. Licking and teasing the bud with my tongue, she tips her head back moaning as a jolt of pleasure rushes through her body. Pulling me away, she grabs my hair in her fists to yank my lips towards hers and kisses me so hard I'm breathless.

"Trav, I'm dripping," she whispers in my ear, licking down my neck and smirking at me like a she-devil.

Dana is deliciously sexy, and never shy when it comes to sex, but seems so sweet and full of inhibition in every other way. It intrigues me and turns me on so bad.

Grabbing her by the waist, I pick her up and instinctively she wraps her legs around my arse.

I kiss her as I walk backwards towards the massage room.

Thankfully the door is one you have to push to open, so pressing my back into it, it opens and we stumble backwards into the room.

Turning around, Dana is facing the massage table, and I put her down with her arse on the edge. Her skirt pools at her crotch, and seeing her arousal dripping down her leg I lick my lips, eager to taste her cream.

I run a finger up her thigh, with my eyes locked on hers, "You sure are wet, baby," I tease, reaching her clit and flicking it with my finger. She squirms in pleasure, and her hips wiggle on the edge of the table when I slide a finger inside her wet pussy. Plunging it in and out, her folds make a glorious squelch sound and her lips part as she moans with increasing pleasure.

"Mmm, Trav, that feels good," she purrs, making my cock jolt.

I want to fuck her with her legs spread wide over the massage table, but first I need to spread her legs, take off the skimpy skirt and taste her.

She lets out a delightful whimper when I unhook the clasp of her netball skirt, flinging it open. It falls to the side and when she stands up to move back onto the massage table more it falls off her completely.

Her eyes glare at me with lust as she sits up on the massage table, pressing her hands into it.

"Spread your legs, baby," I demand, lacing my voice with lust.

She doesn't speak, instead scissors her legs open, her knees falling to either side of the massage table. Again I slip a finger inside her wet pussy, bringing it out and pressing it to her lips as she stares at me. I want nothing more than to taste her, but the look in her eyes as she licks my finger clean makes me want to pound my cock into her pussy like a bull out of the gates.

"Trav, taste me," she purrs, making my cock jolt, precum already dripping from the tip.

"Only if I can bareback you hard, baby," I taunt, fisting my cock in my hand.

She nods, "Oh yes sexy," she purrs again.

Pulling her down to the edge of the massage table, I bend down a little, pressing my face between her legs. Licking her pussy up and down in teasing strokes, I deliberately avoid her clit making her moan, as well as purr my name, "Travis, Travis, fuck, fuck, that feels good.

I don't respond, instead bite her clit, feeling her lift her arse off the table, her cream dripping all over my face and its delectable, candied glory.

I lap it up, pulling away just as she's about to scream out her orgasm.

She pouts at me, mischief in her eyes. Laughing I spear my hard cock into her, making her hiss in pleasure as I thrust in and out of her soaked pussy. Her legs wrap around my arse, locking my cock inside her, pushing me deeper inside.

"Fuck, Dan baby, you...fuck...your pussy is tight, baby," I scream out, pounding in and out of her, balls deep, our skin smacking against each other.

It's sweet, hot torture, and her words are more so, "Fuck, Travis I'm going to come sexy, fuck me harder."

I respond, pounding into her so deep I feel her clench around my cock, her release hard, making her whole body shake as she collapses against the massage table in front of her. My own release spurts into her, her body spasming around my cock, milking me.

Pulling back, she turns to face me, kissing me hard, taking my breath away.

"Fuck, Dana," I moan, taking a step back suddenly when I hear footsteps and voices.

"Did you hear that?" Dana asks, looking at me confused, her whole body blushing.

"Yeah, it's probably the cleaners, stay here and get dressed."

"My guernseys out there Trav," she says concerned.

"Stay here, I'll grab it," I reply pushing the doors open and bumping straight into the cleaner.

She looks at my nakedness, covering her eyes and muttering, "Oh I'm so sorry, I um...didn't think anyone was in here."

"All good, I was giving myself a massage, but couldn't find any towels," I inform her with a cocky grin.

She blushes, grabbing a towel from her cart and shoving it at me, not able to meet my eyes.

"Um, is there anyone else here?" she asks meekly, stirring my cock a little.

I laugh, leaning down to whisper in her ear, "My fuck buddy, so best to hand me that Guernsey you have there or I'll take you right here for a threesome."

She gulps, blushing more and tripping slightly, falling backwards against her cleaning cart.

"Oh um, well um...here," she mutters again, handing me Dana's Guernsey she'd picked up from the floor by my locker.

She turns to leave and wrapping the towel around my waist, I watch her sashaying away like a temptress. My cock tents again, as she turns to look back at me with a sweet smile and crimson cheeks. If Dana wasn't still in the next room, I'd fuck the cleaner, dirty.

Clutching Dana's guernsey in my grip I push the door open to find her sitting on the massage table in her netball skirt with her legs wide open, like an invitation to fuck her again.

I throw her the guernsey, "Put this back on or I'll fuck you again Dan."

She catches it, jumping down from the table, slipping it over her head before I can even think. Stopping right in front of me, she grabs my cock through the towel, kissing my lips fiercely and so teasingly I moan against her mouth, grabbing her around the waist, pulling her against my arousal.

Just as I'm about to slide a finger underneath the skirt to touch her pussy again, she rips her mouth from mine, standing on her tip toes to whisper in my ear, "Until next week sexy."

She walks away then, without even looking back at me. She crashes through the door and I wait until I can't hear her footsteps before I head to my locker to get dressed.

Shoving all my footy gear in my bag, I pull on some trackies and a t-shirt, before slamming my locker shut.

I'd come in after the game with a hard on, and I'm still fucking leaving with a hard on. Even fucking Dana isn't enough anymore.

I brace myself for the cool evening air as I walk out, finding it to be a little balmy as the sun is setting. Cursing myself for not bringing my wallet and credit card for a cab home, I head to the tram stop. A tram pulls up just as I get there, and flagging it down to stop I curse under my breath to find it's packed with hot bodies, all shoved in like sardines. Clutching the pole by the door, the tram rattles away and I fall against, face first in the biggest set of tits I've seen on any sheila.

Stupidly I lick them, and the blonde beauty they belong to lifts my head up, locking her eyes on mine.

"Hey, nice rack you got there," I taunt, flashing her my cockiest grin.

"Hey, and thanks," she replies in a husky tone that is damn sexy. The tram jolts as it stops and our bodies are forced even closer together, as people scramble to get off at the stop while others get on.

I can smell the floral, earthy scent of her perfume and it's fucking intoxicating. I'm getting a fucking hard on just looking at her. She's looking at me like something about me is having the same effect on her and I'm imagining her knickers are soaked through.

"Where are you heading tonight?" I whisper in her ear.

She giggles loudly, grabbing my cock through the front of my trackies.

"Your bed," she whispers back, running her hand up and down my length.

"Fuck, yeah," I groan, so tempted to kiss her when the tram stops, thankfully at my stop.

I grab her hand, pulling her off the tram and against the nearby tree. Frantically I smash my lips to hers, kissing her, tasting her and fuck it's good.

Breaking the kiss a moment later, I press my forehead against hers, "Sorry, fuck gorgeous, I didn't even get your name before I fucked ya mouth."

She laughs, "That's ok, it's um...Alice."

"Alice...nice to meet you, and I'm..."

She cuts my words off, again gripping my cock in her hand, this time actually shoving it down the front of my trackies.

"I know your name, Travis 'hot as hell' Banes."

"Oh fuck, Alice, you're getting me hard."

"Then take me to yours," she suggests with a devious hot as sin smirk.

I didn't normally go for blondes, but fuck me I'm going to take her home and see her delicious tits up close, watching them bounce as she rides my cock until she screams.

It's definitely a night for some after game mischief.

Two | Bouncy Flouncy Playtime

Dragging Alice inside my apartment I groan, shutting the door and slamming her against it as I take her mouth with mine again.

She kisses like she wants to swallow me whole and it's making my already hard as fuck cock throb in my trackies.

Her moans are raw, I'm devouring her mouth, grabbing her hands and forcing them above her head, still with our lips playing.

Reaching down between us, I yank her mini skirt down and she bites my lip before breaking the kiss. I take a moment to gaze at her underwear, if you could even call what she is wearing underneath her mini skirt underwear. It's a scrap of lacy fabric with elastic sides, that barely covers her bare pussy.

Her cheeks flush when I lick my lips, "Fuck Alice, your pussy looks delectable."

She bites down on her lip, short on words and it turns me on.

She's a mix of innocence and she-devil and essentially crack for my cock. I want her, now, but need to see her huge tits free. I want to bury my face in between them and also into her glorious pussy.

Fuck, my cock wants to dive into her pussy lips.

Slipping a finger into her barely there g-string I let out a groan, feeling her arousal coat my finger.

"Damn Alice, you're wet as girl."

She doesn't reply, just moans, as I start to finger fuck her, one finger plunging in and out of her soaked core, my thumb rubbing slowly over her clit. Still teasing her, I kiss her again, loving how she can't help but moan out her pleasure. With my free hand I take hers down from behind her head and she fingers my hair, pulling my mouth even closer to hers. Laughing against her lips I pull back, "Don't come Alice."

She shakes her head, locking her eyes with mine, reaching down to her waist to lift her tank top over her head. My eyes boggle, focusing on her perfect huge tits that are threatening to spill out over the top of her lacy bra. The edge of the lace grazes the pink buds that have risen to attention. "Take it off Alice, and ya g too."

Slipping the bra straps off her shoulders she looks me up and down, "Only if you get naked as well."

"Oh fuck yeah," I moan, realising my finger is still between her thighs. Taking it out, I bring it to my lips, licking it and fuck does she taste good. I grip my t-shirt and lift it over my head, not wanting to take my eyes off her as she drops her bra to the floor, "Whoops," she tuts, hooking her fingers into the elastic at her hips and sliding the g-string to the floor.

She's standing naked against my front door, and fuck, she is the hottest fucking woman I've had in months. Her tits, up close and free of the constraint of a bra are perfect, perky round mounds. Groaning I yank my trackies and boxers down to my feet and my cock springs forward, eager to have her right there against my front door.

"Mmm, Travis, your dick is spectacular."

I laugh, "Haven't heard that one before."

"Um, well it is," she says, grabbing my cock in her hand and stroking it.

"God, Alice, fuck!" I groan before taking one of her hardened buds in my mouth, circling my tongue over it to make her moan in pleasure. My cock is throbbing in her grip, and I can't take a moment longer without taking her pussy as mine.

I look up at her, "You safe for bareback?"

"Yes, just fuck me," she hisses as she presses a kiss to my lips.

Wildly kissing her, I grab her arse cheeks lifting her up and straight onto my hard cock. Instinctively she wraps her legs around my waist, pulling me closer, pushing my cock deeper inside her slick pussy. Her hands wrap around my neck, her kiss meeting my lips again whilst she bounces up and down on my cock. Her pussy is slick, not a tight grip around my cock like I love, but still, it feels fucking good to pound hard inside such a hot sheila.

She's screaming moans of pleasure, my name on her lips as my cum rockets out of my cock, filling her as her orgasm makes her shake in pleasure.

Jumping out of my arms she kisses me, "Damn Travis, that was hot. I've never fucked a guy against his front door before."

"Yeah, glad you loved it. You rocked my world, girl."

I didn't mean my words, I'd had better sex before, right in that very spot, but I wasn't going to tell her that. Stepping out of my daks at my feet I head towards the kitchen, "Wanna drink?"

I'm reaching up to grab down a glass and a bottle of scotch, turning to find her leaning on the bench on her elbows. Her tits practically touch the stone bench top and my cock throbs again just looking at her and the devilish smirk on her face.

"Yeah, sure, and then maybe you could show me your bedroom."

I gulp hard, not sure if having her stay the night is a good idea. The last sheila to stay over was Dana and things are different with her. Having Dana cuddle up next to me in bed feels safe, but I don't know Alice from a bar of soap.

"Um, yeah Alice, I...um...I..."

"What?" she says, a seductive purr in her tone when she comes around to my side of the bench.

Fuck she's gorgeous. Maybe I should fuck her again, doggy, or cowgirl so I can watch her tits bounce. Pulling her close, I kiss her hard, palming her taut round arse.

"Mmm, ok, you convinced me girl, but you're gonna ride my cock."

She doesn't reply, instead grabs my hand and pulls me down the hallway. Once at my room, and she's sprawled out across my tangled bed sheets I dive towards her kissing her, telling my mind to shut the hell up. I'm going to regret this decision in the morning but fuck it, I need some bouncy flouncy playtime.

Three | Morning After Crash

Nightmares plagued me and waking up in a cold sweat with the doona cover sticking to my body I jump out of bed like a fire has started. I pull on the sleep shorts at my feet and sit on the edge of the bed, my head in my hands.

My head is pounding, thoughts of Meaghan filling my mind. She's torturing me in my dreams, two years down the track. She has no idea where I live, but I still can't shake the feeling that she's watching my every move.

The doona moves beside me, and shrieking I leap off the bed in shock when the blonde head pops out and looks up at me.

"Morning, sexy," she coos at me.

Panic is rising in my chest. Meaghan is in my fucking bed! I'm dreaming right? This is a fucking dream! No! Wait! No!

"Get out of my bed! Get out!" I bellow as she sits up in the bed, not caring that the sheets fall into a pool at her waist.

I look her up and down, realising it's not Meaghan in my bed, but some other blonde sheila who I can't remember a thing about.

"Travis not up for a morning romp now?" she teases climbing onto to her hands and knees and crawling across the bed towards me. Grabbing my sleep shorts she daks me, about to put her mouth to my cock when I yank her away by the hair.

"I said get the fuck out! I don't do morning sex with strangers from the night before."

She looks hurt, but I don't give a fuck. She obviously was forgettable as my cock isn't springing to attention and I can't for the life of me remember if her name was Ami or Alicia, or something else.

Clutching my sheets, she wraps them around her body as she stumbles to her feet, screaming at me, "You're an arsehole!" She's giving me dagger eyes, a look that could no doubt kill a man with a weaker soft heart, but my hardened heart takes no shit. Heading towards the bathroom to shower I taunt her, "No girl, I'm a player...and you were more than willing to partake in whatever game we played last night, but I don't do mornings."

She scoffs at me, "You...you...I...I..."

"Cat got ya tongue huh?" I taunt as she hobbles towards me with the sheets still wrapped around her. It's actually a pretty fucking hilarious sight, but I don't dare laugh. "How about you just leave girl, before you make a fool out of yourself?"

This time she huffs, shuffling away and leaning against the door jamb of the bathroom I call out to her back, "Leave my sheets here, thanks!"

Looking back at me from the end of the hallway she drops the sheet from her body, smirking as she walks away. I shake my head in disbelief. Every girl, bar Dana is the fucking same. They all think they can snag Travis Banes after one night of sex. I have my reasons for not doing the morning after and I'm kicking myself for not saying goodbye to big tits last night. I can't for the life of me remember if fucking her was any good, which probably means it it's safe to say it was just a release and not at all good.

I wait to hear the click of the front door behind her before I go to lock it and head back to the shower. I still can't shake the thoughts of Meaghan out of my mind, of the last time I woke up with her in the bed like she was allowed to be there.

She'd breached her restraining order, broken into my apartment, stripped naked and climbed into bed next to me. Waking up the next day, I found her glued to my back whilst she stroked my cock so hard bruises appeared the next day. I called her out, telling her I'd go to the cops but all that got me was her screeching protest, a smashed phone from her throwing it across the room and scratch marks down my chest from her nails digging into my skin when she begged me for another chance.

She was toxic, a one night stand who turned into more and ruined my life, shattering my heart and my trust in women.

I don't do love, relationships or morning afters. And for what I'm going to do for the day now, building some Lego and forgetting all about women seems like the best choice.

God, to be a kid again, would be the fucking best.

Four | Rotten Night Play

It's been about a week since I'd picked up the blonde sheila on the tram. I'd blocked out all thoughts of the morning after and I still couldn't remember her name. The sex with her was forgettable, and I'd not even gotten a stiffy from watching porn since.

I need a good root, from a hot sheila, preferably brunette. Ever since Meaghan screwed me over, I'd mostly steered clear of blondes. The tram chick was an exception because I'd fallen into her and her tits were perfection.

I shouldn't have fucked her though, as she brought back all the bad thoughts of Meaghan, just when I thought the nightmares and horror of my three-year relationship with her were gone from my life.

Other than going to training during the week, I'd stayed at home building a Lego house. We'd had a bye this past weekend, so I'd literally stayed inside feeling sorry for myself. What I need is a damn good fuck and there's only one person I can call when I just want a sheila to fuck me senseless. My always dependable, gorgeous as fuck Dana. Sometimes I felt like a tool, using her for sex but she was always down, never able to resist me when I needed a root.

Grabbing my phone from the coffee table I send her text.

Travis: dan baby you down to come over?

Dana: no Travis I'm busy find another girl to service you

Travis: dan baby come on...my cock wants you

Dana: I said I'm busy

I throw my phone on the futon beside me, pissed off and now horny, partly from her being so sassy and also because I've not come in over a week.

There's only one solution to my predicament and that's to go out to get tanked.

Once at Rivera I head straight to the bar, contemplating what choice of alcohol is going to get me tanked the quickest, without making me feel like chundering. The bar is packed and I get a glimpse of a petite sexy looking brunette at the other end of the bar who looks exactly like Dana. She turns away just as I'm ordering a vodka straight up. I down it the moment the bartender puts the glass down, signalling for another and handing him a fifty dollar note.

After downing the second glass, I contemplate texting Jairus but shake the thought away knowing he's probably at his fucking penthouse naked in bed with his fiancé riding his cock. Sometimes I hated hearing about my best mates sex life, especially when I wasn't getting much action myself, but I'm beyond happy for him. He'd found the perfect girl, and as much as I don't believe in love, at least for myself, I can see that he loves her with all his heart.

Thinking about getting another drink I look towards the dance floor, spotting the same petite brunette from the end of the bar. She's dancing with a group of girls, her back towards me. The way her hips sway, I know it's Dana and it makes me fucking furious.

I cross the dance floor, eye fucking her friends when I step up behind her and wrap my arms around her waist, grinding my groin into her sweet arse. Her skinny jeans are so tight, hugging her body all over, so tight that I can feel my straining cock brushing between her arse cheeks.

She turns her head to look at me, and I squeeze her tighter for a moment, thinking she's about to lean in for a pash when she pulls back from me. Even in the dark club surrounds, I can see her pupils are dilated, her eyes showing a mix of anger and lust.

My cock throbs in my jeans when she leads me over to a booth. Sitting down beside her, I taunt, "So you're busy huh, baby?"

She looks at me again, scoffing, "Yes Travis, I'm out with friends."

"And I couldn't have tagged along? I'm not a friend?"

Shaking her head, she meekly replies, "No. You know we aren't friends Travis." Her words kinda hurt, but she's right. We aren't friends. She's a fuck buddy. I kinda hate myself for only wanting sex from her, as I know she deserves better. But I can't be that guy. I'm not worth any sheilas time. Meaghan made me feel like a worthless piece of shit, and the scars still plague me.

Emotional and physical scars, but at least the physical scars I'd been able to cover with tattoos. I'd not told anyone, not Jairus or even my Dad about what happened with Meaghan and the real reason we broke up. Dad had loved her, but that was only because she put a sweet innocent lamb act on whenever we were together around him. Mum would've seen through her act, and thinking back it made me miss her like crazy.

Dana's now looking across at me, sipping on her pink cocktail. "Travis, are you ok? I..um..didn't mean to upset you."

I look at her, straight into her sweet brown eyes.

"Yeah..um. I'll be fine if you pash me on the dance floor babe."

She glances at her friends, who sneakily wink at her and then me. It's a pity they're blonde as I'm certain I could get one or both of them to head home with me for the night without much convincing.

"Fine, but just one dance," Dana huffs at me when I stand up. She takes my hand, leading me out to the middle of the dance floor. I don't hesitate to pull her close, rocking our bodies together like I'm fucking her to the beat of the song. She's practically putty in my arms, and it's taking a hell of lot of restraint to not drag her out of the club and back to my place. Turning in my arms, she wraps her arms around my neck and smashes her lips to mine in a hot brazen pash. She's fucking my mouth, licking my lips and sucking on my tongue. Her sex is brushing up against my cock, her hips still grinding to the beat as we pash. It's fucking torture. I needed a gobby earlier, and now if I don't get off before the end of the night, I'm going to have a bad case of blue balls.

The song changes, and Dana jumps back suddenly, racing back to the booth to her friends. I don't even bother covering my hard on, walking awkwardly back to the table and pulling her to her feet to kiss her hard, not giving a flying fuck that her friends are watching. She breaks the kiss, staring daggers at me. "Seriously Travis," she snaps at me.

"What Dan? You left me out there with a fucking hard on."

"I said one dance Travis," she spits at me with anger in her tone. Her friends are giggling behind us and I can see Dana is becoming even more ticked off.

I lean in to whisper in her ear, "You up for a quickie in that private booth?"

She scoffs at me, but then smirks before leaning into my side to whisper in my ear, so her friends don't hear, "Maybe just a hand job tonight."

I want more than to just be jerked off under the table, but at least I'll come and not have blue balls. I lead her away towards the back of Rivera, to a booth that faces away from the rest of the club. It's secluded and was often a place where you'd find a couple moaning whilst they engaged in a quick fuck. I'd fucked Dana there a year or so ago and damn did I want to do it again.

Sliding into the booth, trying to not look at the sticky white marks on the seat, I ask, "Are you sure we can't fuck baby?"

"No, Travis, please, not tonight," she practically begs me.

"Fine, so am I just getting a hand job or could I be so lucky to get a gobby?"

She doesn't reply, sliding into the booth next to me and pushing me back against the side as she begins to undo my belt. Before I can think she's unzipped my jeans and has freed my aching cock from the confine of my boxers. Her hands are stroking my already hard cock and it feels damn good. Still stroking me she stretches up to kiss me teasingly.

I moan against her mouth and she lets out a little giggle when she breaks the kiss and licks down my abs, all the way across the trail of hair that points to my crotch. Looking up at me she takes my cock into her mouth, circling the tip with her tongue before taking me deep. Her gagging noises when I hit the back of her throat make my cock pulse in her mouth, and she sucks it furiously, taking it out and back in, licking it all over in teasing circles like it's a delicious lollipop.

I can't help but moan. Dana sucking me off is delicious torture.

"Fuck Dan, baby, you know how to suck a cock, girl."

She holds a hand up to my mouth, to stifle my scream as she takes me deep again. My cock spasms, filling her mouth with my salty warm seed. Once she's removed her mouth from me, she swallows hard, wiping her arm across her lips.

"God Dana, that was amazing baby. Come home with me, I can return the favour."

Without helping me fix up my daks, she stands up and shakes her head.

"Not tonight Travis. I need to get back to my friends."

"Um, ok. You know my doors always open for you though, baby, yeah?"

"Yeah," she mumbles, sauntering away without giving me another look.

I'm fucking confused, as she's never rejected me before. And if I'm being frank it hurts like a slap to the face. She was my go to and I honestly didn't think she had any issues with being my fuck buddy. Granted we'd not ever actually talked about it, but I'm not always the one to make the first move.

Fixing up my daks, I grab my phone from my back pocket to check the time, seeing it's only just gone ten. Again I contemplate texting Jairus, and I hesitate for moment unlocking the screen with Face ID.

Standing up holding my phone I wander out of the club, not even daring to look at Dana as I leave. I don't do feelings, but my ego is bruised and I'm hurt. I need a drink with my best mate.

Travis: Jai the man, are you up for a drink?

I don't expect a reply, shoving my phone in my pocket as I head down Bridge Road, loving the cool night air brushing against my bare arms.

Only a minute or so later, I feel the vibration against my arse cheek.

Fishing it out, Jai's replied.

Jairus: yeah sure. Anni's out. Where you at?

I smirk, thinking about asking him to crash Annika's night out, as the gorgeous as fuck Bella is probably out with her and I could take Bella home for the night instead.

Travis: heading to Punt road inn.

Jairus: no worries...be there asap

Putting my phone back in my pocket again, I head inside the pub, which is surprisingly quiet. Sitting on a stool at the bar I order a whiskey straight up and wait for Jai to arrive, whilst thoughts of both Dana and the equally gorgeous Bella fill my mind. I need to ask Jairus for her number for real this time.

Five | Regretful After Thoughts

Dana

After giving into Travis and sucking him off, I feel dirty. I know I shouldn't keep giving into everything he asks of me, but when he looks at me, kisses me ,I just can't help it.

He's like a puppy dog, pretending to be so innocent and he makes me melt every time. Striding back to the other booth, I don't turn back to look at him, knowing I'll not be able to resist his offer to go home with him.

At the booth, my friends Britney and Shanna are giggling as they sip cocktails and try to discreetly point out who they think is hot on the dance floor. They shuffle another cosmopolitan towards me on the table when I sit back down.

"Seriously, girl, spill!" Brit shrieks excitedly.

Shaking my head, as I take a quick sip of my drink I tell her, "Nothing to spill."

"Oh come on Dan, don't give us that shit," Shanna interjects giving me a dirty look.

I'm silent, sipping on the drink and trying to not meet my friends pleading gazes.

"It was him, yeah? What's his name?" Brit says, looking at Shan for a clue.

This time I reply, "Travis."

"Yes, that's it. Travis, the hot as fuck tigers captain, right Dan?" Brit asks, licking her lips.

"Yeah, and don't even think about going there Brit. He's a tool."

She looks at me with a sorrowful look on her face.

"Who cares Dana, he's hot as sin and I bet he's hung."

I feel my cheeks flush, thinking back to minutes ago when I had his long dick down the back of my throat.

"Ooo, Dan's blushing! You must be right, Brit," Shan teases.

"Mmm, so where is he now?" Brit asks a hint of teasing in her tone, her voice rising as she finishes her loaded question.

"Still in the back booth, probably pulling up his daks."

They both giggle, and Shanna asks, "Did you have a quickie in the back booth?"

I shake my head, blushing again, "No I...um...sucked him off."

"Damn, Dana! You dirty girl!" Brit shrieks again.

"Yeah, I shouldn't have though."

"Why?" Shanna asks, looking at me grinning.

"Because like I said, he's a tool. He just wants sex and stupid me, I give in every time."

My friend's mouths drop open in shock, and Britney speaks, "Seriously you've actually fucked him?"

Taking the straw from my drink, I pick it up and pour the rest down my throat, swallowing hard as I mutter, "Yes...and not just once."

"Oh my god girl! Tell us the details!" Shanna screams.

"I can't believe you've been holding out on sharing, Dan."

"Well, I um...I...um...go down to the change rooms after the games and sometimes he booty calls me," I confess, not meeting their eyes on me.

"God Dana, I had no idea. Why don't you make things official?"

"I told you, he doesn't want a girlfriend and doesn't feel that way about me."

Brit reaches across the table to touch my arm lightly, "How do you feel about him though Dan?"

"Um...I don't know."

"Don't tell us that you're in love with him and you haven't said anything?" Shanna asks, concern in her tone.

"God, no...I...I'm just confused. I keep wondering if things could be different if we just went out on a date or something other than just hooking up. But I...um...I've...."

"What girl? What else are you hiding?" Brit teases, laughing.

"I'm kinda interested in someone else."

"Ooo, really?"

"Yeah I bumped into this hot redhead at Uni a couple of weeks ago and I can't stop thinking about him."

"Do you know who he is?" Brit asked eagerly.

"No, I think I've seen him at a game like last year with Annika, maybe but I don't know."

"Remind me, who Annika is again?" Shanna interjects and Britney nods in agreement.

"Jairus Brooks's girlfriend, well fiancé now. He's actually Travis's best friend. And I kinda did have a mega crush on him."

"Oh right, the blonde one. Pity he's getting married."

"I know Shan," I muse.

"Well, girl, maybe you should track down your redhead hottie and make a move on him," Brit suggests, smirking at me.

"Yeah, not going to happen. I'm honestly to shy to do anything like that."

They both don't reply, smiling for a moment before nodding. I stand up, grabbing Brit's hand to pull her up with me.

"Let's go dance bitches, I'm sick of talking about guys."
Britney laughs and Shanna follows us both to the middle of the
dance floor. A few guys turn to look at us when we start to dance
against each other. My thoughts wander to my redhead hottie and
I close my eyes thinking about dancing with him instead.

Six | Drunk Mates Unite

After downing a few more drinks, I'm relieved to see Jairus strolling into the pub. He pulls up a stool next to me, signalling the bartender for a drink. After ordering a beer, he greets me, "Hey bro, how many have you had and why?"

Lifting my own glass of beer to my lips, I stare at my best mate over the rim. He's giving me dagger eyes.

"Don't fucking remember how many I've had, don't give a shit, but I'm getting tanked."

"Come on Trav, we've got a game tomorrow night. If you show up drunk again, coach will be furious."

"Yeah...well...I'll...be...f..fine," I stammer before letting out a loud belch.

"Sure Travis," Jairus laughs, sipping his own beer. I give him a look, laughing myself.

"I'm only drinking so I don't take some random sheila home."

"Oh right, so I'm your booty call tonight, huh?" He teases me, smirking like a cocky bastard.

"Yeah, I fucking love you. I've always wanted you man," I taunt him, laughing.

He downs more of his beer, trying to hold in his laughter.

"You really are drunk, Trav. If you of all people turned out to be gay, I'd probably die laughing at how crazy that is."

"Yeah, so um, who's Anni out with tonight?"

"Not Bella, if that's what you're asking," he informs me, reading my mind.

"Oh right, and um yeah I was asking. Is she still with that skinny fucktard we met at your party awhile back?"

"How the fuck would I know Trav? She's Anni's friend, not mine and I hardly ever see her so I'm not privy to all the details of her love life."

"Ok, well regardless, maybe you could hook a brother up with her number?" I ask winking at him as he finishes off his beer and signals for another.

"To be honest Trav, I don't have her number."

"Well, fucking get it for me bro. I need to fuck her sideways into tomorrow."

He laughs, "Keep dreaming Trav. I don't think Anni will let you near her."

"Yeah, you're probably right," I muse signalling for another beer, thoughts of ways to get in Bella's daks running through my mind.

"Do you really need another?" Jairus asks me almost accusingly.

"Yeah, mate I do. And no I don't want to talk about it."

"Ok, but at least let me drive you home when we finish the next one?"

"Yeah, thanks mate. I'd appreciate it. And next week, I'll take ya for a spin in my Jag."

"Shit man, fair dinkum, when are you picking it up?"

"On sundee, so fucking ready to get it."

"Sweet as!"

We clink our glasses together, and I cheer, "Bloody oath, it's sweet as."

We down our beers, and head out of the pub to Jairus' red Kia Stinger that he's managed to park right out the front.

Heading towards my place, he asks, "What's up with you and Dana these days?"

"Don't even ask, man. I saw her tonight, and she gave me a gobby, but yeah..." I cut my words off when I look across at him, gaping at me in shock.

"She what? Gave you a gobby at Rivera?"

"Yeah, you know, in that private booth at the back."

He shakes his head, pulling up outside my apartment, "Um, no. Are you serious, Trav?"

"Dead serious Jairus," I taunt mockingly.

"Well, I don't know Trav, you..." he gives me an odd look like he's short on words.

I open my door, stepping out and leaning in holding the door frame to ask, "Pick me up tomorrow before the game?"

"Yeah sure, see ya around three."

"No worries," I reply shutting the car door and heading to my apartment as he drives away.

Since getting with Annika, Jairus had changed and it was hard to admit to myself that it was in a good way. We used to be so alike, getting with any willing sheila, getting way to tanked to remember what crazy stuff we'd done the night before and when he officially became a rookie for the Tigers with me and he'd moved in with Anni he changed. Part of me wanted to change my life for the better as he had, but if that meant falling in love, then I'd stay single, even if that meant my life was going to fall apart around me when my football career ended.

Once inside, I flopped down on my bed after stumbling down the hallway. Thoughts of love gone wrong plague me as my eyes close, but I'm too drunk to give a shit.

Fuck my life.

Seven | Game Day Slump

The forlorn looks my teammates gave me as they left the change rooms, after our twenty point loss to the Crows, hit me right in the damn feels. I'd played a horrible game, barely touching the ball for a minute and when I did have it I fumbled it, ruining a few easy shots at goal and failing to support my teammates.

Slamming my locker shut, I slip trackies up my legs and I'm about to slip my t-shirt on when Jairus comes in from the showers, a towel around his waist and rubbing his hair with another.
I try to smile at my best mate, but he can see straight through it.

"Trav, mate, what's eating ya today?"

I sit down on the bench in the middle of the change rooms, sighing as Jairus heads to his locker. The silence in the room is deafening, I'm waiting for him to say something else, telling myself to open my damn trap and confide in my best mate.
I hear the towel drop to the floor and look up to see his bare arse practically in my face.

Again he turns to look at me, "Trav?" he asks, pulling tight boxers on.
"Yeah, I um...I..."

He seems annoyed, sitting down next to me, "Travis, you played shit out there today. Are you seriously still hungover or something?"

"Nah...well yeah...my head hurts like a bitch. Had no fucking Nurofen in the house and I...fuck it....I"

I stand up, slamming a fist into the lockers in front of me.

Jairus doesn't stand up, but even with my back turned I can tell he's angry and staring daggers at me.

"You're the team captain...you should take better care of yourself, man."

Again I slam a fist into the lockers, anger boiling up inside me.

"You don't fucking know the half of it Jairus."

"Then tell me, Travis. We haven't been best mates for long, but I got ya back," he says standing up, taking a step towards me.

He tries to wrap his arms around me in a hug, but I shake him away.

"Don't fucking hug me, I'm no pansy."

"Never said you were, but I hate seeing you like this man."

Sniffing I try to not give in to the tears I can feel stinging my eyes, pansy tears. Guys shouldn't cry about anything, let alone the scars left by ex-girlfriends.

Turning to look at my best mate, he's slipped on a T-shirt and is still glaring at me with a genuine look of concern on his face.

"I...ah...haven't been sleeping right lately."

"Yeah, what's going on?" He asks concerned, pulling his trackies on, giving me a sideways glance.

"Nightmares," I mutter, biting my lip.

I'm not sure if I'm ready to tell him, tell anyone the horror of my relationship with Meaghan. He's surely noticed the scars, even though my tattoos cover most of them. Dana had, and I'd straight out lied to her face that they were from an accident as a kid.

I hated lying to her and knew if I honestly opened up to Jairus, there is no way I could hold back the truth.

He touches my arm lightly, "Shit man, what about?"

"Um nothing really, just stupid shit, you know, playing a shit game and stuff."

"Hmm, yeah that sucks. Well, I'm here for you man."

"I know Jai, and thanks for not ratting me out to coach."

He gives me a lopsided grin, "Um, about that."

"What?" I spit, slight anger in my tone.

"I might have already said something earlier when I saw him after the game."

"What? Are you trying to fuck me over man?"

"No, he just asked me if you were alright."

"And what you'd tell him?" I snap, so annoyed at my best mate for ratting me out.
"That we went out for a drink last night. Seriously Trav, that's all. Lighten up."

He shakes his head at me, grabs his bag and glares at me as though he's waiting for a reply to a question he hasn't asked.
"I'm sorry man, I didn't mean to get angry at you."
"All good," he laughs, pulling me into his side in an awkward but kinda nice bro hug, "Are you coming now or staying for a bit?"
"Staying, but…"
"You don't need to tell me Trav. I don't wanna know," he laughs again, turning to leave.

Not even a minute passes when I hear footsteps coming into the change rooms. I'd decided on leaving and heading home to shower, slinging my bag over my shoulder walking out when I bump straight into the cleaner.
The contents of her cart in front of her flies everywhere, all over the floor; towels, soap and other toiletry items.
She bends down to pick them up and I follow, helping her pick up the soaps scattered across the floor.
My eyes dart to the open buttons at the top of her khaki green blouse, her tits small but perfect mounds barely hidden from my eyes when it falls forward.
Under my breath, as we stand up I mutter an appreciative mmm, looking her up and down more, her curves not hidden under her work attire at all.
If anything they are accentuated by the tight pants she's wearing.

She looks straight at me, an apologetic look in her eyes, "oh Mr Travis….I'm…I'm so…sorry….I…"

"No need to apologise Sofia…it was my fault."

"No..no…it…" she mumbles again, reaching out to touch me tentatively. It doesn't give me tingles or any of that bullshit, but it's kinda arousing.

"So, I best be going then Sofia," I inform her, waiting for her to cut the tension, to beg me to stay and fuck her senseless.

Every time I'd been alone, the last one in the change rooms, Sofia would come to clean them and the flush of her cheeks when she was around me wasn't something she could hide.

"Um, ok, Mr Travis, I will just clean shower now, on my own."

She's looking at me oddly, her cheeks flushing more than they ever have.It's practically an invitation, a dangling of bait that I have to take.

I chuckle, bending down to whisper in her ear, "Want some help getting the shower clean, Sofia?"

She giggles like a naughty schoolgirl, making my cock jolt to attention, "Mr Travis, we can't," she moans with a seductive hint in her tone. I take a quick look around the hallway, making sure no other cleaners or people are in sight before grabbing her by the hips, slamming her against the cleaning cart and taking her mouth in a hard kiss.

The cart careens back into the change room, crashing against the bench in the middle. I'm still kissing her, and it's so damn arousing, the rush of being caught out sending my cock high and ready to take her completely.

Breaking the kiss, she looks up at me expectantly, her lips red and swollen from the stubble on my chin. "The shower, Mr Travis?" she asks, stepping aside and walking backwards towards the communal showers as she slowly strips from her hideous khaki work attire.

Fucking the cleaner is so wrong, but Sofia is stunning, fiery red hair and curves for days. I need to fuck her now and get all thoughts of any blonde beauties out of my head.

Eight | Clean Dirty Shower

Sofia is standing against the shower wall, her arms above her head, her completely bare naked body on show for me. Stepping towards her, I'm ripping my clothes off, throwing them behind me.

Turning the taps on next to her, my hand brushes the skin of her hips and she lets a delightful giggle as she squirms at the contact. *Fuck she's hot.*

The water is warm and Sofia steps under it. I lick my lips watching the water cascading down her body. Her eyes look up to me, with a mix of fear and lust in them. Her lips part, as though she wants to say something, but instead she darts her tongue in and out between them, running it along her plump lower lip. My cock jolts, ready to take her hard and fast.

Pushing her back against the wall, I crash my lips to hers in a hard kiss. She grabs my cock, rubbing it up and down in her grip. The tip is pressing into her hips. All I want is to pound her hard, make screams emerge from her sweet plump lips.

Stopping the stroking of my cock, she tears her mouth from mine and utters words that make my cock throb, "Fuck me please, Mr Travis, now."

"Mmm Sofia," I moan grabbing her thigh and hoisting her leg over my shoulder. Lining our pelvises up I admire her bare pussy before slamming my cock into her, balls deep. Her moan is loud and bounces off the walls.

Our bodies rock together, moans and dirty as sin screams of pleasure pour out of her mouth like honey. I've never fucked a sheila so vocal, and it's damn hot, but I also want her to shut her damn mouth in case someone hears us.

Her pussy is gripping me, and I can feel her peak is edging closer. Reaching down I drag a finger over her sensitive bud, smashing my lips to hers at the same time to kiss her silent. Her whole body shakes violently as her climax takes over and I pull my cock out of her.

Lifting her leg from off my shoulder, I push her against the wall, taking her mouth in another hot kiss.

She breaks it, taunting me, "Mr Travis, you did not come."

Smirking I fist my cock, pumping it hard, before spurting my white warm release all over her belly. She looks down at it, smiling and running a finger through the sticky liquid before she runs it over her lips and licks them clean.

"Damn Sofia," I groan, running a hand through my hair before stepping under the water to wash away what I've just done.

Fucking her felt damn good, but it was incredibly fucking wrong. Fucking random sheila's won't help block out the past. All it does is make me feel good in the moment, and then when they look at me with that lust in their eyes, all I feel is guilt.

Guilt like I'm cheating on Meaghan, which is so fucking laughable but it still feels like it.

I'm a complete douchebag and as I step out of the shower, leaving Sofia covered in my cum without another word or glance back I feel like I have no choice but to go and visit Meaghan.

Being with her is all a guy like me deserves.

Nine | Guilty As Charged

For the past couple of weeks, I'd avoided everyone, only seeing Jairus and my other mates at training and games.
Just dragging my sorry arse out of bed to go there was bad enough, and I specifically made sure I was out of the change rooms long before Sofia would come in.

I still felt so guilty about fucking her, and even more so when I found a note from her inside my locker.

Mr Travis
Have not seen you since our shower. Been thinking of your cock.
Text me 0412 312 453
Sofia xxx

I'd saved her number in my phone but vowed I'd never use it.
I'm an idiot, but not that stupid.
Fucking her was a one-time thing, that I do not plan on doing again.
I need to fuck someone though, my hand really does nothing to make my cock come to the party. Porn is definitely not a turn on, I need to touch to feel pleasure, with a woman.

Flopping down on the couch with a beer, aimlessly scrolling through Facebook I practically jump out of my skin when a message pops up at the top of my screen.

Dana: sexy, help me!
Travis: what with baby? Need a good fucking?
Dana: no you dirty boy. But I need to get out of this hellhole tonight
Travis: why baby? Roomies getting it on again?
Dana: they're having a party
Travis: join in baby
Dana: I'd rather not. Come take me out dancing?

I look at the word come and back at her name. And my cock throbs in my pants thinking about the last time Dana made me come with her lips wrapped around my cock, it deep down her throat. Fuck it.
I'll take her out dancing for the night, bring her back here and fuck her brains out, to forget and just feel.

Travis: ok baby..I'll pick you up in twenty
Dana: thank you xxxx

Twenty minutes later, I'm at Dana's doorstep, being a gentleman by actually going to the door. About to knock, she opens it and looks me up and down as she closes it behind her.
I'd thrown on a long sleeved button up shirt with my jeans, and watching Dana lick her lips as she admires the way it hugs my abs has my cock throbbing.

Heading to my brand spanking new convertible Jaguar I watch Dana's eyes as she follows behind.

"Is this yours?" She purrs, seeming a little giddy.

"Yeah, baby, all mine. Get in."

Sliding into the front seat her short dress creeps up her thighs, giving me a glimpse of her black lacy knickers. Starting the engine I reach over to touch between her thighs, and looking across at me she bites down on her lip.

"Dan, baby, keep giving me that look and I'll christen the back seat by fucking you."

She opens her legs for me and driving off I run a finger over her slit, feeling that her knickers are already soaked.

"Take me dancing first, sexy," she taunts shifting on her seat as I rub my thumb over her clit.
"Dancing then fucking baby, you're already wet for me."

She moans, filling the whole car with her exhaled breath when I slide my finger into the knickers and straight into her wet core. Teasing her for a couple of minutes, I watch her out of the corner of my eye as she writhes on the seat in pleasure.

Just when she's about to cum I pull out my finger licking it clean, "Mmm Dan baby, you taste divine," I taunt slipping the Jaguar into a carpark a few blocks away from Rivera.

Her hand is on the door ready to open it when I touch her arm pulling her back towards me for a quick pash.

"Leave your knickers in the car, baby," I demand, lacing my tone with lust.
"I can't Travis. This dress is really short."
Her face is still close to mine, so I nibble on her ear before whispering, "Exactly, baby."

Staring at me she lifts her arse off the seat, gathering up the back of her dress and hooking her fingers in the elastic of the lace.
Biting on her lip she slides the fabric over her pert arse, down her thighs and to her knees before she sits down again kicking them off her feet.
Smirking at her I get out of the car and wait for her on the curb.
Snaking an arm around her back as we head to Rivera I cup her bare arse cheek in my palm. She jumps slightly at the sensation but the sweet smile she gives me as we head inside tells me my dirty Dana is out to play tonight and my cock is aching to have her.

~~

After we grab drinks, quickly downing them I pull Dana onto the dance floor, slamming our bodies against each other.
My cock is straining against the front of my jeans, the friction as we rock against each other to the music has me on edge.

She seems a little edgy herself, and I'm not sure if its because she's commando and my hands are squeezing her arse cheeks as we dance or if something else is bothering her.

I mouth the words *'relax baby'* to her before taking her mouth in a hot pash. She takes control of the kiss, and I wish for a moment we weren't in the middle of a crowded dance floor, as thoughts of plunging my daks to the floor and pounding hard into her wet pussy fill my mind.

God, I fucking want her.

I shouldn't fucking want her but damn. Still kissing her I slide a hand from her arse to the space between us to her clit. She moans into my mouth and breaks the kiss, tipping her head back when I slip a finger inside her pussy. The club is silent for a moment, and I whisper-yell in her ear, " I want you to cum, baby."

She moans, smashing her lips to mine again in a fierce kiss that's turning us both on. I can feel her arousal dripping down her thighs as I slip another finger inside her pussy, still thumbing her clit. It drives me fucking wild when she lets go. She rips her mouth from mine, my name on her lips as she comes all over my hand.

I don't give her a moment to collect herself, don't say a word, instead, I grab her hand dragging her straight out of the club and practically sprinting to the Jag. She's following, her sandals slapping against the concrete.
Reaching the Jag I push her against the door, kissing her so hard she pants for breath.

When she breaks the kiss I finally speak, "That was so fucking hot, baby. Please come back to mine? I need to fuck you so bad."

She nods her reply, grabbing my cock in her hand for a moment before she slips away and around to her side of the car.

I unlock it, and we both slide in, eye-fucking each other as I gun it home.

Ten | Indecent Provocative Nooky

Dana

Barely a minute passes after Travis parks his Jaguar before he's dragging me upstairs to his apartment. He fumbles with the keys to unlock the door, pushing me inside and against the wall.
He pins me on the spot, his cock pressing against me and his hands either side of my head.

"Fuck Dan, baby, you turn me on girl."

Laughing, I kiss him and he moans against my lips when I pull him closer, fisting his unruly ash blonde locks in my fingers.
The kiss is hungry, fierce and sending a rush of damp to my naked core. I whimper in pleasure when he bites my lip and teases my tongue to lace it with his.
I shouldn't want him.
I know wanting him is bad for me, but Travis is like a drug, an addiction that I can't let go of.

Breathless he breaks the kiss, "God Dan, you know how to fucking kiss."
"Mmm, you too sexy," I taunt him, giving him a smirk.
"That look again huh?"

"What look, sexy?" I taunt him again, giggling.

"You know exactly what look Dana, so the only question is where am I fucking you tonight?"

I lean in, nibbling on his ear before I whisper, "Wherever you want me, sexy."

He lets out an audible groan stepping back from me with a cocky smirk on his lips. We've practically fucked on every surface in his apartment and every time the sex is off the charts good.

Sometimes I wonder if I do have feelings for him, but I always shake those thoughts away knowing he would never feel that way about me. We never talk about our past relationships, and never really talk in general unless it's dirty talk while we fuck each other senseless.

He's still looking at me, with the sinful smirk and feeling brazen I gather my dress up and pull it over my head.

I'd only worn a lacy bralette that barely covered my boobs, and it exposes my nipples through the lace. His eyes dip from my face, all the way down my practically naked body and he licks his lips before he moans and grabs me around the waist.

"You have a fucking hot as sin body, baby," he groans when he effortlessly picks me up one-handed throwing me over his shoulder. He slaps a hand against my bare arse cheek, making me hiss in pain and pleasure.

I can't help but giggle, as he carries me so confidently towards his bedroom. "Stop, Travis put me down!"

He chuckles, throwing me down on the unmade bed and crawling over me to pin me down with his still clothed body.

Running my hands up the back of his shirt, I kiss him hard and it makes my body ache for him. He breaks the kiss, looking down at me as he unbuttons his shirt. His eyes are full of lust and teasingly I grab his cock through the front of his jeans.

"Fuck Dan, baby," he groans when I fumble to undo the zipper of his jeans. He snatches my hand away, holding it with his whilst he uses his other hand to free his hard cock from the confines of his jeans. He's not wearing jocks and his cock is so hard it's pointing straight at me, ready and eager.

His eyes lock on mine, he plunges a finger inside my wet core, teasing my sweet spot when he stretches over my body to kiss me, so hungrily I moan feeling as though my peak is coming like a bullet train.

"Travis, fuck! I'm gonna come!" I scream out after breaking the kiss.

"Oh no...you fucking aren't," he bellows pulling his finger out and shoving his cock into me forcefully. My body clenches around him, drawing him deeper and deeper with every thrust.

"Mmm, Travis," I moan, wrapping my legs around his arse to push him deeper, against my g-spot. He stretches over me to kiss me again, rocking our bodies together in a fast rhythm that he mirrors with his tongue in my mouth. The bullet train of my climax is coming faster, and I can feel his cock pulsating inside my core, his release building.

"Dan, baby, I fucking love your pussy," he teases, "come for me."

On his demand, I let the bullet train dock at the station, my release humming through my body in a sudden jolt.

I feel Travis let go, deep inside me, his cock throbbing as he fills me. In a too sweet gesture, he brushes a stray hair from my cheek and kisses me softly.

"God Dana, I...," he stutters, looking down at me for a moment before he rolls off to lay next to me, kicking his jeans from his legs to the floor. I'm completely lost for words, wondering if he was about to confess his feelings for me. That would be a complete shock and way too good to be true.

Pulling the sheet up over us, I look at him a little worried, "Sexy, are you ok?"

"I'm fine, baby. But can you stay the night? Snuggle with me?"

"I guess if you want."

"Come here then, baby," he urges me stretching out his arms, "and take off that barely there bra. I want you naked in my arms."

Lifting my arms I take off the bralette, shifting on the bed until our bodies are pressed together and his arm is pulling me closer.

He kisses me suddenly taking all the air from my lungs. It makes my heart hammer in my chest and I mentally tell it to shut the hell up. All I can expect from Travis is hot as hell sex, and maybe after some cuddles like this, even if it's just a once off it feels beyond amazing.

Eleven | Coffee Slosh Down

Pulling up into a car spot on Bridge Road, Jairus is smiling at me like a giddy kid as he runs his hands over the dashboard of the jaguar.

"You were right Trav, she drives like a dream."
"Yeah, purrs like a kitten to huh?"
"You said it, man," he laughs opening the door to get out.

Following him out, I lock the doors with the key fob and step up onto the curb to head to the coffee shop.

"So tell me again why we're going out for coffee like two pansies?"
"We're not going out for coffee Trav, I said I need coffee and here we are," he laughs, practically sprinting down the footpath.

Grabbing his arm I pull him back, "Slow down man. You're like a damn ram, charging for its prey."
He laughs, "Sorry, I...I...just need to get this coffee before I meet Anni for some wedding stuff."
"Yeah? Sounds stressful?"
"Yeah, Nah, I just want everything to be perfect for her you know?"

"Not really. You know I don't do love, man. Weddings aren't on my radar. I'd have no idea what to do, how to plan a shindig like that."

We're just outside the coffee shop, and he looks at me with a sad look in his eyes.

"Anni's been planning her wedding since she was a little girl, wanting to be the princess for the day."

"Yeah, most sheilas do that, what's that got to do with you, man?"

He smiles slightly, "I don't want her to feel like a princess, but a Queen."

"You've gotta stop with this sappy shit man, you're so whipped it's scary."

Again he laughs slightly, "Whipped isn't the word, Travis. I'm absolutely in love with her. Life without Annika wouldn't be worth living, but you'd never understand."

He's dead wrong. I'd been in his boots, years ago before I met him with Meaghan. Before all the shit went down with her, I had been planning on proposing to her. I had it all planned for the ultrasound appointment when we were going to find out the gender of our baby, but I found her on the bathroom floor in a pool of blood, crying wretched uncontrollable tears.

In her hands, she had a sharp pair of scissors that she was holding against the soft skin of her belly, about to slice into herself.

I still remember the haunting scream that came from her lips when I reached out to her, and still remember the sting of her carving a line across my abs with the edge of the scissors.

Seeing my own blood as well, spurting out from the deep cuts across my skin was enough to make me black out and when I came to, it was as though nothing happened.

"Travis, Travis!" my name is being called, and a hand is on my shoulder, shaking me slightly.

"Huh? What?" I mutter looking at my best mate who's looking at me concerned as we stand outside the coffee shop.

"You ok mate? You disappeared on me there for a minute."

"Um, yeah, I'm...fine," I stammer, shaking my head to clear the foggy feeling.

"Ok, I'm just going in, you coming?"

"Nah, I'll just wait here."

He turns to the door of the coffee shop, about to head inside when a gorgeous brunette rushes out with a cup in one hand. Her head is down a little bit and she's not looking where she is going as she rushes away.

I'm about to open my mouth to speak, about to take a step aside when she bumps straight into me, sloshing her piping hot coffee down the front of my t-shirt. I hiss at the heat against my skin.

"Oh my god, I'm so sorry...I...I..." she apologises stammering when she looks up at me.

Her hand brushes the front of my t-shirt, as though she's trying to wipe the coffee away, and for a moment I want to step back from her, but at the same time pull her close to kiss her soft pink lips that she's taken between her teeth.

I'd not seen her for nearly a year, but I knew it was her. Anni's gorgeous as fuck friend Bella, and yes I should ask her for her phone number, but her touch is sending a jolt of electricity through my entire body.

The intensity of her touch and the look in her eyes is scaring the shit out of me, but I can't move or look away.

"It's ok, no need to apologise gorgeous," I tell her smirking.

"Um, thanks," she says, biting on her lip again, and fuck if that is not one of most gorgeous sights I've ever seen. She smirks at me then, "Travis, yeah?"

"Yeah, and you're Bella?"

"Yeah, and I'm also really late for work."

I run a hand through my hair, unsure of what to say when just standing next to her is making my blood hot with lust.

"At least let me grab you another coffee?"

"Nah, it's ok, I clearly don't need it since I'm such a bumbling idiot. I'll...um...see you around," she says sweetly, smiling at me and walking away before I can even say another word.

I don't get tongue-tied around any sheila, and sure as hell don't offer kind gestures like buying coffee unless I know it's a sure way to get into her knickers.

But fuck, Bella has me all knotted up like some pussy whipped idiot and I want her so fucking much.

She looked as hot as sin in jeans and a t-shirt, so without a doubt out of them her body would be delectable.

My cock is straining in the front of my jeans just thinking about seeing her curves up close.

"Travis!" Jairus bellows at me again.

"Oh hey man, I..."

He laughs at me and my lack of coherent words.

"Was that Bella?"

"Yeah, and fuck man, she does something to me."

"I can see that," he laughs, nodding towards my crotch as he takes a sip of coffee.

I don't attempt to cover up my hard-on.

"Anyway, man, I gotta go meet Anni. Thanks for taking me for a spin. I'll catch ya."

He gives me a sideways glance, looking at me like he wants to bro hug me, but doesn't want to feel my wood against his stomach. I laugh before replying, "Yeah, yeah, I'm going to go deal with this thinking about fucking Bella."

"Thinking about her is all that's going to happen if you want to live," Jairus suggests with a hint of malice, but also lightheartedly. I pat him on the back, as he turns to walk away, "Message received man," I laugh.

I head to the Jag then, sliding into the driver's seat and unbuttoning my jeans to let my cock spring out.

My cock is hard as fuck, and all she did was touch my abs through my coffee soaked t-shirt.

I've never had this reaction with anyone, it takes more than a simple touch from Dana to get me this rock hard.

I want Bella, I need Bella, and despite my best mates warnings to keep my distance I'm not going to until I've fucked her and hopefully that will stop these feelings of something more popping into my brain.

I'll just play it cool, tell my best mate all is peachy with Dana, if I can lie to him.

Twelve | Suited Up Appreciation

Jairus

Standing in the suit shop I feel so overwhelmed with all the choices. Annika's words about what kinda suit she wants me to wear are playing in my head on repeat.

She wants me to wear a skinny tie, with a white shirt and black pants. The groomsmen are not going to wear ties which I think is a little odd, but whatever my Anni wants, goes.

Travis is standing next to me, pulling a suit off the rack and glaring at it and then glaring at me like he wants to say something.

"Trav, what's bothering you? Ya giving me stink eye."

"Dana is acting weird," he replies heading towards the changing area.

"How so?" I ask, grabbing a black suit off the rack and following him.

Sliding the curtain across, he says, "She's not down."

I start to strip out of my trackies and t-shirt, laughing when I reply, raising my voice a little so he can hear through the partition, "Maybe she saw through ya shit."

"What ya mean man? He yells back.

Again, I laugh, "That you're a tool, who won't commit."

I can hear him stumble as he pulls up his daks, and he says, "She doesn't want a boyfriend, Jai."

We both step out, and looking at him I taunt, "Are you sure about that?"

Spinning around to check out his arse in the mirror he replies, "I don't know...we don't talk much...unless it's dirty talk before we fuck."

I scoff under my breath, tugging on my sleeves, "So that's your problem...you need to talk to a girl before you rip off her daks Trav."

"How the fuck are you so wise?" he taunts, laughing.

"I'm not...just found the right girl who takes my sass," I reply, looking at us both in the mirror.

"Yeah, I don't think that's Dan...she's to fucking shy when I'm not between her legs."

I laugh, admiring the suit I'm wearing more. I snake the tie around my neck, fixing it into a perfect knot.

Travis elbows me in the side, "You look ripper man, Anni will cream her pretty lace knickers seeing you in that suit."

I slap him jeering, "You disgust me!"

"You love me, brother," he taunts back looking at me as we both look in the mirrors.

I wipe an arm across my cheek, tears stinging them from his words.

"You crying man?"

I sniff back the tears, "Yeah, Nah, I...I..."

Travis lets out a slight chuckle, pulling me against his side in a bro hug.

"You're like the brother I never had Trav," I inform him, smiling.

"Likewise brother and I'm sorry for being such a dick," he says sincerely.

"All good," I reply, turning back to the mirror.

"We look good huh? Who's the other groomsman?" he asks, admiring himself.

"I don't know...haven't decided," I tell him, biting down my lip. I'm worried about finding another groomsman since my other friend bailed on me.

"You better get to it.... I'm sure Anni's on ya back."

I laugh, "Yeah just a little, she's already becoming a bridezilla and we've only been engaged for a few months."

Travis laughs back, taunting me, "Fuck it out of her. I bet she purrs when she comes too."

I scowl at him, biting down on my lip as I think about fucking my beautiful fiancé'.

"Oh yeah she does," I mutter under my breath, the words coming out of my mouth sounding like a moan.

"I fucking knew it!" he exclaims, patting me on the back.

"You better not have thought about fucking my fiancé brother," I taunt him with a hint of cheekiness in my tone.

"Well, I might have before she was your fiancé, but she's not my type you know?"

"Not ya type? Beautiful, sexy and sassy as fuck is not your type?"

He looks at me with an odd look on his face, as though he doesn't know what to say.

"Yeah Nah, I meant blonde is not my type, gorgeous, sassy and dirty are for sure."

"Right," I laugh going back behind the curtain to get changed.

Travis does the same and after when he's about to head out, whilst I pay the deposit for the suits he says, "So what's the deal for your bucks night?"

"I'll get back to you on that..." I tell him as a thousand thoughts are running through my head. I just want to head home and chill out.

"Ok...catch ya tomorrow then to smash the hawks," he tells me, opening the door of the shop to leave.

Once everything is in order I head out to the Stinger parked just outside. Getting in the driver's seat I gun it home, desperate to see Anni and tell her I have a ripper suit picked out that will meet her approval.

Thirteen | Take Her Out

Opening the door I'm shocked to find Dana standing in front of me in a short arse hot to trot halter neck dress. It brings out her eyes and I'm salivating thinking about taking it off her.

I usher her inside, "Damn baby, why wear something so hot if I'm just taking it off you?" I practically groan, looking her up and down, taking in the short blue dress, all the way down to the thongs on her dainty feet.

"Because you're not taking it off me Trav," she informs me with a hint of teasing in her voice.
"What do you mean, baby?" I ask pouting at her.
"I want you to take me out on a date, a proper date," she declares eagerly.
"You know I don't do the whole date thing, Dan," I tell her defiantly, my hands against my hips in protest.
"Yeah, well I want to Trav...I miss stuff like that."
I stare at her for a moment, contemplating what she's asking, and sigh, running a hand through my hair when I tell her, "Fine, come in...give me a minute."

Scooting down the hallway to my bedroom, I grab a discarded t-shirt from the pile on the floor, slipping my arms thru the t-shirt sleeves as I head back to Dana.

At the door, I pull on some sneakers and smile at her.

"Ready, baby?"

"Yeah," she replies meekly.

Grabbing my wallet and keys I snake an arm around her side as I lead her out of my apartment to the Jag parked on the street.

"Top, down or up baby?" I ask, pressing the key fob and smirking at her.

"Down sexy, down," she says teasingly but so sweetly it gives me a sick feeling.

What the fuck is wrong with me to be feeling that.

We slide into the Jag and I put the top down. It slides back and as I'm reversing out into the street I ask her, "So baby, where are you taking me on this date?"

She laughs softly, "I'm not taking you anywhere Travis, you're taking me out on a date."

"Fine, at least choose the tunes then," I tell her, smiling at her and reaching across to touch the bare skin of her thigh.

She cranks the stereo up as I drive off, revving the engine and slipping the gears effortlessly. Driving a manual car makes me feel invincible and I love how the Jag purrs when I slip into each gear. Dana starts singing sweetly, looking over at me, eye fucking me and it's making my cock ache.

"Fuck baby, you're turning me on, god you're so fucking gorgeous," I tell her, smirking.

We drive for a bit and thoughts crash into my mind about how Dana makes me feel. Her sweet innocence but dirty mind, turn me on so fucking bad and the way she fucks me so hard I pretty much think of her when my cock is inside any pussy.

I know this feeling isn't love, but its lust and I sometimes, just as I am now wondering if I could fall in love with Dana if we did shit like actually going out on dates.

Pulling up at the beach, near Luna park I shake away the stupid, sissy thoughts and look around, winking at Dana, asking, "So does car sex count as a date, baby?"

She shakes her head at me, getting out of the car.

My cock is painfully hard and mentally I tell it to calm down as I get out of the Jag, sauntering around to Dana's side.

"Are you up for the ghost train?" she asks when I take her hand.

It feels cold in mine and it sends an odd tingle through my body. If she's cold I want to warm her up, all over, not to mention seeing if her body has goosebumps all over it that I can kiss away.

"Are you baby? You can hang on to me anytime," I tease squeezing her hand and giving her a wink again.

"Not funny Travis, I'm no chicken," she snaps with defiance.

"Never said you were baby, but what if I am?"

She laughs at my tease. When we get to the gates, I drop her hand, stepping up to the ticket booth to pay.

From her handbag, she tries to hand me a fifty dollar note, but I brush her hand away tapping my credit card on the machine to pay.

Taking her hand again I wave the unlimited ride tickets in my other hand. She snatches hers from my grip, as we walk through the open mouth into the park.

"You didn't have to buy my ticket, Travis," she says sweetly smiling at me.

"Yeah I did, Dan. I might be a dick most of the time, but I know what being chivalrous is."

She smiles at me, before kissing my cheek. This side of her is so damn cute, her shyness is a touch endearing, but it's not exactly the type of personality I go for in a sheila.

I want someone who is just as feisty outside the bedroom as they are in the bedroom and Dana might be a firecracker in bed, but she can be an unlit match outside of it.

And making her come out of her shell, that is way too much damn effort.

After nearly three hours of rides and silliness like crazy teenagers, we're heading back to my apartment.

I'd never usually kiss her in public, or show any kind of affection towards her in public but I'd pulled her close, hugging her multiple times, and I'd held her hand the entire time, plus given her cock aching kisses on the ghost train and rollercoaster.

I could tell she was wet for me, she never could resist my kisses and I wasn't letting this night end without fucking her until she screams.

Pulling up outside my apartment, I cut the engine, reaching over to touch her thigh again.

"Baby, come in please?" I beg, locking my eyes on hers.

"Trav please, I don't think we should."

"Oh come on Dan, you've teased me all fucking arvo," I bellow, edging my hand higher, right at the edge of her lacy knickers that are soaked with want.

"Trav, I...I," she stammers, as I start to tease her with a finger through the lace.

"Come on Dan, baby, you're wet as fuck for me."

She groans, and it's clear she's battling with the temptation.
She gives in when my finger slips beneath the lace to flick her clit as I smash a kiss to her lips.
I start to pump my finger in and out of her dripping pussy, the kiss is hard and possessive, and I tease her tongue with mine in rhythm to my finger fucking of her pussy.
Panting she breaks the kiss, "Trav, fuck...um..."
"What baby? You can't tell me you're not loving that."

I pull my finger out of her pussy lifting it to my lips and closing my eyes as I lick it. I moan deeply, loving her sweet nectar.
It's so fucking delicious.

When I open my eyes she speaks again, "I um...did love it but I'm about to come all over your seats."
"Well, we can't have that. Get inside now so I can fuck you until you purr baby," I taunt, laughing.
I jump out of the car, rushing around to her door, opening it with a hand outstretched for her to take.
Taking it she stands up and I pull her up out of the car, into my arms.

She's leaning against the car when I smash a kiss against her lips, and I moan reaching up under the hem of her short dress.

Cupping her arse cheeks in my palms she whimpers in pleasure, the kiss is dirty and arousing and considering we're still outside its fucking naughty, but that makes me love it even more.

Still kissing her, I slip my fingers beneath the elastic, starting to edge them over her hot arse. Feeling her soft skin against my fingers is making my cock scream. She pulls back from the kiss, cursing, "Fuck Trav, what are you doing?"

"Taking off your soaked knickers baby," I tell her sniggering.

"I can see that Travis, but have you lost your mind? We're still outside!"

"I realise that Dana and I'm going to take them off you and you can leave them in my car to remind me of you practically coming all over my seat."

She scoffs, and I look at her with a teasing look.

"You disgust me sometimes Travis."

"You love my dirtiness, baby. Now, are you gonna take them off? Or do I have to?"

Again she scoffs, stepping aside and hoisting her skirt up a little to slip the lacy knickers down her legs.

When they reach her feet, she kicks them and her thongs off. Bending down to pick them up she holds them up to me on one finger, and I flash her a cocky smirk when I grab them from her finger, sniffing them and moaning in delight at the smell of her pussy on them.

"Fuck Dan baby, you soaked these knickers real good."

She blushes, and she looks so damn hot I can't but help kiss her again. Deepening the kiss, I throw her knickers into the open car and pull her aside so I can shut the door.

Breaking the kiss, not saying another word, I drag her inside.

We're barely inside the door when I smash a kiss to her lips backing us towards the futon couch in the middle of the room. Pushing her down on the couch, it screeches along the floorboards a little when it moves back against the wall.

"You could clean up Travis," she complains.

"I wasn't exactly expecting company tonight, baby."

"Hmm, whatever," she mumbles, when I bend down in front of her diving under the hem of her dress.

Before she can say another word I flick my tongue over her clit, and she whimpers at the pleasure.

Making her squirm in pleasure is such a fucking turn on, so I continue rolling my tongue over her clit and into her pussy, lapping up all the delectable cream she's offering me.

Licking a sheila's pussy is most definitely a turn on, the odd, sweet taste like nothing else. I grip her hips in my hands, continuing to lick her pussy and pushing her dress up to see more of her naked body.

Stopping a moment, I look up at her, smirking.

"Dan, baby, can you take this tight little dress off? I want to fuck you naked."

She huffs, sitting up a bit on the couch so I can gather the fabric up towards her boobs.

When the dress reaches her boobs, she pulls the halter neck over her head, keeping her arms up so I can pull the dress off her completely.

I rake my gaze over her naked body, not able to hide the lust that is pulsating through me.

"Damn Dan...baby...your body is hot as fuck...you fucking sexy minx not wearing a bra."

She mutters an 'mmm' in response, staring at me and I want to rip my clothes off and slam my cock inside her dripping pussy as though my life depends on it.

"Trav, you're still dressed," she says so innocently, I want to laugh, but I keep my lips sealed and stand up, my cock bulging and practically poking her in the eyes.

"Then undress me, baby," I taunt pushing my cock closer to her face.

Standing up, she stumbles a little falling into my arms. I wrap my arms around her, pulling her closer and smashing a kiss to her lips. A smile crosses my lips as I deepen the kiss.

Pulling back from the kiss she giggles and I bunch up my t-shirt, yanking it over my head before throwing it on the floor.

Her eyes take in my bare abs, her eyes locking on the new tattoo I'd gotten the week before.

Her fingers brush against it and she asks softly, "Is this new?

"Yeah, and still a little tender baby," I hiss through gritted teeth.

"Sorry," she apologises reaching down between us to undo the belt of my jeans and fumbles with the buttons and zip.

Something is definitely bothering her, as her hands are shaky and she seems like her mind is elsewhere, not focusing on the sex we're about to have.

Finally, I'm free of my jeans, only in tight red boxers that are bulging with my hard cock. Without giving her any warning I grab her hand, shoving it down the front of my boxers.

"Touch me, baby, make my cock hard so I can fuck you into next week."

Not responding, she squeezes my cock in her hand, running her dainty hand up and down my fatty which grows longer in her tight grip.

Lust is coursing through me and groaning I push my boxers down my legs.

"Mmm, Dan, baby, just like that," I grunt, glaring at her with lust.

"Mmm, you like that huh?" she taunts me smirking like a minx.

Again I grunt, kissing her and pushing her back down on the couch.

I don't give her a moment to think, instead, I shove my cock inside her pussy, moaning as it grips me and takes all of my length inside. Running my hands down her sides, I start to thrust in and out, deep, hard and wild.

"Fuck, Dan, baby! You grip my cock like a fucking animal."

Crushing my lips to hers, I kiss her fiercely, driving my cock just as fiercely into her pussy.

Her moans of pleasure when I hit her g-spot are so fucking hot, making my cock throb inside her.

She closes her eyes, her pleasure increasing.

I moan, murmuring her name, her sweet name like butter on my lips.

My release is building, my cock throbbing and to prolong fucking her I slow my thrusts, "Dan, baby, come with me."

Like my words are a switch, she starts to tremble beneath me, her climax building. My release is sudden, filling her pussy with my cum. As her release rips through her body she screams out, "Austin, oh fuck!"

I jump off the couch in shock, screeching at her, "What the fuck Dana? Who the fuck is Austin?"

She shrinks back on the couch, slapping a hand against her mouth. She's looking up at me innocently. My chest is heaving in anger and I bellow at her, "Well? Who the fuck is he?"

I damn near want to punch someone and ball my fists when she bites down on her lip a moment like she's scared I'm going to hit or slap her.

She mutters, "He's...um...he's...a...friend."

I slam my fist against the couch, "A friend! A fucking friend! Really Dana? You've got to be fucking shitting me!"

Again she stammers, "I'm...I'm...not...Travis. Austin is just a friend."

I don't believe her words, you don't call out friends names during sex, and I have a feeling I know who this Austin is but I not going to think about it. I don't want to think about anyone else fucking her.

Still looking at her I'm trying to stop myself from seething with anger when she stands up, picking up her dress from the floor. She still looks so scared, and I'm cursing myself for my reaction.

But I don't need that shit from her. We might not be together, but she's pretty much my exclusive fuck buddy, well most of the time and I kinda feel like she's cheating on me. And fuck does it hurt. It makes my thoughts rush back to Meaghan confessing about cheating on me, after her miscarriage when they told us the DNA results that absolutely shattered my already broken heart.
The child she was carrying wasn't mine and it felt like I lost it twice.

Dana is slipping her dress back on and I can't look at her, can't look her in the eyes when I scream at her in anger, "Get the fuck out Dana, you're a fucking skank."

She rushes out of my apartment, not saying a word, but it's clear she's crying as I hear her sniffles. When she shuts the door behind her I sense her looking back at me, but my head is in my hands, looking down at the floor so I can hide my tears from her.
I'm such a fucking pansy for still being this shattered over something that happened four years ago, but love is a feeling that never really leaves you.

Fourteen | Little Sweet Attire

Annika

It's been a couple weeks since Bella had dropped her bombshell on me, after I'd chosen my wedding dress. I felt stupid that I hadn't noticed the little pooch peeking out at the top of her jeans, but now I know she's pregnant it's plainly obvious.
She seemed so down, like she was hiding something else from me and her confession about being in love with Austin shocked me just as much as her pregnancy news, but there's something else.

All the talk of Austin is making me miss him so much, and I wonder if he's feeling the same way about her that she does about him.
Walking into Baby Bunting she sighs, clutching a hand against her bump, "God Anni, I don't even know where to look first."
"Yeah, baby stuff overload," I reply, looking down at my feet.
I'd been feeling really clucky the past couple of months and finding out Bella is pregnant hurt a little.
I not about to confess that though, keeping my cards close to my chest.
I follow her as she heads towards the clothes section.
Stopping in the boys section she ran a hand along the rack of tiny blue outfits.
"Bel, is something up?"

She sniffs back tears, "I um...I don't know what to do Anni."

"About what, Bel?"

"Everything," she replies looking at me, sniffing back more tears before continuing, "I'm so in love with Aust, but he barely speaks to me now and Jaxon is being all over the top like this baby is going to change things between us."

The tears have broken through now, and it hurts my heart to see my friend feeling this way.

"Oh Bel," I coo pulling her into a hug.

She sobs against my shoulder, and when a sales assistant strides over to help, and ask what's wrong I shake my head at her whilst giving her dagger eyes for being so damn rude.

Bella pulls back from my a hug a minute or so later, wiping her arm across her face, "I'm sorry Anni, these damn hormones."

I laugh and love the smile that turns up at the corner of her lips.

"You don't need to apologise Bel. I get it."

"I know. I'd be lost without you, Anni."

"I'm always here," I promise, picking up the cutest pair of overalls I've ever seen, "Have you told Austin about the baby?"

She shakes her head, "No, I want to but I'm afraid I'll confess how I feel about him."

Her eyes don't hide how anxious that is making her feel.

"Would that be a bad thing? Maybe he feels the same way and is to afraid to tell you because of Jaxon?"

Again she shakes her head, "He doesn't Anni. Trust me. I'd say it's more likely he's still in love with you."

I laugh, "Probably, but Austin never could seperate sex and love. He wants to put feelings aside but he's not capable of that."

She lets out a deep laugh then, "Yeah true, but trust me,Austin is not in love with me."

"Ok, but please tell him about the baby soon?"

"I will," she promises, turning to walk deeper in the abyss of Baby Bunting.

After about twenty minutes, she holds back a sob when she looks at me, "Anni, I....I don't think I can afford any of this right now."

I touch her arm lightly, "Let me buy you what you need. Tell me what you want, Bel...all of it and I will get it for you."

Again tears are streaming down her cheeks,

"You...you...don't...have to...do...that...for...me," she wails.

"It's the least I can do, Bel. You're practically my sister," I tell her, putting an arm around her and leading her out of the store.

In my head, I'm making plans to come back and buy her anything and everything she'll need for her baby.

I drop her back at Jaxon's and getting out of the car she says softly, "Thanks Anni, for everything. I love you."

"I love you to Bel, and don't worry about anything. I've got it all sorted."

I toot the horn, waving at her as I drive home. The overwhelming sense of being clucky is taking over again and my mind is wandering to making love to Jairus.

I hadn't told him, but I'd been missing taking my pills.

I want a baby with him so much. He would make the most wonderful father.

I can only hope it will happen soon.

Fifteen | Baby Crap Heap

Bella

After a long day at work, trying to stop myself from retching every five seconds from the overwhelming smell of bath products I stumble into Jaxon's house, tripping over a massive pile of baby stuff that's somehow appeared in the hallway.

There's at least ten outfits, a pram, a bassinet, a box that has a picture of a cot on it and a change table.
Tears well in my eyes looking at it all, my heart leaping in my chest when I think back to Anni's words about getting me everything I need.
I don't deserve a friend like her, and I wish the baby growing in me was hers instead. She deserves all the happiness in the world, and I know now she's in a happy relationship that she wants a child.
Her kids with Jairus will be stunners, no doubt, just like their parents.

Stepping around the baby stuff I'm heading to the kitchen when Jaxon pulls me aside, harshly grabbing my arm to drag me back to the hallway.

"Care to explain why this pile of baby crap got delivered earlier?"

"I...um..don't know," I stammer, shuffling my feet on the floorboards, not able to meet his eyes that are glaring at me in anger. He wouldn't believe me if I told him that I think Anni bought it for me, for us.

"What do you mean you don't know? You obviously bought all this crap!"

I'm about to protest when he bellows, "Well, you can take it all back Bella. We can't afford this right now."
"I can't," I snap, "I didn't get a receipt."
"You're shitting me?"
"No, I'm not. Plus we need this stuff. Were you expecting the baby to sleep on the floor?"
"No, but Bella, I can barely pay the rent, and buy food and you're hardly working and go spend all your money on stuff we don't need right now."
"But we do need it," I protest, tears starting to stream down my cheeks.
"Oh for fucks sake Bel, please don't cry," he says, pulling me close and kissing my hair.

I look at him, and can tell he's sorry for his outburst.
"Sorry, it's just these damn hormones."
"I'm sorry to gorgeous, but take it easy with money yeah? Just until I'm back at work."
"Ok," I reply sniffing.
"I love you Bella," he says softly, not letting me say another word as his lips crash against mine. His kiss is sweet, but even with

pregnancy hormones raging through my body his kiss doesn't
have the same effect on me it did months ago.
It's partly because I know I'm in love with Austin but also because
of seeing Travis again a month or so ago.

I hadn't said anything to Anni about bumping into him outside the
coffee shop, but touching him, his hard abs through his white
T-shirt sent shivers rushing through my body and every time I
think about touching him, or of doing something more with him I
practically soak my knickers. I know we are being partnered up for
the wedding, but I also know that nothing can happen between us
even if I want it to.

Sixteen | Giddy Girly Time

Bella

Anni looks over at me smiling as we head down Bridge Road.
"You still haven't told me where we're going, Anni?" I bleat at her.
"It's a surprise, I'm treating you to some girl time."
"You don't have to do that...you've already bought so much for me. I'm never going to be able to pay you back."

She lets out a sweet laugh, as she pulls into a car space outside 'The Jam Factory'.
"You don't have to pay me back Bel, don't be silly. I'd never expect that, ever. I have the money now and I want to spend it on you."

We get out of the car and she grabs my hand leading me inside to the shops. I find it hard to keep up, even though I'm not that big yet I still find myself walking like I've got a basketball between my legs.
She stops in front of a hair and beauty parlour, the biggest grin on her face as she drags me inside up to the counter. "Booking for two under Anni," she says to the overly made up girl behind the hightop counter.
"Great, this way please," the girl says softly.

We are led to seats near the back that have foot spas set up and all manner of nail polishes and hair products behind them.
I feel a little giddy when I sit down in one and the girl standing behind asks me 'what I'd like done to my hair'.
I've not had a haircut for months, probably over a year and I have no idea what is on trend.
I look at Anni, who is sitting back in her own chair, waving her hands about as she talks to the girl who is washing her hair. She'd cut her long blonde locks shorter recently, and sitting against her chin they frame her heart-shaped face beautifully.
As always she looks stunning and I feel a little jealous.
I can see why Jairus fell in love with her, she has a sweet prettiness that is only enhanced by her caring personality.

Her smile fades when she looks at me, "Bel, are you ok?"
"Yeah I'm fine...just don't know what to do with my hair."
"Just trim it. I like it that length and you'll be wearing it down for the wedding so shoulder length will be super pretty."
"Yeah, ok. Yours looks stunning that length Anni. It suits you. You always look so pretty."

I hang my head, not able to meet her eyes looking at me.
"Bella, you're every bit as beautiful as your name implies. And I know someone who thinks just that," she says sweetly winking at me.
"Oh...yeah, I know Jaxon thinks that, but I don't feel it."
"Not Jaxon," she says shaking her head, "and not Austin either, obviously."
"Then who, bitch! Tell me!" I laugh snorting.

She laughs when she replies, "Travis."

"As if, Anni. He's like sex on legs, just like your gorgeous fiancé'. He'd never be into me."

"Well, he is, Jai told me...but I'd stay away Bel. He may be Jai's best friend but I don't think he's boyfriend material."

"Yeah," I muse softly thinking back to bumping into Travis outside the coffee shop. Just touching him through his white cotton t-shirt had sent a rush straight to my core and left a giddy feeling in the pit of my stomach that surfaced every time I thought of him.

I'd felt it months ago when I first met him to but shrugged it off thinking there was no way he'd be single.

Seeing him again had only made my confusion surface again. Feelings always make me so mixed up, but what Travis makes me feel when he's near is different to anything I've ever felt around a guy and it scares the shit out of me.

Biting down on my lip I try to shake the thoughts of him from my head so I can enjoy the pedicure, manicure and hair treatment but getting him to leave my mind isn't easy.

I'm screwed, as being partnered up for Anni and Jai's wedding in the coming months means I'm going to be seeing a lot more of him. It's making me excited, but nervous as hell.

Seventeen | Wait For Later

The last few weeks had been pretty uneventful, aside from training and games I'd done jack shit. Thankfully I'd not been plagued by any nightmares, but I'd also not picked up in weeks, nor gone out to drink with the flies for weeks either.

I'd had wank material, as every time I thought of Bella my cock tented my daks and I'd have to jerk off thinking about fucking her to tame the beast. Still, though, I missed sex so a night out with my best mate is needed. I pick up my phone, pressing speed dial one.

He answers without it even ringing, "Hey Trav, bro, what's up?"
"Hey Jai man, I need to pick up. You down for a sesh?"
"Yeah, let me tell Anni and I'll see ya in twenty. Same stomping ground as usual?"
"Yeah, sounds ripper."

I hang up, heading to my room to locate some clean clothes. There's a mountain of laundry by the basket and I dig through it for a pair of jeans, giving them the sniff test.
They don't reek of spoof so they're good to go. I slip them on before heading to the wardrobe for a shirt. I yank a white rugby top off a coat hanger and slip it over my head before putting my feet into some Adidas sneakers.

Scooting down the hallway to the bathroom, I tousle my hair slicking it back with a handful of gel before splashing on some Creed Aventus cologne. It cost a packet, but it smells fucking divine and never fails to make a sheila fall to her knees for me.

After grabbing my wallet, phone and keys, I head downstairs, contemplating taking the Jag.
I decide jumping on the tram is a better option, as getting tanked is on the cards and I not down for risking my licence.

Fifteen minutes later I stride into Punt Road Inn, happy to see Jairus already sitting at the bar, sipping on a beer.
Pulling up a stool beside him, we clap shake our hands in greeting, and he asks, "What's ya poison tonight?"
"Something strong," I tell him, signalling the barman.
I order a whiskey, and down it the second it's on the bar top in front of me.
"Whoah, Trav, bro. Take it easy," Jairus warns as I signal for another.
"I need a few stiff ones to pick up tonight, bro, so lay off."
He laughs, as I take the second whiskey a little slower.
"Who's got you so wound up, man?" he asks.
"Do you even need to ask that?"
He shakes his head, "You've been jacking off thinking about Bella again, huh?"
"Damn straight I have. I can't stop thinking about her."
"So things didn't go well with Dana last time you hooked up?"
"No!" I screech, "She screamed out some other cunts name when she came."
"What? You're fucking shitting me! Who was it?"

"I don't remember, started with A I think."

"Fuck, man, that's shit. But...um..."

"What Jai man? You're acting loopy."

"Just um...stay away from Bella."

"Why?" I ask, looking down at my cock that has sprung to attention just from the mention of her name.

"It's not a good time. Just wait until the wedding."

"God, fuck Jai! That's months away. My fucking cock will fall off by then if I don't get to fuck her."

"Just trust me, Travis, please. I can't tell you any more than that."

His tone is pleading, and I contemplate his warning, a thousand thoughts running through my head of why he'd be warning me away. Nothing makes sense and nothing other than being with her is going to make this longing feeling go away.

I down the whiskey before asking Jairus, "Want another beer?"

"Yeah sure, you want one?"

"Yeah, a Carlton Draught."

He orders one for us both, taking a big swig of his before he glares at me.

"What you staring me down for now?"

"Nothing," he laughs.

I laugh when I reply, "I'll heed your warning, but after the wedding, well fair game, I'll fucking have her screaming my damn name."

"Whatever you say Trav, man."

"Yes, whatever I say, whoever I want I'll have.

Just like I was now going to have the sheila down the bar who keeps giving me bedroom eyes.

I beckon her over with a finger and she saunters over with a seductive hip wiggle.

"Hey gorgeous," I greet her when she's standing next to us.

"Hi, I'm Alyssa," she coos, licking her lips.

"Nice to meet you, Alyssa, I'm Travis and this is Jairus."

"I know who you both are, and I..."

She's tongue-tied like they all are. She's not blonde, so she's fair game. Jai stands up, putting his empty beer bottle down on the bar top.

He gives me dagger eyes when he says, "Trav man, I'm going to call it night, and head home to Anni."

"Ok, bro. Catch ya at training."

He replies quickly, "Yeah catch ya then, and nice to meet you, Alyssa."

"You too Jairus." She smiles at him as he heads out.

I turn to look at her, and she has a cheeky smirk on her face. "I'd thought he'd never leave."

I chuckle slightly, thinking that she definitely has balls for being so forward. I'm not able to reply before she's kissing me and cupping my fatty in her hand. I kiss her back and inwardly thank my lucky stars that I have a bed buddy for the night.

Eighteen | Guilty Dirty Escapades

After some rather hot kisses, and nearly being dakked on the dance floor by Alyssa we are back at my apartment. She's something fierce, pashing me and barely saying a word or coming up for air.

It's hot as hell, but I also just want to fuck her and get it over with. Once inside my apartment with our lips still locked together, I lead her to the futon, pushing her body down against it.
She whimpers against my lips and I break the kiss, giving her a smirk as I yank my rugby top over my head.
Her fingers run down my abs, and I try not to shrink back from her touch. It's not doing anything to my body, not making my cock spring to attention at all, which is so not like me.

She's glaring at me, like she's tongue tied so I tell her, "Take ya dress off. I only fuck naked."
She giggles, sitting up on the futon and pulling her pink dress over her head. Her bra is lacy, hiding her smallish perky tits and her pussy is bare, not hidden beneath the scrap of fabric she's calling underwear.
I glare at her, a silent take them off stare, as I take off my jeans and slip my boxers down my legs. Her eyes shift to my cock, which isn't even hard yet and her mouth falls open.
Her obvious shock and her lack of words are pissing me off.

"Well, suck it, bitch," I roar, edging closer to her on the couch.

Still she doesn't speak, instead takes my cock into her mouth. Her tongue runs over the tip, licking the slit, making circles over my shaft that's now beginning to grow. It feels so good, so fucking good to have a sheila giving me a gobby, but I'd rather sink myself inside her bare pussy.

Yanking on her ponytail I pull her off my cock, and she smiles at my forcefulness. She's responding to my being rough, so I continue by gripping her thighs and spreading them open. Bending down I lick her from the bottom of her pink pussy up to her clit. She's so fucking wet, and I'm desperate to fuck her, desperate to release all the pent up emotions that have been racing through my mind.

"Are you clean?" I ask.

"Yes," she hisses, "fuck me please Travis."

I groan, loving when a sheila begs. I don't give her another minute, before I hoist her legs up in the air, slamming my cock into her tight pussy. My thrusts are hard and I watch our bodies slamming against each other.

"Oh yes, oh yes," she screams out, finally finding her voice.

I just want her to shut up, so I can imagine that I'm fucking Bella instead. It's the only way I'm going to get off from this mediocre sex. Alyssa seems to be enjoying it so I pound into her harder, balls deep.

"Oh fuck Travis," she calls out, biting down on her lip as her climax starts to build.

Her pussy is tensing up, squeezing my cock. "Fuck, I'm coming!" She moans, spasming and shivering as her climax rushes through her body. She looks at me with an odd look that I can't read. Withdrawing my cock I fist it, closing my eyes to not look at Alyssa so I can think of Bella.

Mere moments later my hot cum spurts out all over Alyssa's belly. Opening my eyes she's smiling and runs her fingers over the white mess I've left on her stomach. She licks them clean and moans an appreciative hum that stirs up a sick feeling in my stomach. Standing up I grab my boxers, slipping them up my legs before I pick up her underwear and practically throw it at her.

Her eyes are still on me as she dresses, a stupid smile on her face like she's just had the best sex of her life and I feel so guilty for the way I just treated her like an object. The guilt is also plaguing me that I thought about Bella whilst fucking someone else.

God do I want her.
And damn do I want to fuck her, to cream inside her pussy.

Alyssa is now dressed, so with a hand on her back, I usher her towards the front door.
"Thanks for tonight Travis," she coos, kissing my cheek.
I'm not sure what to say, I've never had a sheila thank me for sex before.

"You're welcome, Alyssa."
I curse myself for my stupid response. And before I say something even more stupid I kiss her to make it seem like I had a good night as well.

"Can I give you my number?" she asks when she breaks the kiss.

"Yeah, sure," I reply grabbing a pen from the table by the door. Holding out my palm to her with the pen in the other hand, she grabs it and writes her number and name in scrawly handwriting.

"There," she says as she draws a little heart next to it, "call me."
"I will," I promise with fake sincerity as I open the door.
She steps out, blowing me a kiss as she heads down the stairs.

Shutting the door behind me, I spit on my hand and scrub off her name as I head down the hallway to my bedroom.
I may have fucked someone and found release but I'm still so wound up I'm wishing I'd just jerked off instead.
The only way forward now is to keep my cock in my pants, unless it has the chance to be inside Bella's pussy, it's going to be celibate.

Nineteen | Bump Love Celebrations

Annika

Bella is giving me an incredulous look and seems pissed off that I've picked her up, bought her back to the penthouse without as much as a hello.
She's tapping her foot impatiently when we step into the elevator, "Anni, please tell me what's going on?" she begs me when the doors slide open on level thirteen.

Shaking my head I walk out of the elevator, backing towards the door. My key card is in my back pocket, it clicks open the door and I depress the handle.
Opening the door, Bella follows me inside, her mouth dropping open when she sees her co-workers, Dana and some other friends gathered in the middle of the penthouse.

"Surprise!" they all chorus. Bella is grinning from ear to ear, with silent tears dripping down her cheeks.
She elbows me, before hugging me, "You shouldn't have Anni. You've already done enough."
"Don't be a silly billy, you deserve it."

Pulling back from my hug she looks around the room at the banner with the words 'Happy Baby Shower' on it hanging over the dining table, which has a spread of party food and a massive cake in the centre. On the top is a bathtub with a pregnant woman in it.

"It's all so beautiful, the cake, Anni, wow...that must have cost a fortune."
"Not telling," I giggle, ushering her towards a seat.

The girls start chatting, fussing over her and her grin is so sweet. It does hurt a bit though, as a part of me wishes it was me being doted on. Excusing myself to go to the bathroom, I head down the hallway to our room, where Jairus is just getting out of the shower to head out so us girls can have the house to ourselves for the arvo.

Standing in the doorframe of the ensuite I look him up and down, "Mmm," I moan, biting my lip.
"Hey sweetheart, why aren't you out there with the girls?"
"I missed you, and I just needed a moment."
"Aww, sweetheart I know. But our time will come soon," he says stepping towards me and kissing my forehead.
"I know, baby, but it doesn't make it any easier, especially when my period is always late."
"Yeah, how about we make an appointment to see a doctor? Make sure nothing is wrong?"

I don't reply, instead stretch up on my tiptoes to kiss him. He wraps his arms around me, pulling me closer as he deepens the kiss and I melt into him.

Breaking the kiss, he brushes a stray hair from the side of my face, "It will be ok, sweetheart. I promise."

Smiling, this time I reply, "I know. I love you Jairus, you'll be an incredible Dad."

"I hope so, and I love you too, Annika."

My heart skips hearing him say my full name. I never get tired of hearing it from his lips, in his deep sexy, but sweet voice.

"I should get back out there. Are you heading out soon?"

"Yeah, I'll be leaving in ten, after I get dressed."

"Ok, baby. Don't miss me too much," I jeer leaving the ensuite. He slaps my arse playfully as I leave and I giggle, fighting the temptation to run back into his arms to fuck him.

Back in the dining room, the girls are eating and chatting. It warms my heart to see how happy Bella looks. I know I've done the right thing in planning this, even though Elyse and her Mum couldn't be here, its still a wonderful celebration of love.

Twenty | Boys Not Allowed

Jairus

Walking out of the bedroom, I catch Anni for a moment giving her a sweet kiss, "Text me when you're done, sweetheart."
"I will baby. Have fun."

I blow her a kiss from the door, opening it as I'm shrugging my jacket on. I'm shocked to find Travis standing in front of me, his fist up as though he was about to knock on the door.
His fist instead meets my chest, as I screech, "Trav, man, what the fuck are you doing here?"
"You weren't replying to my damn text, so I'm here."
"Right, so um," I start, trying to close the door without him sidestepping to see what's happening.
"What's going on bro? Can't I come in?"
"No, Anni is um...naked," I lie, biting on my lip and still trying to shut the door. Travis is pushing me aside, laughing, "Yeah right. Just let me take a squiz at your digs."

This time I push him out into the hallway, and the door slams behind me.
"Later man, I'm just heading out."
"Fine, your driving," he snaps.

He follows me into the elevator, and down to the parking garage level. We slide into the Stinger and I start the engine, driving out to head to the local shopping strip.

Travis is pouting at me, and I can't help but laugh.
"Why are you pouting like a chick?"
"Am not. You could have just let me squiz at ya digs, man."
"Why are you being such a damn kid, Travis?"
"Just got a lot on my mind."
"You know I'm here for you, no matter what. You don't have to act like a damn kid."
"I know, I'm sorry. I just feel guilty about something."

I pull into a car space outside my favourite coffee shop, cutting the engine and getting out. Travis gets out and looks at me like I'm mad.

"Seriously, coffee again?"
"It's barely past breakfast Travis."
He laughs, "It's five o'clock somewhere."
I nod, "True, but now, here, it's not so I'm getting coffee and if you want to spill whats got a stick up your arse you'll join me."

In a huff, he follows me inside and reluctantly orders a latte after I order my extra-strong cappuccino. I'd been feeling extra tired lately, practically full lethargy like my legs and arms were dead weight attached to my body.
I hadn't mentioned anything to Anni, I didn't want her to worry. And I hadn't told coach or Travis either. It's probably nothing so there isn't any reason to tell anyone.

We sit down at the back of the coffee shop to wait for our orders. Travis is still pouting, so I ask, "Seriously what's up with you?"

"I fucking want her man. And you're cock blocking me big time for some fucked up reason."

Our coffees arrive, and I stir sugar into mine, looking away from Travis's glare.

"I wouldn't tell you to stay away if I didn't have a reason to."

"That's great Jai, but you haven't exactly told me what this reason is."

I take a big sip of my coffee, staring at him over the rim of the mug. "And I'm not going to Travis. It's not my place to tell you."

"What's that supposed to mean?" he snaps at me.

I'm not liking this obsessive side that Bella is bringing out in him. It's possessive and it worries me that he might not be telling me something about his previous relationships or lack thereof.

"If Bella wants everyone to know, that's her call. But you need to trust me and give her some space. That's if you really want her as much as you say you do."

He doesn't reply, instead, gulps down his coffee. I quickly finish mine, and we both stand up heading out just as I get a text from Anni.

Twenty-One | Pretty Knocked Up

Jairus is still giving me dagger eyes, death stares all the way back to the penthouse and it's stirring up a sick feeling in my gut.
I can't possibly think of any reason why I need to keep my distance from Bella. His refusal to tell me is making anger rise up in my chest and it's a wonder I haven't knocked him out for how much his refusal is infuriating me.

"Are you coming up?" he asks me after he parks the car.
"So I'm allowed to check out your digs now?" I taunt, emphasising 'allowed'.

"Yeah, Anni text me that everything was done."
"Right, done," I mutter under my breath when we step into the elevator.
The silence is absolutely fucking deafening but I have nothing to say to my best mate, nothing good to say at least.
The elevator doors slide open and their penthouse front door is wide open. Anni is hugging Bella goodbye and seeing us arrive they step apart.
Looking at Bella, I'm sure I'm hallucinating.
Her belly is round, she's clearly and very obviously pregnant.
We're all standing in the hallway, looking at each other, waiting for someone to say something or move.
I turn to look at Jairus, "What the fuck? Why didn't you tell me?"

Jairus balls his fist, shrugging, "Because I knew you'd react like a fucking tool Travis."

"That's fucking low Jai," I snap turning to Bella who is looking at the floor like she wants it to swallow her whole.

No one else is going to tell me anything so I ask her directly, "Bella who knocked you up?"

She looks up at me, whimpering slightly as she bites down on her lip. Words spill from her mouth that make absolutely no fucking sense, just screaming and yelling, a bunch of expletives and then she bursts into hysterical tears.

I'd only asked her a question and she's falling apart at the fucking seams.

Anni's giving me dagger eyes as she puts an arm around Bella's shoulders and leads her back inside the penthouse.

Jai stops me from following, and again I ask, "Why didn't you just fucking tell me?"

He scowls at me and says, "I didn't tell you because I thought it was best to stay away from her and her being pregnant is why."

"That's a fucking lame reason, man. I'm an idiot sometimes when it comes to sheila's but I'm not an arsehole. And I fucking like her."

"Then just give her some space to deal with being pregnant. Keep ya cock in your pants."

"God fuck Jairus, do you really think that low of me...." I start, continuing before he can get a word in, "No...um..don't fucking answer that. I'll see you at training. Obviously, I'm not welcome here."

I turn towards the elevator, ignoring him when he tries to apologise. He's my best mate, but him thinking so low of me that he didn't want to tell me Bella was pregnant seriously hurts.
I'd never intentionally hurt any sheila and certainly not Bella.

As I head to the pub, I can't get over how fucking pretty, and how fucking sexy she looks pregnant.
It doesn't make me want her any less, in fact, I kind of want her more, to care for her like I wish I could have done with Meaghan.

Twenty-Two | Booty Call Denied

The pub is dead, hardly a hot sheila in sight and after a few drinks, I'm buzzed, but not feeling the vibe in the pub at all. I gulp down the rest of my beer, slamming it down the bar before I head home.

Driving after I've had a few is a risk but I'm not going to leave the Jag in South Yarra overnight. My cock is still aching for release, and I can't get Bella out of my mind.
Fucking her whilst she's pregnant would be wrong, but I still want her so bad. She's fucking gorgeous, beautiful actually and I can tell she feels the same as I do.
Her brown eyes glow when she looks at me, and it's fucking crazy but it makes my heart skip.

But love is bullshit, just a chemical reaction in your brain.
What I need is a damn good fucking from the one who makes all thoughts go out the window of my apartment.
Pulling up into my car space, I cut the engine getting out of the Jag as soon as the engine stops.

From my pocket, I fish out my phone, typing a text to Dana as I bound up the stairs.

Travis: Dan, baby…. I need you…you down?

Unlocking my front door, I undress awkwardly, still holding my phone in my hand. I kick my jeans across the room and throw my shirt on the futon. My cock is aching, tenting the front of my jocks. Sitting down I grab it out of the confines of my jocks, starting to jerk off when Dana replies.

Dana: no Travis I'm not down
Travis: why baby? My cock is hard for you

Holding my phone face down towards my body, I open the camera, taking a photo with my cock out of my jocks, sticking my tongue out in a dirty tease. I send it to her.

Travis: see baby? Come play with me
Dana: seriously Travis….a dick pic

I can picture her scoffing as she types the words.

Travis: you love it, baby….come over and play with it
Dana: I can't….
Travis: why baby?
Dana: I've started seeing someone

I don't reply then. If she's got a boyfriend, she's not going to fuck me again and it practically makes my cock shrivel up in protest. I know it's the guy she called out the last time we fucked, but I can't remember his name and frankly, I don't care. I'm only pissed that he has taken my go to booty call away. Absentmindedly I start to scroll through my phone contacts to find a random hookup.

My finger slips, accidentally dialling Sofia. I quickly press end, but I'm sure it's probably too late. I hope like hell it didn't connect on her end. She knows where I live and she's honestly the last person I want to see after our awkward sex in the change rooms, but I have a feeling that she's going to be down for another session. I'm just not sure if I am.

Twenty-Three | Down For It

After a quick shower, I'm in the kitchen attempting to cook something to eat other than baked beans on toast, which had been my go to lately.
Ordering in was too much hassle and meant I had to wear more than just jocks whilst I waited for it to be delivered. And in my own home, generally, even jocks were an optional garment.
I much prefer my birthday suit and when alone in my own house walking around naked is my right.

Tonight though I have jocks on and I'm pottering around the kitchen stirring the tinned soup on the stove. It's probably not edible but it was the only thing in my cupboard that looks half decent.

I'm startled by a knock on the door, not expecting anyone but panic flares in my chest when I think of my dialling Sofia earlier.
Grabbing my shirt from the futon I shrug it on, not bothering to do up the buttons as I head to the door.
Opening the door, my panic is confirmed as Sofia is standing in front of me, wearing an oversized coat and high heels that accentuate her calves and make her a lot taller than the petite woman I'd fucked in the shower in a moment of weakness.
She's smiling at me sweetly, and I look her up and down noticing she's dyed her hair brown.

It suits her, making her hazel eyes stand out against her olive skin. I think about kicking her out, but she holds up a plastic bag of takeaway that smells absolutely fucking delicious, the smell of fried rice and some other delectable Chinese food hits my nostrils.

"Hi Mr Travis," she coos at me, smirking, "I bought you dinner."

How can I fucking resist a good feed of Chinese?

"Um hi Sofia, it smells delicious but what are you doing here?"
"You call me Mr Travis. I come for you." She bites down on her lip, looking down at my crotch and the image of her coming for me in the shower last time I fucked her flashes in my mind.
She's here, she's bought food and she's clearly down for another fuck.
Who am I to deny a woman who wants to come?

From the kitchen, I hear my shitty soup bubbling over. Racing back to it I don't say another word to Sofia, but I hear the door close as she enters my space.
I turn the stove off, turning to find her leaning on the bench. She's put the food down and is smirking at me, a glint in her eyes like she's not hungry for food at all.

"Mr Travis, you ok?" she asks standing up and pushing her chest out.
"I'm fine Sofia," I tell her heading around to the other side of the bench, "are you wearing anything under this coat?"

She shakes her head at me, "No, Mr Travis," she purrs seductively, making my cock tremble a little in my jocks.

"That's naughty Sofia," I taunt her.

"I naughty girl for you, Mr Travis," she coos, parking her arse on the stool behind her.

The way she continues to call me Mr Travis is so odd, but kinda sexy at the same time. She's looking at me now with a seductive 'I want to eat you' look, her hazel eyes drinking me in.

I lock my eyes on hers, leaning on the bench with one hand and invading her personal space by stepping closer to her, so my lips are only a breath away from hers.

"Why did you really come over, Sofia?" I ask, almost kissing her but waiting for her answer.

"To fuck you, Mr Travis," she replies huskily grabbing at the front of her coat and fumbling with the buttons a little before she opens it wide. She wasn't lying, she's completely stark naked underneath. Completely bare, her nipples hard telling me she's ready and is probably dripping her desire onto the leather stool.

"Mmm, fuck Sofia," I growl, crushing my lips to hers in a hungry kiss. She moans against my lips, her hands running down my back to cup my arse cheeks in her small palms. They slip beneath my jocks and she slides them down so they fall off, down my legs to the floor. Breaking the kiss then, she looks at my cock appreciatively, licking her lips as she stands sliding the chair back a little. She smirks, taking off the coat completely and throwing it aside.

I can't think when she then drops to crouch on the floor, and slowly edges my cock into her mouth, between her pretty full lips that still have a touch of red lipstick on them.

Her hair moves, bouncing brown curls, as she sucks my cock, taking it in and out of her mouth and circling the tip, down the length with teasing licks. God, does it feel good to be getting a gobby, but I need to fuck her.

Snatching a handful of her hair, I yank her off my cock and she fists it, looking up at me puzzled.

"Stand up, Sofia. Sit on the stool and spread your legs for me," I instruct her. She obeys, standing up slowly with her eyes locked on mine the whole time. Sitting back on the stool she clamps her legs together. Stepping closer to her, gripping her thighs I pull them apart.

"Sofia, I told you to spread your legs, girl," I taunt. She smirks and then giggles.

Without another word, I plunge my cock into her bare pussy. A hiss escapes her lips at the sudden contact and I pull out, teasing her clit with the tip of my cock. "Mr Travis, please fuck me," she begs, fisting my hair and pulling me down to crush her lips against mine again.

She kisses like a hungry animal, who wants to fucking devour me whole. As the kiss intensifies, her tongue lacing with mine my cock fills her again and I thrust into her harder, faster, so much so she tears her mouth from mine and moans so loudly I swear the neighbours will hear her.

Her pussy is so damn wet my cock slips out, and I pull her into my arms for another hungry kiss, wrapping my arms around her tiny waist to turn our bodies around. I sit back on the stool then, putting her on my lap.

In her ear I whisper huskily, "Ride my cock, Sofia."
She doesn't say a word, just sits on my cock, sliding herself up and down whilst she leans back using the bench as a support for her back and clutching it with her hand. Her other hand has a death grip on my thigh, but her slick pussy bouncing up and down on my cock is making all thoughts of pain fly out of my brain. She leans back for a kiss, moaning appreciative hums against my lips.

When she breaks the kiss, her mouth opens in an 'o' as her climax starts to build. Her pussy is clenching around my cock, and I want to tell her to get off me before I blow my load inside her, but when her whole body twitches as she screams out her release with a bellowing, "Oh fuck!" I thrust my crotch hard into her, my cum filling her.

She looks at me with a smirk as she climbs off, and puts a finger into her pussy, bringing it up to her lips to lick it. "Mmm, Mr Travis, you cream in me."
"I'm so sorry Sofia," I reply, biting my lip worriedly.
"No be sorry Mr Travis. I on birth control pills."
"Oh right," I mutter standing up and picking up my jocks.
"I go now Mr Travis," she says scuffling her high heels on the floorboards as she saunters over to grab her coat. She won't even look at me, and I feel so bad, so guilty for thinking with my fucking cock again.

"Sofia, are you ok? I'm sorry we didn't even eat the dinner."

"I fine Mr Travis. I eat already. The food for you."

"Well, thanks, for the food and the sex. I needed both, gorgeous."

She blushes a deep crimson, as she slips her coat back on. "I here anytime for you, Mr Travis," she purrs at me with that naughty seductive tone her accent laces her voice with.

"Thanks Sofia, but you deserve better."

"Yes, Mr Travis. But you do too."

I shake my head at her, "I don't know about that Sofia, but thanks." I smile and she tightens the tie around her waist as she steps closer to me. A sweet smile on the corner of her lips makes me curse myself more for what I've just done. Her soft lips kiss my cheek and she turns to walk out of my apartment, not looking back at me or saying another word.

After she's gone I stare at the food still on my bench. I'm such a tool, I basically just paid her for the food with sex. I can't eat it, even though my stomach is screaming for some decent food. I pick up the bag, depress my foot on the pedal of the bin at the end of the bench and dump the food straight into the garbage.

Brushing my hands together, I head down the hallway to shower, to wash all traces of Sofia from my body, to hopefully wash away the guilt so I don't feel like a fucking idiot.

Twenty-Four | Old Man Chat

Waking up after I'd stupidly fucked Sofia again I feel out of sorts, not myself and completely foggy. It makes me think of Dad and I feel damn guilty for not seeing him in forever, especially with Tessa now living overseas.

Yes, I'm happy for my sister, glad she met her strapping English lad Ryan, but I miss her so damn much.

I have the money to go see her, but not the time and it makes it even harder to not let the guilt get to me.

I know she feels guilty too, but her life isn't here anymore with Mum gone and Dad in the nursing home.

I make a promise to myself to call her as soon as I can if I can get my head around the damn time difference.

Getting out of bed, I pull some jeans and a t-shirt, not giving them the sniff test so I hope they don't reek. In the bathroom, I spray some deodorant under my arms and tousle my hair with water to settle it down.

I rush out of the apartment then, grabbing my phone, wallet and keys in a hurry.

Just the thought of seeing Dad after way too long is making my heart pound, but I know I also need to tell him about Meaghan. His stroke and subsequent dementia after Mum's passing made opening up to him hard, as I could never be sure if he'd remember the next day. I dread the day he doesn't even remember I'm his son. It will seriously break my fucking heart.

Twenty minutes later, I'm at the nursing home, being led to his room by a sweet older nurse who gives me an odd look that is kinda creepy considering she's probably twice my age.

Dad is watching TV when I softly knock on his door. He looks up through the glass and a twisted smile spreads over his face.
The stroke had affected his muscle use on his left side, so his smile now is a little lopsided.
When I enter the room he flicks off the TV, and says slowly, "Ah my boy...I...i've mm...missed you."

Pressing a kiss to his forehead, I reply, "Hey Dad, i've missed you to. Sorry, it's been so long."
"I...I...www...watch you, my boy."
"Glad to hear it Dad," I reply smiling as I pull up the chair to the side of the bed.
"I'm...p..p..p..proud o..of...you," he says with his lopsided smile again.
"Thanks, Dad, but I need to tell you something," I tell him taking his hand and holding it in mine.
He doesn't stutter this time, "Like what son?"

I gulp, swallowing the lump that's crept up into my throat from deep within my guts. He squeezes my hand comfortingly, urging me to speak.
"About what really happened with Meaghan."

His eyebrows raise in a questioning look and again I gulp before I let the words start to roll off my tongue, "She attacked me, Dad, with a knife when I didn't help her with dinner and she was pregnant with our baby and I....' I stop a moment, feeling tears stinging my eyes. He lifts a hand to my cheek, brushing his thumb under my eyes, "Ohhh, d...ddear boy," he says.

I continue, sniffing hard, "I was going to ask her to marry me, but I found her bleeding on the bathroom floor and she sliced my skin so bad I passed out. And when the knife attack happened after that I called the police."

"Dd...did...tthey hhelp?" he asks, a scowl on his face.

"No, painted me as the perpetrator, not the victim. She got off on it Dad, she was sick. I woke up with her in the bed one morning when I hadn't realised she'd stayed over and I panicked and she ended up pulling a gun on me."

"Oh Tttravis," he whimpers, seeing the pain in my eyes, the tears that are dripping down my cheeks.

"I still have nightmares about that. I can't escape her even with the restraining order."

Dad says clearly, "She sounds like a batty bitch."

Even though what I've just told him is horrible, he as always manages to find humour in the situation and I laugh softly when I reply, "Beyond batty, but I can't move on Dad. She haunts me, even though she's not a part of my life anymore."

"You... ww...will son," he stutters, taking a deep breath to finish his sentence clearer, "when the right woman comes along."

I don't respond to that, as thoughts of someone flash into my mind. I want her to be the right woman, but she's not mine to have and it hurts like a slap. Standing up I kiss his forehead again, "I gotta go, Dad. Get in a run before training. I'll come back soon, I promise. I love you and I'll pass on your love to Tess."

"I...lll love yyou, sson," he replies, cupping my cheeks and giving me a peck on the lips, "tttell Tteess to ccall mme."

"I will, bye Dad," I add as I leave.

I hadn't gone for a run in ages, and it wasn't easy to run in jeans but heading across to the park hearing my feet pounding against the concrete is definitely clearing my head, just not taking away the thoughts of Dad's words about the right woman.

Twenty-Five | Shot Him Down

Bella

Work had been kicking my butt, constant chundering and a basketball sized bump protruding from my front didn't exactly go well with so many product displays.

I spent most of my day apologising to my colleagues and customers as I knocked bath bombs and soaps to the floor, that I couldn't then bend down to pick up.

It was utterly fucking exhausting and heading back to Jaxon's on the tram, my eyes are fighting a battle to keep open. I don't want to fall asleep, afraid I'll miss my stop and end up who knows where. Baby brain is killing me, I've done so many stupid things like putting my phone in the fridge and turning up a day early for a shift.

After twenty minutes of fighting to keep my eyes open on the tram, I jump off, very unladylike, nearly tripping up on the curb.

I fall against a warm body, looking up to find Jaxon. He wraps his arms around me, hugging me close, "Hey sexy," he drawls at me, "You ok?"

"Um hi, Jax. How did you know I was on this tram?"

"You text me that you were leaving work. Don't you remember?"

I shake my head, laughing, "No, damn baby brain."

"All good, let's go home. I've got a surprise for you."

My heart lurches in my chest, my palms feeling sweaty when he takes my hand with his as we walk the short distance from the tram stop to his house. I don't like how he says home. I still feel like it's his home and not mine.

I haven't officially moved in with him, the thought of giving up my freedom after Jace kicked me out is too damn scary. They're brothers after all, and even though Jax is practically the polar opposite of his twin, I'm sure the apple doesn't really fall far from the tree.

Arriving back at his house, ten minutes later, he has a wide smile on his face that's got my stomach in knots about what his surprise is going to be. He opens the door, ushering me inside with a hand on the small of my back and the moment I step inside my heart drops to the floor.

Flowers, roses of all things, are scattered across the floor and a banner is strung over the kitchen bench which has a bottle of non-alcoholic champagne and two champagne flutes on it.

Jaxon has crossed the room in front of me and dropped to his knees. My heart is pounding in my chest, anxiety rising from my gut. I don't want this, I really fucking don't want this.

He reaches into his pocket, plucking out a small velvet box and holding it up to me. I want to turn and run out the door but my fucking feet are glued to the floor.

Opening the box, a sparkling tiny diamond ring glints when the light from the skylight catches it.

"Bella, I know this ring isn't much, but it's all I could afford. It is no measure of how much I love you. So my beautiful, will you marry me?"

Um fuck no Jaxon, how, what, why would you even ask?

I look at him, scowling, "Stand up Jax, please."

I'm completely tongue-tied and when he stands up, shutting the box the look on his face shatters me.
"I'm sorry Jaxon, but I can't marry you."
He's sobbing,"Why not Bel?"
"Because....I...I...don't love you as much as you love me."
My words are lies, I don't love Jaxon at all, not even a little bit.
He's possibly my baby's father but my heart doesn't beat for him.
It still beats for Austin.
Jaxon looks angry now, he throws the box on the floor seething at me, "For fuck's sake Bella, we're having a fucking kid together and I...I..."

I bite down on my lip, feeling the baby kick me hard. Words are tumbling in my head, but I can't get my tongue to cooperate.
Tears sting my eyes.
I feel like such a bitch, but marrying Jaxon is so far from the right thing. I never trust my gut instincts, but my baby kicking my belly repeatedly is sure telling me something, so this time I listen.

"I really am sorry Jaxon, but you don't want to marry me."

He's still seething, his chest rising and falling rapidly. But he also has tears in his eyes and his voice comes out muffled, "Yes I do want to Bella, I love you, so fucking much and I want to be a father to our baby."

He puts a hand on my belly, but I brush it away, "Don't Jax, don't touch me, please."
"Why the fuck not Bella?"
"Because...because...arr...fuck it!" I scream out, finally getting my feet to cooperate.

Without saying anything else I trudge out of his apartment.
Once outside, I sprint back towards the tram stop. My breath is catching in my chest, tears starting to stream down my cheeks, but still I run, waving down the tram and jumping on.
Collapsing into a seat I take breaths to calm myself, but the tears are still cascading down my cheeks, now coming out in sobs.

~~

Still crying wretched tears, I stumble off the tram and into the now very familiar apartment building. I don't know why I'm here, but I need to escape for a while and don't want to go to see Austin.
Once in the elevator I depress the button for level thirteen and wait to get to the top floor, hoping that no one else comes in.
When I reach their front door I tap on it lightly, and Anni opens it. She takes one look at me, not saying a word as she wraps me in a hug and pulls me inside as she closes the door behind us with a little kick.

Pulling back from the hug, I see they have Travis and some other teammates and cheer squad members, including Dana over for dinner.

I look at Anni apologetically, "Oh Anni, I'm sorry. I'll go...I didn't um..."

She puts her hands on my shoulders, "It's fine Bel. What happened?"

I'm about to tell her, when Travis stands up from the table, heading to the kitchen with a whiskey glass in hand.

He locks eyes with me, and my heart skips.

The look in his eyes is giving me butterflies, but they're all tangled up in my belly.

"You ok?" he asks coming over.

I bite down on my lip, muffling my sobs and for some reason, I want to tell him and not Anni.

Twenty-Six | Hold The Girl

Bella's eyes lock on mine when I stand up to grab Jairus a drink. Her eyes are red from crying and her mascara is dripping down her cheeks.

Still, she looks utterly mesmerising and seeing her so obviously upset is stirring up an odd feeling in my stomach.

If some fucker has done something to hurt her, or her baby I want to punch his fucking lights out.

She looks between me and Annika, opening and closing her mouth about to say something.

Striding over, after putting the glass on the bench I ask, "You ok?" Her chest rises and falls pushing her tits up in her sweetheart neck t-shirt. I want to look away, feeling like a dirty tool for looking at her tits in the current situation, but I can't.

She mutters something incoherent and I look at Anni who shrugs her shoulders at me. Her sobs increase, and she bites down on her lip looking at me with some crazy mix of fear and lust in her eyes. I know I shouldn't but seeing her falling apart again, is breaking me and I pull her into my arms.

Her tears fall onto my cotton shirt and I'm awkwardly standing there in the middle of the hallway holding her. Her sobs are wails now, muffled words against my chest and I look at Anni again, whispering, "What the fuck am I supposed to do?"

"I don't know Travis, I don't even know what's wrong. Just comfort her."

Right. Just comfort her. How the fuck do I do that?

Holding Bella still, I press a kiss to her hair, rubbing my hand up and down her back. She lets out a whimper and it makes my cock stir.

Fuck she turns me on.

She looks up at me a moment, and says, "He proposed."
"Who?" I ask, wondering one why she'd be so upset and two wanting to tell whoever this fucker is to back the fuck off because I want her to be mine.
I'm shaken from those thoughts, when she meekly says, "Jaxon."
"Right, and you said?"
"No. I don't love him." Her words are meek and she rests her head back against my chest again. I'm glad I don't have to fight some other fucker for her.

It seems like hours pass, my chin resting on her head whilst I hold her in my arms, when Jai hobbles over on his crutches.
He nudges me, forcing me to let go of Bella. She moans as I let her go and fuck is that not a mega turn on.
I want to hear her moaning just like that with my cock buried inside her.

"Take her home Trav," Jairus tells me.
I give him a cocky grin, and reply, "Yeah, i'll take her home."

Jai scowls at me and says, "Her home Travis...not yours."

Again I flash the cocky grin, "Yeah, yeah," I agree.

I'm a douche, and damn horny from the last fifteen minutes holding Bella in my arms, but I'm still a gentleman and I'm not going to take advantage of her.

I take Bella to the jag, asking her, "Do you want to go home?" as we slide in.

Doing up her seatbelt, she shakes her head, she says, "No. Can we go back to yours?"

We're heading down St Kilda Road now and I fight with my body, mentally telling my cock to calm down when I reply, "I really don't think that's a good idea Bella. I can pay for a motel room for you for the night if you want?"

Again she shakes her head, looking across at me. I can see the lust in her eyes and I hope for a moment that she begs me to pay for a room for the night, and asks me to stay with her, to make her feel better with kisses all over her body.

Of course she doesn't say that, instead she licks her lips, still locking her eyes with mine, "You don't have to. I'll just go back to Jaxon's."

"Ok, if you're sure," I reply, touching her thigh.

I can feel her skin heat at my touch, even through the fabric of her leggings. Snatching it back, I ask for directions and she tells me to head towards Hawthorn, rattling off an address that seems pretty easy to find on Camberwell Road.

Driving is pretty difficult, as I can't help but stare at her.

I don't honestly know why I'm so attracted to her, but when she's vulnerable she is so fucking beautiful.

To cut the tension inside the Jag, I decide to make small talk. "So who is ya baby daddy?"

"I don't know," she replies frowning.

"Shit that sucks, it's not Jaxon?"

"It could be, but I don't think so."

"Oh well, I hope it works out," I reply pulling up to the house, hoping it's the right address.

Her hand grabs the door latch, and she looks at me one last time, "Thanks for the ride."

Mmm fuck, I want her to ride me. And I want to pull her back into the car and kiss her but she gets out and I watch her go inside. A light comes on and she gets wrapped into a hug, so it's clear she's forgiven for her rejection.

As I drive away I curse myself for not giving her my fucking phone number but also for the wicked thoughts that are plaguing my mind about her.

I want Bella, any way i can have her and right fucking now.

Twenty-Seven | Eyes See Double

Jairus

Watching Anni driving down the city streets towards the Epworth, I can't help but smile, staring at her. She's singing along to a song on the radio, tapping her fingers on the steering wheel to the beat.

She catches me staring, giggling when she asks, "What, baby?"
"Nothing. Just admiring you, sweetheart."
She blushes, replying, "What's to admire? I'm already so fat."
"You're not fat sweetheart. I'm seriously in awe of you, how you're handling being pregnant and you look stunning."
"Whatever you say, baby."
I laugh at her, squeezing her thigh, "Are you excited to see our baby?"
"Yeah, but nervous to."
"Me too, sweetheart, but I'm sure everything's fine."

She nods, pulling into the Epworth underground carpark.

Ten minutes later we're in the elevator heading up to the maternity part of the hospital. Only bringing in one crutch I'm hobbling along, and leaning on Anni as we head down the hallways. We could have gone to our local GP, but as soon as Anni found out she was pregnant she wanted all her prenatal care and birth to be at the hospital that had helped me with my Meningitis. She was also planning on completing her make up practical in the new year so it would be great for her to be so close in case something goes wrong.

Stepping up to the nurses' station, she greets the nurse as though she's an old friend and I know we've made the right decision in coming here.

We take a seat in the waiting area, and she nervously bounces her knees. I put a hand on her thigh to calm her down, "Sweetheart, look at me."

Her gaze turns to look at me, her eyes fearful. "It will be fine, Anni. There's nothing to worry about. We're going to see our baby."

"I know, Jai, but I'm so worried because I haven't been as sick the past week or so."

"Don't stress about that, sweetheart. It probably doesn't mean anything."

I brush her hair out of her face and press a kiss to her forehead, then one to the tip of her nose and then I gently kiss her lips. She murmurs softly, before breaking the kiss and smiling sweetly.

"I love you Jairus," she says, her smile growing wider.

"I love you, Annika," I tell her taking her hand in mine when her name is called from a doorway down the hallway a little.

She stands up, helping me grab my crutch to follow her. Her hand is still laced with mine and she squeezes it hard, giving me another sweet smile. My heart swells with love for her, and I'm mega excited to see our baby on the screen, even if it's just a blip.

Stepping into the room, Anni's mouth drops open when she sees who the attending doctor is.

"Um hi, Doctor Thompson. Are you doing my ultrasound?"
"Yes, Annika. When I heard you were coming in, I pulled a few strings. I'm so excited for you both." He smiles and nods at me.
"Thanks," Anni replies meekly. Doctor Thompson laughs a deep chuckle.
"I knew there was something going on with you both when you were admitted the first time Jairus."

It's my turn to laugh, "Yeah, I finally got her to admit how she feels about me."
"I'm glad to hear it, you've got a good one here and your baby will be lucky to have such great parents," he says looking at Anni before he continues, "Annika, if you could step behind the screen there and take off your pants and underwear, we can get started. There's a gown to put on."

Anni follows his instruction and steps out a moment later in an ugly blue hospital gown. "Great, now hop up on the bed, and put your knees up, legs open for me."

I'm leaning against the wall, as I can't sit down in the chair without falling to the floor. The room is so silent, I can hear Anni's breathing, so I hobble over and take her hand.
Doctor Thompson is holding the ultrasound wand in his hand, ready to start when he says, "So Annika, how far along do you think you might be?"

He slowly starts to insert the wand, and a blurry image comes up on the screen. "Um, I'm not sure, maybe six weeks or eight, I don't know." She turns her gaze to me for a moment, and I shrug. Doctor Thompson is glaring at the screen and it's making me nervous, my heart is pounding hard, and I'm sure Anni's is pounding harder.

"Well, I'm thinking you're right about being around six weeks, but..." his voice trails off and I almost shriek out, so worried he's about to give us bad news.

"But what?" Anni bleats out, biting her lip between her teeth in nervousness.

Doctor Thompson points at the screen, at the two blobs, "You're not having one baby."

"Sorry what?" Anni asks, squeezing my hand.

"Annika, you're pregnant with twins."

"Really? Twins?" Her voice raises in excitement.

"Yes, here is baby one," he points to the screen again, "and baby two."

Her gaze turns to mine, "Oh my god Jai! Twins!" she shrieks excitedly.

"I know sweetheart, so amazing," I reply, bringing her hand to my lips to kiss.

Doctor Thompson finishes up, doing all the measurements and says, "So congratulations. We'll schedule a follow-up ultrasound for around week eight to ten, but until then Anni continue taking your prenatal and rest up."

Sitting up she says, "Should I be worried that my symptoms have settled down a bit?"

"No, don't worry about that. Everything looks on track for the moment."

"Ok, thank you," she replies, jumping down off the bed.

"No worries, Annika. Take your time getting changed and I'll leave some pictures at the nurses' station for you. I'll see you when you come in for your next ultrasound."

"Thank you, Doctor Thompson." She smiles at him as he leaves.

Once he closes the door behind him, she giggles pushing me against the wall.

"Twins, Jai! We're having twins!"

"I know, sweetheart. I'm so excited!"

I grab her arse through the gap in the back of the gown and crush my lips against hers in a hot kiss. Again she murmurs before pulling back.

"Wait, you dirty boy. We can celebrate at home."

"Oh yeah!" I bellow, spanking her arse cheekily when she slips behind the screen to get dressed.

~~

Having a cast up to my knee made everything damn difficult, especially sex. Since I'd broken my ankle, we'd pretty much only had sex a couple of times. It was partly because Anni was afraid of hurting the baby but also because most positions were awkward with a leg I can barely move.

Ever since we left the hospital, Anni has been teasing me, smirking at me and giving me bedroom eyes. My cock is throbbing in my shorts and there is no way I'm not fucking her now. Stepping into the elevator, she leans against the railing, beckoning me closer with a finger.

Hobbling over I fall against her, and before I can even think she smashes her lips to mine in a hot lust filled kiss full of pent up emotions.

The elevator dinging out our level forces us apart, and I groan, "Damn sweetheart, god I want to fuck you right now."

She giggles, snaking an arm around my waist and I put mine around her shoulder so we can hobble out of the elevator.
I lean against the wall at the front door whilst Anni opens it and I hop inside watching her as she starts stripping her clothes off, not caring where they land on the floor.

Stopping halfway across the room, all she has on is her cheeky black g-string.
"Mmm, sweetheart, fuck you're beautiful," I drawl out, biting down on my lip as I hobble towards her.
Wrapping my arms around her I pull her close, kissing her lips hard. She moans against my lips, and I slide a hand down to cup her arse cheek in my palm, giving it a little squeeze. She whimpers breaking the kiss.

"Jai, baby, please, I want to fuck you," she begs with a seductive tone in her voice.
"Mmm, sweetheart, I want to fuck you too, but it's so damn awkward right now."

"I have an idea, baby," she says winking at me and taking a step back closer to the dining room table. She pulls out a chair, turning it around so the back is against the table. She saunters back over to me, pulling me gently over to the chair.

"Sit down, open your legs, and take off your shorts," she instructs me. And damn if her authoritative tone is not the sexiest fucking thing ever.

I shuffle towards the chair, yanking down my shorts and boxers down to my ankles before I plonk my arse down.

Anni stands in front of me then, between my legs, and slips her g-string down her legs, leaning forward and kissing me as it drops to her ankles.

"Mmm, fuck sweetheart, I can smell how wet you are," I tease, reaching forward and inserting a finger into her aroused core.

She whimpers at the contact, again bending forward and kissing me again. My cock is rock hard and i'm so ready to be inside her. Breaking the kiss, I bring her finger to my lips to taste her.

She's looking at me like she wants to devour me, her eyes darting from my face down to my hard cock. Yanking my t-shirt off, I taunt her, "Are you gonna suck my cock, sweetheart?"

She nods, falling to her knees between my legs. Her pretty pink lips take my cock in, and she starts licking it up and down in teasing strokes. It feels fucking incredible and I want to blow my load into her mouth, but more so inside her wet core.

I fist her hair a little, pulling her off my cock, and turning her gaze to mine. "Sweetheart, that felt incredible but I really want to fuck you."

She doesn't say a word, instead, she turns around leaning back a little and puts a leg either side of me. Grabbing my cock at the base in her hand she holds it steady and impales herself on me. "Oh...oh...fuck!" she moans out as she starts to bounce up and down on my length.

"God, Annika, fuck!" I call out, wrapping my arms around her, running my hands over her gorgeous baby bump and up to her tits. Her moans have turned to pants, so loud and so damn hot.

To tease her, I reach down to flick her clit and she screams out an illicit moan of carnal pleasure, leaning back against me so her tit is right at my lips. Still teasing her clit, I bite her nipple, licking it with my tongue.

"Oh Jai, fuck, fuck fuck!" she screams, still riding my cock like she can't get enough. It is seriously amazing, watching, feeling her reactions. Panting, still with her back pressed against my chest she says breathlessly, "Kiss me Jai, please kisss me."

Moaning I give in, taking her lips with mine for an intense kiss that makes my whole body throb with need.

I can feel her body tensing up, her climax building. She breaks the kiss, panting and presses her body down on mine again, a delicious moan escaping her lips as the wave of her intense orgasm hits her. Her grip on my cock as she rides it out makes me fill her up with a load so big its dripping down her leg when she climbs off my lap.

"Damn, sweetheart, that was fucking incredible."

"I know, baby," she replies, bending down to kiss me again, "I'm ready for bed. That was so exhausting, but in the best way possible."

"Oh yeah," I reply, taking her hand so she can help pull me up.

Wrapping my arms around her we stagger towards the bedroom and I whisper in her ear, "I love you Annika and I can think of a lot more dirty positions to hear you moan like that again."
She pulls me down to the bed, "Sounds like heaven, baby. I love you too, Jairus."

Laying down beside her, I kiss her, thinking about how I'll never get tired of hearing her say she loves me.

Twenty-Eight | Dressing Bumps Pretty

Bella

Anni is dragging me into the dress shop, a cheeky grin on her face. I'm not really in the mood to go shopping for the bridesmaids' dresses, but Anni insisted as their wedding is fast approaching.

She'd been stressing as it was, so I start to pull dresses off the rack holding them against my bump.
I'm still worried about the possibility of being pregnant for the wedding, but I shake the thoughts aside pulling a pink flowing gown off the rack.

"What about this one?" I suggest, swishing from side to side.
Anni shakes her head, scowling at me. "I don't like pink. Will clash with Amanda's hair."
"Yeah I didn't think of that," I reply, frowning as I put the dress back. Anni hasn't told me much about the wedding party, other than my being partnered with Travis 'hotter than sin' Banes and I'm a little curious.
"So who is Amanda partnered with?"
"I don't know. Some other friend of Jai's."
"You didn't ask Austin when you saw him the other day?"

She pulls a red dress off the rack, touching the silk fabric but turning her lips up at the corner when she puts it back and replies, "I wanted to, but I thought it would be awkward enough just having him there."

"Yeah, I guess. I'm really glad you asked him to come though Anni. You would have regretted it if you didn't."

"Yeah, I know. I'm so glad we made up. I missed him heaps. Are things over between you guys?"

"Oh yeah, that ship sailed. He's so damn confused about how he feels right now. Wouldn't surprise me if he ends up with Kaden."

She gapes at me like I've let a big secret slip.

"That's not going to happen Bel."

"Why? What do you know that I don't?"

"He's seeing Dana. Things are pretty serious between them."

"What?" I spit out shaking my head.

"Yeah, he's going to bring her to the wedding."

"Well, there you go. But fuck...I totally didn't see that coming at all."

I laugh and smile at Anni when she pulls an ankle length flowing emerald green dress off the rack. It has spaghetti straps and a rolled neckline.

She holds it up, eyeing it and I can tell it's the one by the sparkle in her eyes.

"Do you like this one?"

"Love it, let me try it on."

Taking it from her I slip behind the change-rooms curtain.

"Bel, I'm really worried my dress isn't going to fit. The wedding is only a month or so away and the twins are already making me feel like a goddamn elephant."

With the dress on, I slide the curtain across, wondering if I heard her right. "Did you just say, twins?"

"Yeah, didn't I tell you?"

"No, you didn't, bitch," I reply laughing and touching a hand to her rounded belly.

"Well, yeah we found out before I saw Austin."

"That's great Anni. Imagine if they're both boys and look just like their gorgeous Dad."

"Yeah, I know. I can't believe I'm having twins Bel. What if my dress doesn't fit by the wedding?"

"It will Anni," I soothe, swishing the dress I'm wearing from side to side, "what you think?"

"It's perfect Bella. It fits over your baby bump, just in case you're still pregnant."

"I damn hope not, you think you feel like an elephant now, just you wait, girl!" I tease smiling at her as I slip behind the curtain to get changed again.

She pays for my dress, and orders one in for Amanda. Linking arms, we practically skip out of the shop.

"Ready to get some shoes?" She asks, a giddy smile on her face.
"You bet," I reply, as we head down Bridge Road.

I want to talk to her more about how bad things are going with Jaxon, but she's so damn happy I don't want to bring her down, so instead, I follow her into Novo and keep my trap shut as we look at all the pretty shoes.

Twenty-Nine | Dirty Leg Up

Annika

It seems as though all Jai and I have done lately is go to doctors appointments, some pregnancy-related and others for his ankle. Thankfully the time has finally come for him to get his cast off. I didn't have to worry about him wearing it for the wedding, but I'm still worried about his recovery. He'd been doing extra physiotherapy with his good ankle, so he could get back to playing quicker. I could tell he was feeling down in the dumps about sitting on the sidelines for so long and he's definitely itching to get out on the field again.

Hobbling behind me, on his crutches I hold the door open and he follows me in, kissing my forehead when I close the door, "Thanks, sweetheart."
I smile at him, helping him sit down in the waiting area, "No worries, baby. I'll just check in."

Watching him as I head up to the reception desk, I can see he's worried and he's bouncing his good leg nervously. After speaking to the receptionist I sit down in the chair next to him, taking his hand. "Baby, what's wrong?"
His gaze turns to mine, "I'm worried it hasn't healed. I can't deal with this cast anymore."

"It will be fine, baby. You've had it on for six weeks and it was only a mild fracture."

"I hope so, sweetheart. I can't marry you with a fucking leg cast on."

I'm about to reply when his name is called to go through for his x-ray. Helping him up, he leans into my side, hopping on one foot down the hallway. He follows the technician into the x-ray room and I blow him a kiss that he catches and presses against his leg for good luck.

The x-ray is super quick, and he comes out with a wide smile.

"All good, baby?"

"Yep, need to go into the other room and wait for the nurse."

Handing him the crutches for the last time, we head into the other room to wait for a nurse.

A sweet older nurse comes in, "So Jairus, you ready to be rid of this?"

"Most definitely, my leg is so damn itchy."

"That happens," she replies, getting to work on removing the cast. It's off in barely a minute and Jairus sighs in relief, raking his nails down his leg in sweet relief.

"Feel good, baby?"

"Oh yeah," he laughs.

"You'll have to wear a moon boot for two weeks and do some daily exercises to help get it back in shape."

Of course he asks, "And when can I get back to playing footy?"

The nurse laughs, "When you're longer wearing the moon boot, but some light training will be fine for the next two weeks and you

can resume all other daily things, as long as you're wearing the moon boot when out."
"Ok sounds good." He smiles, lifting his leg as the nurse straps the moon boot on.

Helping him stand up, he waves to the nurse as we leave.
"How's it feel baby?"
"So much better. I'm glad to have the cast off, and when we get home I'm having my wicked way with you."
"Oh really?" I tease, taking his hand as we head to the car.

As soon as we're in the penthouse elevator Jairus pushes my butt against the railing, taking my mouth in a heated kiss. I could kiss him forever and never tire of the way he makes me feel.
Being pregnant makes the desire burn in me harder and as soon as the elevator opens I drag Jairus out, straight inside our penthouse.

He laughs, "Wait, sweetheart, wait...let me take this wretched thing off, so I can fuck you properly."
I giggle, watching him wrestle with the straps on the moon boot. Finally getting it off, he throws it across the room limping over to me and grabbing me around the waist. Locking his eyes on mine, he goads me, "So sexy pregnant fiancé, what can I do to make you moan like you did the other day?"

Breaking free from his arms, I lift my dress over my head, exposing my crop top bra and lacy knickers. Lust flares in Jairus' eyes, "Mmm, sweetheart, you're fucking beautiful."

"You're handsome, baby, so get undressed and meet me in the bedroom."

Frantically he starts stripping from his clothes, dropping them as he follows me down the hallway to our bedroom.

He stops, standing in the door jamb completely naked and his dick is already hard.

Winking at him I slip my knickers down my legs and lift the crop top over my head, throwing them both aside.

Climbing onto the bed I beckon him to me with a finger, smirking at him cheekily.

"You're so fucking sexy, sweetheart," he teases, limping into the room and kneeling on the edge of the bed.

He grabs my hips pulling me down closer to the edge. I love him taking control in the bedroom. The thought once before we got together scared the shit out of me, but when Jairus takes control during sex he is so gentle the love he has for me shines through.

"Spread your legs, sweetheart. I need to taste you, so damn bad."

I obey, scissoring my legs open and lying back on the mountain of throw pillows on our bed. Before I can even say anything or pull him up to kiss me, he's in between my legs flicking his tongue over my clit. It feels divine, and I'm just about at the precipice just from that, when his tongue glides down, deep inside me and as he licks all my arousal he moans.

He stops a moment, looking up at me, "Damn sweetheart, you taste like heaven."

I blush, cupping his cheeks in my palms, "Kiss me, baby, I wanna taste too."

"Fuck, Annika, that's dirty sweetheart," he taunts before edging up over me and kissing me hard, sliding his dick straight inside my folds.

I hiss in pleasure as he fills me, rocking in and out as our tongues start to lace together. Sex with Jairus always feels amazing, whether it's hot dirty fucking or sweet, slow making love kinda sex. He was made for me, and as my mind wanders to marrying him soon, I feel my climax building. Taking my mouth from his I whisper, "Jai, I love you."
"I love you too, Anni, and I love making you come. So let go for me, sweetheart."

He pushes deeper into me, I wrap my legs around his firm arse, pulling him in and feel his release spill inside me as I hit my peak. Softly he presses a kiss to my lips, not making a move to slip out of my body, "Annika, god I love when we come together."
"Me too, Jairus."

Pulling out, he lies down next to me, smiling.
I toss the throw pillows aside and slip under the covers. He does the same, before pulling me against his side and kissing my forehead.

Thirty | Crushing On Red

Annika

It feels so strange to be back at a game, waiting eagerly to watch Jairus play. He'd been giddy for weeks now that his ankle is all healed and the physio gave him the all clear to play.

It's a big game at Marvel stadium against Carlton and being back in the cheer squad is just as exciting. I couldn't wear my guernsey though, as my belly has swelled, partly bloating and the twins starting to grow heaps.

Dana is standing next to me, preparing for the runout and I can't help but smile. Since I'd started coming to games, we'd become quite good friends and I could see why Austin seemed taken with her. I really wanted him to be happy, and Dana seemed perfect for him. A little shy at first, but once you got to know her, she was a lot like me, no inhibitions and definitely not shy.

Ten minutes or so later when the game is starting, and Travis bumps into the barrier in front of us she presses a hand to his chest to push him away laughing. He gives her a playful wink and kicks the ball back onto the field. It kind of rubs me up the wrong way, considering my last conversation with Austin, so I elbow her in the side and she looks across at me.

"Hey Dan, I saw Austin the other day."

"Yeah?" she replies, not meeting my eyes and blushing.

"Yeah, and we're friends again. He mentioned you."

"Yeah, what did he say?"

"That he really likes you. And for Austin to say that things must be getting serious between you."

She gets all shy, looking down and shuffling her feet on the concrete. Her blush increases.

"It seems like you really like him too?"

"Yeah,I do. But I want to take things slow. Things with Travis were always so intense and I don't want to get myself mixed up with feelings for someone who doesn't feel the same."

"Yeah I get that, I'm just glad you've found someone. And trust me, Austin wouldn't have told me that if he wasn't feeling something for you. He doesn't do feelings lightly."

Dana laughs, "I know, but I still need to take things slow."

"What about Travis? Nothing going on still with you guys?"

"Oh no, I told him to back off. All he wants is sex, and I'm not giving into him anymore."

"Yeah, I sometimes don't get why Jai and him are such good mates. They seem so different."

She laughs, "Yeah, not really. Jairus was a lot different before he met you. Like pre Sara days I mean."

"Right," I laugh, "I don't wanna know. You don't still have feelings for him to do you?" I ask, a knot in my stomach.

"No, I'm not crushing on your gorgeous fiancé anymore. He's so in love with you Annika," she replies as speak of the gorgeous devil he bumps into the barrier.

He takes a deep breath.

"You ok baby?"

"Yep, ripper, sweetheart," he replies giving me a quick kiss, that gets displayed on the big screen with the word 'score' underneath it.

"I love you, Jai the man!" I call out as he kicks the ball back in, straight to Travis who sends it via handball to another player who then kicks it straight back to Jairus.

He then runs in, kicking it straight through for an easy goal and the roar around the ground erupts, the words 'Jai the man!' flashing up on the big screen.

I feel giddy.

My man is back in the game!

Thirty-One | For My Queen

Jairus

Getting the text from my high school mate Luke that he couldn't be a groomsman for our wedding really fucking shitted me and had me panicking.

I knew Anni was planning on having Bella and Austin's sister Amanda as her bridesmaids.

Without a doubt, Travis was my best man, which was good in some ways but bad in the fact he was going to be partnered with Bella and there was some weird thing going on between them. I'd told him to keep his distance, but I didn't doubt for a second that would make him more eager.

He'd made his intentions clear on more than one occasion, but I had to keep shutting him down for now.

Anni is still lazing in bed, barely getting any sleep with her pregnancy and also her nursing degree being quite intense in the last few months. She never complained, but I knew the lack of sleep and demands of uni were getting to her. Leaving her in bed, I head into the kitchen to make a coffee and some pancakes for breakfast.

Her phone is charging on the bench, and I know I shouldn't look but there's a message on the screen from Austin.

Before grabbing a coffee cup, I pick up her phone and laugh that my trusting Anni doesn't have a lock on her phone.

I open the message, thankful it appears he doesn't have an iPhone so he won't see the message has been read.

Clicking on his name I grab his number, typing it one-handed into my phone at the same time.

From behind me, I hear Anni shuffling her feet as she enters the kitchen yawning.

"Morning, baby, what are you hiding?"

"Nothing, sweetheart," I reply, turning around after putting her phone back on the bench behind me.

"Who are you texting this early?" she asks me, rubbing her bloodshot eyes and taking another gasp of air in an even bigger yawn.

"Just Travis," I lie, my gut turning that I'm lying to her, but I have to keep this a secret.

I want it to be a surprise on our wedding day. "Do you want some pancakes for breakfast?"

"Oh yes please, baby. I'm sure I've got baby elephants growing inside me," she says giggling, crossing the kitchen towards me. She wraps her arms around me, trying to pull me close but her belly gets in the way and she has to stretch up on her tiptoes to kiss me.

"Sit down, sweetheart, breakfast will be ready in a jiffy."

She waddles over to the table and when her back is turned, I grab out the things for pancakes, getting started quickly before quickly typing a text to Austin on my phone.

Jairus: hi Austin, it's Jairus. Got your number from Anni's phone. Hope that's ok. I need to ask you something.

His reply is almost immediate, and I nearly drop my phone when it vibrates in my palm.

Austin: hi Jairus. All good. What's up?

Quickly I pour some batter into the pan, checking that Anni is still engulfed in her book.

Jairus: I wanna ask if you'll be in our wedding? Prolly partnered with your sister.
Austin: I'd love to man. Does Anni know?
Jairus: Nah... I want to keep it a secret for the big day
Austin: no worries...all in...let me know when I can get fitted for a suit and shit
Jairus: will do...thanks man I owe you
Austin: I'd do anything for her
Jairus: I know...me to...she's my queen

I put my phone down and flip the nearly overcooked pancake onto a plate, grabbing the butter, sugar and strawberry jam to carry them over to the table.
Putting them down, I smile at Anni, "For you my queen."
She giggles again, "I don't feel like a queen. And wouldn't that mean you're a king?"
I smirk at her, "Oh sweetheart, I'll be your king any day. Eat up, yeah? We have a big day with the final viewing of the venue happening."

She doesn't reply, just forks a large bite of pancake into her mouth. She laughs and pats her belly, looking down at it and talking to the twins.

I can't make out what she's saying as I head back to the kitchen to cook myself a pancake, but just the thought of her talking to the twins whilst they're growing inside her makes my heart swell with love, for them and for her, my queen.

Thirty-Two | Pre Wedding Jitters

Time just seems to be slipping away, as though it was literally March yesterday and I'd just helped Jairus plan his proposal to Annika.

Now we're only a month and bit away from their big day and before the Bachelor and Bachelorette parties they've decided to treat us all to a Pre-wedding get together.

I not exactly sure where it's at, so getting dressed is a challenge.

Rummaging through my drawers, I pull on some dark, almost black denim jeans and a white Mossimo T-shirt.

Heading out the door I shrug my arms into my black leather jacket, shoving my phone, keys and wallet into my jean pockets.

Since I'm the best man, and I know everyone is going to be at this shindig including Bella, I decide that getting tanked is not a good idea so I slip into the Jag and gun it to the restaurant as I'm already fashionably late.

I park outside the restaurant in Clifton Hill. It's pretty quiet for a Saturday night, so when entering I wonder if Jairus booked out the whole place.

Glancing around the room I see familiar faces at a large table at the back. There are other diners on tables near the front.

Wandering over, Anni catches my eye, waving me over.

Reaching her, I give her a kiss on the cheek, admiring the maxi dress that stretches over her figure and baby bump.

"Hey Travis, Thanks for coming. Take a seat, I'll get Jai to get you a drink."

"Of course. You look amazing. How are the twins treating you?"

"I feel like I'm growing baby elephants," she laughs when Jairus steps up behind her, wrapping his arms around her waist and kissing her hair.

"Hey, man. Glad you finally made it. Don't be late on my wedding day yeah?"

"I won't be," I jeer, looking around the table as I take a seat, "who's the redhead sheila?"

"Amanda; Austin's older sister. She's my other bridesmaid," Anni replies, sitting down next to me, with Jairus on the other side.

Jairus leans on the table, turning to look at me, "Don't even think about it Travis," he warns like he can read my mind.

Yes, I was thinking she's gorgeous, long wavy red hair and a soft sweet smile, but my gaze doesn't stay on her long when I look to Bella sitting next to her.

I swear my heart fucking jumps in my chest when she sees me and her pink lips curve up into a sexy smile. She's sitting next to a guy I don't know, not her boyfriend I met last time.

He tries to grab her hand she has resting on the table but she snatches away.

There's an odd distance between them if they're together and he keeps giving sideways glances to Amanda, smiling when she locks eyes with him.

I can see Bella is holding back her emotions, trying to hide the fact she looks like she's about to break down into tears.

I just want to rush to the other side of the table, to pull her aside and comfort her like last time she was upset and fell into my arms.

But instead, I strap myself into the seat, daring myself to not move unless I need to piss.

Food comes to the table, garlic bread and some kind of antipasto platters with salami, sun-dried tomatoes, roasted peppers and olives. Taking a bit of everything I look towards the other end of the table watching Dana. She's feeding some redhead guy a piece of salami and giggling with the biggest smirk on her face.
He bites down on it, eating it before kissing her.
It turns my fucking gut, that she's so cosy in public with someone else. I'm confused, she was never like that with me and I wonder what he's giving her that I never could.

After about twenty minutes, I've downed two lemon, lime and bitters and ordered a chicken parmigiana to eat.
The food is yet to arrive, and the drinks have gone straight through, so I'm bursting for a leak.
A few minutes earlier Bella had gotten up from the table. She still looked upset. I knew I shouldn't but I get up to follow her to see if she's ok.

Making out like I'm heading to the dunny to drain my snake I head down the narrow hallway near the kitchen. I'm not looking where I'm going and bump straight into someone.

"Sorry," I mutter looking down at the person who is practically falling at my feet, stumbling on her high heels.
My eyes blink furiously, locking with hers as I help her stand up.
"Bella, You ok, sunshine?"

She looks at me a little confused, but replies, "Um yeah I'm...fine... I just..."

Her breathing is shallow, "Just stand here a minute, catch ya breath," I suggest, backing us closer to the wall.

She leans against it, taking deep breaths in and out.

Wrapping my arms around her, she leans into me and sighs against my chest. I hope she can't hear my heart beating a hundred miles a fucking hour.

Holding her close does something weird to me.

I take in slow calming breaths, inhaling how she smells, fruity like apple shampoo and some intoxicating perfume that courses through my nostrils warming my whole body.

God, I fucking want her.

I can't help but wonder what her pussy smells like, tastes like and what her mouth tastes like.

I'm about to find out, about to pull her pretty pink lips to mine when I'm kicked in the belly and I have to pull back from our embrace.

"Someone doesn't want me hugging you," I laugh.

"Yeah, sorry...I um better be getting back...thanks, Travis."

She smiles sweetly at me and kisses my cheek before walking away.

Looking down at my crotch, I notice I have a fucking hard on.

I probably poked her baby with it. I adjust the front of my daks, cursing myself for cracking a fat from just holding her close.

No sheila has ever had that effect on me before and fuck I want her, but I can't.

For one she's pregnant and two, Jai would fucking kill me, especially if I broke her heart, which for me is usually inevitable.

Thirty-Three | Girls Go Out

Bella

Anni had told me to spare no expense for her Hen's day out.
I organised everything, asked her for the cash and she handed it
over without batting an eyelid.
It upset me a little that she was able to throw money around like it
meant nothing. Clearly, Jairus earns a lot more than I thought in
his football career and I hate that I'm super jealous that my best
girlfriend snagged such a hottie, but also a hella rich one.

Arriving at her penthouse in the maxi taxi, with Dana, Amanda
and some of the other cheer squad girls piled in with me I drag
her in and laugh at the grin on her face and the excited giggles she
can't help but let escape from her lips.
She kisses us all on the cheeks, before taking a seat next to me.

"So Bel, where are you taking me?" she asks, not able to hide her
excitement.
"It's a surprise Anni, but firstly it's out of the city a bit."
"Oh, should I be worried?"
"Of course not dufus, but I hope you're hungry."
"Ooo," she laughs elbowing me, "you know these babies make me
forever hungry."
We chat with the other girls about the big day, about how
pregnancy is treating us both and before we know it we're pulling

up outside the Yule Chocolate Factory. Anni's eyes go wide, her mouth falling open in surprise.

"Bella! Oh my God! I always wanted to come here. How did you know?"
"I know how much you love your chocolate."

We head inside, linking arms. At the front door, a bubbly girl greets us, "You must be the Hen's party?"
"Yes, we are!" Anni choruses as I slip the 'Bride to be' sash over her.
"Great, well get yourselves organised and your official guide will take you all through for a chocolate factory tour in ten."
"Sweet," Anni replies, rubbing her baby bump and licking her lips. I laugh at her, slipping my 'Maid of Honour' sash on and handing Amanda her 'Bridesmaid' one.
Minutes later our guide arrives, introducing himself. He's geeky cute and seems just as sweet as the chocolate.
It's clear he's a little taken aback by having to take a group of gorgeous girls for a tour, but he's meticulous and explains everything so well, leading us through the small factory.

Anni gulps down a couple of extra helpings of each sample, absolutely loving the first part of her day out. It makes me so happy to see her excited, but still, jealousy is in the pit of my stomach.
After the tour we sit down in the restaurant, looking over the menu of chocolate delights. They all sound delectable, but I'm feeling a little nauseous so let the girls order and head to the bathroom.

Anni follows me, knocking on the door, "Bel, are you ok?"

"Yeah, just feel a little sick."

"Oh, we can leave if you want?"

Coming out of the toilet cubicle I find her standing with her back leaning against the sink.

"No, it's fine. It's your day, I don't want to ruin it."

"You wouldn't be ruining it, Bella. Please tell me if something else is bothering you."

Washing my hands I sigh and mutter, "I'm so jelly of you and Blondie."

I hope she didn't actually hear my confession.

But of course no such luck. "Why Bella?"

"Because Annika, he's gorgeous as fuck, and clearly hella loaded and so fucking in love with you, it's sickening."

She looks at me, huffing with a scowl on her face, "Well I'm sorry we fell in love and you couldn't have him. Why can't you let me be happy?"

Fuck, I shouldn't have said anything. I put my damn foot in it, big time.

"I want you to be happy Anni and I...I..."

"Seriously Bella, spit it out!" she screams at me so loud I swear every person in the restaurant is going to burst in to see what's happening.

"I don't want Jairus. Yeah, I thought he was hot, but he only has eyes for you Anni. And I'm just so fucking confused, I can't even think straight."

Her eyes soften, partly because I'm obviously not after her man, but mostly because Anni is always the sweetest and can't be angry or hold a grudge for longer than two-seconds.

She laughs softly, "Confused about what?"

"My feelings," I confess, biting down on my lip to not blurt everything out in a flurry of words.

"For who? Aust? Jaxon?"

"Not Jaxon, I seriously can't feel anything for him, even with this baby on the way."

"So Austin then? Are you still in love with him?"

"Yeah, but I...um..." I stammer, getting a picture of Travis in my head from a couple of weeks ago when he held me in his arms and my heart wanted to jump out of my chest.

I barely know the guy, but every time he's near my heart pounds and my core aches. I want him so bad, but it feels like a bad case of lust and I'm sure that's all he wants from me is to fuck me and leave, given what I've heard from Jairus and Anni of his reputation with women.

"Bel? Tell me!" Anni demands touching my arm lightly to make me look up from the floor.

"I...um...think...I...might have feelings for Travis."

Her eyes boggle at me, "Whoa, seriously? Did something happen between you guys?"

"No, nothing...just a couple awkward but sweet hugs."

She giggles excitedly, "But you want something to happen?"

"Yeah, he...Fuck...I don't know."

"Oh I know Bella," she laughs before continuing, "I felt the exact same way when I met Jai."

She winks at me and I know she gets it.

We don't say another word, instead head out of the bathroom to drown ourselves in chocolate bliss for the afternoon.

After gorging on way too much chocolate, we pile back into the Maxi taxi to head back to the city. I'm still not feeling the best, but suck it up as we get to the club for some cocktails and dancing. Anni and I both get virgin margaritas, whilst the other girls order cosmopolitans. We sit down together in a booth, downing our drinks as quickly as we can before we head to the dance floor.

Only a few minutes pass, barely even one song when the first stabbing pain hits. Clutching my stomach I rush to the bathroom, afraid that my drink was laced with some kind of drug.

I can tell Anni has again rushed after me.

The club bathroom is horrible. Blue lights to stop people shooting up, an extremely sticky floor, and the putrid smell of shit and vomit wafts out from the cubicles.

It makes me want to chunder myself, but thankfully I don't.

Stopping at the sink I splash water on my face, concentrating on taking deep breaths in and out when another rush of pain hits.

Anni rubs my back comfortingly, "Bel, are you ok? You felt sick earlier and now?"

"I um...think I'm in labour. It's really bad."

"But you aren't due for like a month."

"I know, maybe it's Braxton Hicks. But Anni, I need to go home...I can't ruin your night."

"Ok, are you sure? Do you want me to come with you?"

"Of course not. Stay here, enjoy your night."

She pulls me close for a hug. "I love you, Bella, you're such a great friend. Thanks for organising things today."

"No worries, Anni," I reply as we head out of the toilets and back to the girls on the dance floor. I apologise to them, telling them I'm not feeling up to any more partying and I head outside, ordering an Uber on the way.

I contemplate ordering one straight to the hospital, but despite my confession to Anni about having no feelings for Jaxon I still want him by my side if it's time for my baby to be born.

I'm still not sure he's the father, but at the moment he's the one who has been by my side the entire pregnancy and I need the support, as I'm scared as hell.

Thirty-Four | Boys Go Wild

It gave me great delight to organise Jai's Bucks night. He loves Annika so much it's fucking sickening but his Bucks night has to be filled with debauchery for old times sake.

He'd been pussy whipped before when he met Sara, but Annika had completely whipped him.

I'm glad for them both though, as he deserves to be happy.

Sometimes I wish I could find the same for myself, but he met me when I was beginning my player lifestyle after Meaghan really screwed me over.

Sometimes I even wondered if Dana could be my girl, but after the night out a couple of weeks ago it's pretty clear she's moved on and I feel so low, like I'm not good enough for anything but being fucked.

Starting the night off, we head to Punt Road inn, myself with Jairus, Dana's new man, and a couple of the boys from the team.

At the bar I order a round of drinks, beers to get us started for the night. I plan to get my boy drunk, but not so drunk he cheats on his girl.

"So, Jai, brother, are you ready?" I ask, taking a sip of my beer.

He looks at me worriedly, taking a sip of his beer before quickly putting back down on the bar.

"Ready for what exactly?"

We all laugh.

"To get married, idiot," I jeer at him.

"Oh yeah, I think so," he replies nervously, taking a big gulp of beer.

"Ok, I'm nervous as fuck. I want it to be so awesome for Anni."

"It will be," Dana's man replies, "I promise you that."

"I hope you're right Austin," Jairus replies and I make a mental note to remember his damn name.

It occurs to me that he's the one she called out the name of the last time I fucked her and it makes me a little angry.

If I was holding a tinny of beer it would have been crushed in my fist, but luckily I can curb my anger and scull my beer down in a few gulps instead.

Ordering another round, we chat for a bit and when I can tell Jai is bordering on tipsy, about to tip over the edge to being tanked I announce our leaving to head to Busty Nights gentleman's club.

Walking in we're greeted by a stunning busty sheila, with purple hair and piercing green eyes. She looks us up and down as though she recognises us, and I sense Jairus tensing up.

"Lighten up man, head to the private rooms at the back."

He glances at me for a moment, as we all head through the club. There are spotlights everywhere, focusing on girls gyrating their pelvises on the floor to ceiling poles to dirty music that pumps out from the speakers.

It's so fucking hot I don't know where to look. Reaching the rooms at the back we're ushered inside where three sheilas are dressed up in various fantasy outfits, one a sexy nurse, another a school girl and thirdly a cheerleader.

Laughing I slap Jai playfully on the back, "So man, take ya pick."

"What the fuck man?" he curses at me, scowling and then laughing.

"You gonna pick the naughty nurse?" I ask, wondering if he ever did get to fuck Annika in her naughty nurse outfit.

"I don't know man. I feel like that would be cheating on Anni."

"It's not cheating, man. Just a little harmless fun. And if you don't come it's definitely not cheating."

"I guess," he replies, looking at the three dancers again before he replies, "I'll take the cheerleader."

He looks to Austin, who says with a smirk, "Well, I'll take the naughty nurse then."

That leaves me with the schoolgirl, who is thankfully a brunette.

They give us all sexy smirks when we step closer, the schoolgirl taunting me, "So you boys wanna play or watch us play first?"

My cock tents a little in my daks, thoughts of them kissing and touching each other flashing in my mind.

I wink at Jai when I reply, "I'd love to watch you kiss each other and touch each other."

"Does the buck want that too?"

"Why not," Jairus laughs, looking at the rest of our mates who are practically salivating.

Without another word being spoken, the three girls step closer to each other, one sandwiched between the other two. The nurse and cheerleader are facing each other, moaning as they kiss each other wildly. The schoolgirl reaches down to touch the nurses pussy, rubbing her own pussy in her super short skirt against the cheerleader's arse.

It's so hot I want to join in and honestly, I want to fuck the school girl.

My cock is rock hard when I step up behind her, whispering in her ear, "Can I kiss you whilst you give me a lap dance, sexy?"

She turns her head back to me, her lips meeting mine in a kiss that is all tongue and not the least bit arousing which is a little odd to me.

Shrugging it off when I break the kiss I step back onto the lounge that runs along the wall, and she's in my lap, a knee either side of me.

I glance across to Jairus who now has the blonde cheerleader sitting on his lap, grinding over him in seductive swirl of her hips. "You good man?"

"Feeling a little guilty, but ok."

"Just enjoy it, man. Then go home and fuck Anni all night."

He laughs, watching the cheerleader in front of him who stands up and shoves her arse in his face. He slaps it and she giggles.

I turn my attention back to the schoolgirl, whispering in her ear, "Touch my cock sexy."

She whispers back, "Will cost you extra."

From my pocket, I grab out a hundy and tuck it into her bra strap. I can't think when her hands unbutton my jeans and is then stroking my cock. I couldn't care less if the boys know what is happening, they seem oblivious.

"How much for a gobby?" I whisper to her.

"How much you got?"

"Enough, sexy. Take me to a private room and I'll shower you in money."

She hops off my lap, taking my hand to lead me away.

I tell her to wait a moment, tucking my cock back inside my jeans when Jairus stands up and gives me a what the hell look.

"I'm heading to a private room for some fun. Go get tanked and watch the show on the main stage."

"Sounds great," Austin replies, heading out the door with the rest of the boys following.

The schoolgirl looks at me then, "We can stay here now if you want to play with all of us?"

God, yes, I fucking want to play with them all.

I nod and they strip down naked, dakking me and freeing my cock that one takes into her mouth whilst the other two kiss each other. I know it's wrong to be enjoying this so much, but I've been so pent up thinking about Bella I've not been out for weeks and my own fist never seems to get me off.

I curse myself for being so damn horny as its barely a minute or seems like it when I blow my load into the brunette's mouth.

I pull up my jeans, thank them all for getting me off, and rush out throwing a few hundy's back into the room.

Spotting Jairus and the boys by the main stage I head over and smile at him when he hands me a beer.

"What happened? Did you fuck them?" he asks me almost accusingly.

"Nah, just got a gobby. Came in like a minute."

He laughs at me. "You need a girlfriend."

"Yeah, Nah, I'll be right," I reply, gulping down some beer.

I just wanted to enjoy the rest of the night, to not think about Bella and focus on making sure my best mate has his last hurrah.

It's clear how much he loves Annika, and as much as I find it sickening I also want someone in my life I could feel that way about again.

Thirty-Five | Don't Panic Sweetheart

Jairus

Early the next morning, close to three am I stumble into our penthouse. I'm already starting to feel a hangover coming on and I just want to climb into bed next to Anni and sleep for the day.

Opening the door however I find her pacing from the kitchen to the sunken lounge, completely beside herself.
Stepping up to her I steady her, stopping her pacing by pulling her into an embrace. She sobs into my chest, soaking my t-shirt with her tears.
Kissing her hair I ask her, "Sweetheart, what's wrong?"

Freeing herself from my arms, she looks up at me, sniffing back her tears.
"Bella is in labour. She started having contractions last night so she went home, but she went into hospital a few hours ago."
"Well, um give me a minute, we can go there now."
She shakes her head at me, "No...I'll wait until she's had the baby. It's her and Jaxon's time now."
My heart swells at how considerate she is, even though she's in a panic for her friend she's still trying to remain calm.

Pulling her close again, I look down at her tear-stained cheeks, caressing one with a brush of my fingers across her flushed skin. "Ok, sweetheart. Let's head to bed and get some rest before then."

She moans a little, clearly tired.

Slowly she follows me down the hallway to our bedroom and sinks into the bed when I pull the covers back.

We lie on our sides, facing each other, our lips barely a whisper apart.

I want to be closer to her but her baby bump hinders our pelvises touching.

"How was your night anyway, sweetheart?"

"It was good, sucked that I couldn't drink though. How about yours?"

"Good, but I really wanted to just get home to you."

"Really?"

"Yeah, being in the gentlemen's club just made me think of you and making love to you, all night."

"All night?"

"Well, all morning now, sweetheart," I reply, leaning forward to press a kiss to her lips.

We kiss a little while, and I slip a hand under the short dress she's wearing, touching her core through the soft lace.

She moans, "Mmm, Jai, that feels good."

"Get naked for me sweetheart, I want to make love to you."

"Can you help me? It's so hard with my bump in the way."

She sits up, lifting her arms above her head so I can lift it off.

Looking over her body I lick my lips seeing her breasts practically spilling over the cups of her bra.

"God Annika, you're so beautiful."

I kiss her belly, "I can't wait until the twins are born as well."

She smiles at me, giggling at the contact of my lips against her sensitive skin, "I can't wait to meet them either, but being a pregnant bride is going to suck."

"You'll look beautiful no matter what sweetheart."

"I hope so baby," she says sweetly rolling over onto her other side.

Hooking fingers into the elastic of her lacy knickers I slide them down her legs, before unhooking her bra.

She grabs it and throws it on the floor, stretching back to press her arse against my cock.

"Mmm, Anni, kiss me sweetheart."

She obeys, crashing her lips against mine, and grinding her arse against me. My cock was hard before, but now its bursting out of my boxers, rubbing against the zipper of my jeans and it's bordering on painful.

Breaking the kiss I stroke the stray hairs from Anni's cheek.

"Sweetheart, please I need you now."

She smiles, watching me as I yank my jeans and boxers off, before pulling my t-shirt off and grabbing her around the waist to pull her close.

I don't say another word when I grab her leg, lifting it up as I slide my throbbing cock inside her.

She's insanely wet and my cock slips out, coated in her juices.

Shoving my cock back in she leans back to kiss me fiercely, her tongue forcing my lips to part and she laces her tongue with mine.

It makes me moan against her mouth, and I grab her growing breasts in my palm, flicking the sensitive tips which makes her tear her mouth from mine, and push her pelvis down further on my cock.

Our bodies are completely one, I'm balls deep inside her and its euphoric. My release is nearing and I'm pumping harder and faster inside her. Her moans grow louder, and she's panting as she starts climbing towards her peak.

My hands wander down her body, and I place one over her belly and the other I rub over her clit in teasing strokes matching the pounding of my cock thrusting in and out.

"Fuck, Jai, fuck, fuck!" she cries out, her whole body shaking in an idyllic rush of a release. She kisses me again and I bite her lower lip, my release filling her before I pull out.

My cum drips down her thighs, and she giggles, "If I wasn't already pregnant I would be now."

"I know sweetheart. That was incredible. Making love to you is better than playing footy."

It's a tease, and I curse myself when she rolls over again to face me, and says defensively, "Not funny, Jai."

"I'm sorry sweetheart. I love you."

I softly kiss her forehead and she smiles wide when she replies, "I love you to, Jairus Kingsley Brooks. I can't wait to be your wife."

"I can't wait to be your husband, sweetheart. I'm so proud of you and it will always be only you, Annika Elizabeth Brooks."

She laughs, "I love the sound of that."

I don't reply, instead pull her to my side when she rolls over again, her bump facing away from me.

Protectively I wrap an arm around her, resting my palm on her belly. My whole world is in this bed, my Anni and my babies.

Drifting off to sleep I wonder if they will be boys or girls or maybe a mini of each of us. No matter what, I feel like the luckiest son of a bitch this side of the Nullarbor.

Thirty-Six | Baby Here Confusion

Annika

The next morning not long after the sun has come up and is pouring in our large bedroom windows I climb out of bed.

"Sweetheart, come back to bed."
"I can't sleep with the light pouring in and I want to check my phone to see if there's any news."
"Ok, let me know. Close the curtains and give me like twenty minutes please."
"Ok, baby," I reply, crossing our bedroom and sliding the blackout curtains closed. The room plunges into darkness and I give my eyes a moment to adjust before I walk out the kitchen to grab my phone from the bench.
Sure enough, there's a missed call from Bella and a voice message. Tapping on it I put it on speaker, "Hi Annika, it's Jaxon. Just calling from Bella's phone to let you know we've had a little girl, born at five am today, weighing eight pounds two ounces. All good here."

I'm so giddy and excited for her, wondering what her name will be. I know Jai wanted to sleep in, but I rush back into the bedroom screaming out, "Jai, she had a little girl this morning!"
He sits up in bed, rubbing his eyes when I flick on the light.

"That's great sweetheart. Can I have a shower before we go meet her?"

"Only if I can join you, baby?"

"Oh you bet sweetheart, can't waste water," he laughs, practically jumping out of bed and running over to wrap my still naked body in his arms.

Together we hobble to the bathroom, stepping into the double shower together and turning the water on.

As it warms up I kiss him.

Laughing and kissing we wash each other's bodies, taking a bit of time to tease each other. His hand slips down between our bodies, and he slips a finger inside me, flicking my clit with his thumb at the same time.

Our kiss grows more intense, his tongue dancing with mine in the same rhythm as his finger thrusting in and out.

Breaking the kiss, I look up at him and the smirk on his gorgeous face that's dotted with light blonde stubble. I love the feel of it against my face when he kisses me.

"Jai, fuck! What are you doing to me?" I moan, pushing my pelvis down hard when he inserts another finger, still teasing my clit.

"Feel good, sweetheart?" he asks cheekily.

"Oh, oh...better than good, baby," I cry out, feeling the rush of pleasure take over my body. Pulling out his fingers he licks them clean, smirking at me when I crouch down so his cock is at eye level.

Grabbing it in a fist I stroke it up and down, making sure it's at full attention before I slide it down my throat, pursing my lips around the base.

Licking the tip teasingly I pull back and forth, on and off his cock.

He falls back against the wall, moaning, "Fuck Annika, you give good head."

Fondling his balls, I continue sucking him off, swirling my tongue up and down his shaft and into the tip.

Barely a minute passes when his salty cum shoots down my throat, his cock spasming as his release fills my mouth.

Swallowing hard as I remove my mouth from his length he takes my hands and helps me stand up.

"Good, baby?" I ask, giving him a cheeky smirk.

"Better than good, sweetheart."

He kisses me, a sweet, but demanding kiss that takes my breath away.

Breaking the kiss reluctantly I turn the water off, taking a step to grab a towel to wrap around my body.

Jai follows, his gaze never leaving mine when he steps out of the shower and wraps a towel low on his waist.

"You're so beautiful, Anni. If we didn't have somewhere to be, I'd fuck you so hard right now."

"Later, Jai. I want to go meet Bella's baby."

"I know, I know," he says, laughing and slapping me on the arse as I walk into the dressing room to find something to wear.

After our sexy time in the shower, we finally head to the hospital. For some reason, I'm feeling super nervous. I can't shake the feeling that Jaxon is going to be heartbroken, that Bella's little girl isn't his.

Walking into the suite, Austin is standing there holding the baby, rocking her from side to side. It warms my heart to see him smiling down at the sweet little girl in his arms, who has a pile of strawberry blonde hair atop her head.

Stepping up to him, I kiss his cheek in greeting, "Hey, you're a natural. And her hair, anyone would think she's yours."

He smiles at me, "I know Anni, but Bella is adamant that Jaxon is the father."

"Yeah, who knows. Are you heading off now?"

"Yeah, I'm meeting up with Dana."

He hands the baby back to Bella, giving her a kiss on the forehead. I'm glad to see there's no bad blood between them, but my heart aches a little for my best friend, as it seems clear he really wants the little girl to be his.

Once Austin has left, I take my turn holding Bella's sweet little girl. We both congratulate her, but I have to ask her, "Bel, where's Jaxon?"

"He went home. He was here all night."

"Oh ok, how's he feeling?"

"He's pretty happy. Glad she's here, even though she's early. It makes it real."

I smile, rubbing a hand over my belly. I can't wait to feel my babies kick and hold them in my arms.

Jairus seems like he's uncomfortable, so I ask him softly, "Baby, want to hold her?"

His eyes light up then, making my heart swell with love for him. Handing her over I question Bella, "Have you chosen a name?"

"Yeah," she smiles wide, "Nora Gwendolyn Mishal."

I'm taken aback by her not using Jaxon's last name, considering she is so adamant that he's Nora's father, but I don't question her.

"Aww, Bel, I love it. So sweet."

Jairus coos at her, saying her name. He looks damn gorgeous holding a baby. I know he's going to make a perfect Dad when our babies come along.

"Well Bella, we need to head off. Get some rest," Jairus says, popping Nora down in the crib by the bed.

"Thanks for coming," she says softly as we leave.

Taking Jai's hand as we walk out, I can't help but smile at him. Nothing is going to make me happier than becoming his wife and having our babies.

Thirty-Seven | Pash Don't Fight

Bella

The last month and a bit has passed by in a complete blur.

It feels like yesterday that Jaxon and I bought Nora back to his place from the hospital.

Half the time I wonder how I'm keeping my damn eyes open, and still standing when I'm not in bed.

Being a new Mum is literally killing me, all Nora does is cry, eat and shit.

I feel like she doesn't even know what the word sleep is.

Jaxon is being a complete tool, expecting me to do everything and I'm about ready to pack up my stuff and move back into the Richmond apartment.

The only thing that's stopping me, even though I'm still paying rent there is that I don't want to face Austin.

Watching him hold Nora tugged at my heart a lot more than it should have.

I blame it on the damn hormones and my still kinda being in love with him. So living with him again just isn't an option.

I can hear Nora's wailing from the other room and its grating me.

I'm standing in front of the wardrobe in Jaxon's bedroom, staring at the little clothes I have here and trying to decide what to wear to Anni and Jai's rehearsal dinner.

I'm as nervous as all hell, knowing I'm going to have to see Travis again after our last awkward but oh so sweet moment together a couple of months ago at the dinner shindig.

He looked gorgeous as fuck then, all casual in black jeans, a white t-shirt that clung to his hard abs, with a black leather jacket open at the front and being so close to him that night before Nora kicked him in the guts sent my libido racing.

I can't help but think of what he might wear for this occasion.

It's at Anni and Jai's favourite restaurant, Terrace, where they went on their first date which is so damn touching, just thinking about it is making tears well in my eyes.

The damn hormones are still getting to me and thinking about Travis is sending them south, straight to my lacy black knickers.

Still searching through the wardrobe, I'm taken aback when Jaxon walks in as I'm pulling out a revealing maxi dress.

It's backless, except for a strip of fabric at the top of my back. It comes to just above my arse and the front dips into a v that shows off my new rack. The neck is a halter style and the black flowing fabric that clings to my bust and down hides the little pooch of a belly I still have.

Thankfully I've lost most of my baby weight.

"No way are you wearing that!" Jaxon bellows at me.

He's holding Nora on his hip, and she's stopped her sobbing for the moment.

"I can wear what I want to wear Jaxon. I've not been able to wear something like this in months."

"Doesn't mean you should Bella, it's so fucking revealing."

I scowl at him for swearing in front of Nora, even though at this point she's unlikely to remember.

"So what? I want to look nice."

"For who Bella? Are you seeing someone else?"

"What do you care if I am? We're not together Jaxon."

"I still love you, Bel. I want us to be a family."

"I'm sorry Jax, but I can't commit to that. I don't feel that way about you and nothing is going to change that."

"Yeah, whatever. Why are you even going tonight? Can't you get out of it because Nora is only a month old?"

I scoff at these stupid questions. "I have to. I'm the maid of honour. And you'll be home with her and at the wedding tomorrow."

"Yeah, but I?" he stutters, looking at Nora in his arms.

He seems absolutely petrified.

"Seriously Jaxon, man up. You want to be a family, you want to be her Dad, then act like it."

He turns and leaves the room to let me finish getting dressed.

Slipping the dress on, I shut the wardrobe door to admire myself in the mirror, before sliding my feet into some strapy black high heels that give me another couple of inches in height.

I feel gorgeous already and I haven't got a speck of makeup on.

Quickly I run down the hallway to the bathroom, wiping a lick of mascara on my lashes and adding a touch of gloss to my lips.

My cheeks are already flushed, partly because this dress is sexy and I'm not wearing a bra, and partly because I'm thinking about seeing Travis.

I leave my hair down, the slight waves framing my face.

Calling out to Jaxon that I'm leaving I grab my purse, phone and keys, rushing out the door before he can reply.

~~

Walking into Terrace, and outside to the large deck, I'm blown away by how beautiful it's been set up. Fairy lights are strung across the beams, and in the middle of the deck, there is a large long table, lavishly decorated with candles and pots of wisteria. It smells divine as well, and I inhale it as I walk closer to the table. Glancing around I try to spot Anni, but instead, I see Travis leaning against the railing, his back to me.

He's wearing light denim jeans with a brown belt, his white dress shirt is tucked in, sleeves rolled up to his elbows and when he lifts his beer to his mouth the shirt flexes showing off the ridge down the middle of his back.

I'm a sucker for back muscles, and Travis certainly has the goods. Swallowing hard I hastily grab a glass of champagne from the tray of the waitress walking around the deck.

Focusing on gulping it down, loving the bubbles and the cool liquid running down my dry throat, I don't realise someone has stepped up beside me until she speaks.

"Bella, dearest, is that you?" I turn to the voice, finding Anni's sweet mother Elizabeth standing next to me. "Yes, Mrs Mathers," I reply softly.

"How are you dear? You look lovely, especially after having your baby not so long ago."

"I'm fine, thanks. And yes, she is nearly a month old now."

"Lovely, is she here? With your partner?"

I gulp down more of my champagne, not sure what I should reply. "Um, no. Her Dad is at home with her tonight. And we aren't together."

"Oh, well it was lovely to see you, dear. Have a great night."

She walks away, and I feel horrible, the champagne hitting me hard but also I feel like she judged me for not being with Jaxon, purely because he's Nora's Dad.

My gut is stirring, not like I'm going to chunder but just an off feeling.

Pushing through the small crowd of people I head inside towards the toilets, but there's a massive line as always so I wander back out onto the deck grabbing another drink on the way.

I'm sure the dinner will start soon enough and all the formalities that go along with that so I take a moment to myself standing by the railing, looking out over the city as I sip the champagne.

There's a slight breeze being high above the hustle and bustle of the city, but that isn't what makes me shiver.

He is next to me, Travis is standing next to me and his hand is at the small of my back, his coarse fingers brushing against my bare skin.

The simple touch makes me shiver in delight, my whole body suddenly feeling alive.

Instinctively we both turn to face each other, our bodies colliding against each other. His hand reaches up to brush my hair out of my face, and I immediately miss the contact from my back, but his touch against my cheek is even more intimate and my heart is racing.

He has a hot as sin smirk on his face, that is dotted with stubble, a little more than a five o'clock shadow.

Fuck, he's gorgeous.

Leaning down a little, I feel his breath against my ear when he exhales.

Again the shiver rushes through me, this time straight to my already damp black knickers.

"Bella, you look hot as fucking sin in this dress, sunshine."

His words are a whisper in my ear, but they're loud in my head and make me tingle with anticipation.

I know I shouldn't want his kiss, shouldn't want anything from him and definitely shouldn't want to find a place to strip him naked and taste more than just his mouth, but I want that and more.

His gaze is locked with mine now, our breath in sync and I taunt him with my words, "You don't look too bad yourself, Travis."

I drawl out his name, hissing the 's' when I reach down between us to cup the bulge in his jeans.

"Fuck, Bella," he groans, pressing his forehead against mine, so close our lips are a mere centimetre apart. I want to close the gap, want to taste his kiss, but we jump apart hearing the tapping sound of a knife on a glass and a booming voice, "Ladies and Gents, it's time to take your seats for dinner."

Heading to the table to find my seat, I can feel Travis's gaze on my arse. Knowing he's looking makes my whole body blush.

I don't know how long I'm going to be able to hold off on the temptation of being with him. Every time he's near me my whole body tingles with need, and once again I curse myself for having a bad case of lust.

Thirty-Eight | Best Friends Forever

Austin

Annika's big day has finally arrived, and I'm feeling giddy for her, as though I'm the one getting married.
It's certainly been a challenge to keep my mouth shut about being partnered with Amanda.
I thought it was super sweet that Jairus didn't want Anni to know, but I'd never been good at keeping secrets.

Now that the big day is here, I'm eager to spill the beans.
Anni is getting ready in a suite at the RACV City club.
It's an absolutely decadent venue, and I feel a pang of jealousy, wishing Dana and I could afford such a lavish place to get married at.
Knocking on the door, I'm feeling a little nervous at what I'm about to do. Yes, we're friends again, but things have still been a little awkward and I'm hoping to mend the bridge some more.
She opens the door, already wearing her wedding gown and she looks stunning.

"Hey Anni, can I come in?"
"Yeah, of course, Aust," she replies, ushering me inside and pulling me into a hug.

Pulling back from her sweet embrace, I glance around the suite, laughing at the makeup and discarded clothes everywhere from the girls getting ready.

"So, what are you doing here so early when the ceremony isn't starting yet?"

"I needed to give you something," I reply, reaching into my pocket to pull out the best friend pendant I'd given her before she moved out, and we'd had the massive fight that crushed my heart.

Her eyes light up when I hold it up to her, smiling.

"Oh Aust, you kept it," she coos at me, turning around so I can put it on her.

She brushes her hair aside and putting it around her neck I clasp it closed.

She looks at me closer, taking in the tuxedo suit I'm wearing.

"Aust, why are you wearing a tux?"

I laugh, winking at her, "Because I'll be standing up at the altar with my bestie when she marries the perfect guy."

She can't hide her happiness, "What? Are you serious Aust?"

"Yeah, babe, dead serious. Jairus asked me a month or so ago. It's been damn hard keeping it from you."

She playfully punches my arm. "I bet. You never could hide anything from me."

"I know, babe," I laugh smiling. She doesn't return the laughter though, seeming a little solemn now.

"Are you ok? Not having second thoughts are you?" I jeer lightheartedly.

"I'm nervous Austin and I feel like a whale with the twins clearly showing."

"Aww Anni, babe, you look stunning. This dress was obviously made for you."

"Really, you think I look ok?"

"You look better than ok. Jairus will crack a fat when he sees you."

She laughs hard then, and I join laughing with her at the thought of Jairus with a hard-on at the altar.

When we've calmed down, I kiss her cheek, "I love you, Anni."

She looks a little shocked at my words, and I have to correct myself, laughing, "Not like that babe."

She chuckles then, "I know sorry, I'm just so anxious for today to go well."

"It will Anni, I promise. It will be perfect."

"I hope so. When's your big day?" she asks, grinning at me.

"Soon...it's your day now," I jeer, poking her belly and making her giggle.

It's so great to have my best friend back in my life.

"Have you seen Am around?"

"Yeah, she's gone to get some food and coffee."

"Ok cool, I'll see you at the altar babe."

I hug her again and turn to leave, opening the door when Amanda comes back in.

I smile at my older sister, "See you soon, Am."

"No worries, Austy. Make sure the groom is ready."

"I will Am," I promise as I head back down the hallway, back to the boy's suite.

Thirty-Nine | Words So Special

Annika

Amanda walks back into the suite, holding three coffees in a tray and some bakery items.

I try to take one, but she shakes her head at me.

"Put a robe on, you don't want to get anything on your dress, An."

I nod in agreement, "True that."

Bella is in the bathroom, so I rap on the door, "Bel, you decent?"

"Yeah, come in."

I open the door, grabbing a robe from the hook on the back.

"Am just bought the coffee and food in."

"Sweet, was that Austin's voice I heard?"

"Yeah, he came to bring me back my best friend pendant and tell me he's partnered with Amanda."

"Oh really? That's pretty special."

"Yeah, apparently Jai asked him like a month ago and made him keep it a secret."

She laughs, "Good move."

"Yeah, come to have some food before you put your dress on. You look like a goddess."

She follows me out, "So do you dufus. Blondie is going to crack a fat seeing you coming down the aisle."

"That's what Austin said," I laugh.

We drink our coffee and eat our croissants in silence for a couple of minutes, our reverie broken when there's another knock on the door.

"Are you expecting anyone else to be here yet?" Amanda asks me, putting her coffee cup down to go and answer the door.

She peeks through the peephole, turning back to look at Bella and I shrugging, "There's no one there."

"Maybe they dropped something off," Bella suggests.

Amanda opens the door, and shrieks in shock and amazement. She bends down, picking something up and shuffles backwards, closing the door before she turns back towards the middle of the room.

In her hands, she's holding a massive bouquet of flowers; lilies, tulips, frangipanis and others in a variety of colours.

It's absolutely gorgeous and smells utterly divine.

She hands it to me, "I'm guessing these are for you Annika," she says sweetly.

I inhale the sweet nectar of the flowers, noticing the envelope tucked into the box.

It has my name on it, in scrawly, manly handwriting. My heart pounds and putting the flowers down I grab it out to eagerly rip it open.

Inside is a letter on a plain white piece of paper. Unfolding it I take a deep breath, sitting down on the edge of the bed to read it.

Time stops the moment I read his words.

MY DEAREST ANNIKA, MY SWEETHEART,

TODAY IS OUR WEDDING DAY AND I KNOW THIS DAY WILL BE THE BEST DAY OF MY LIFE.

UNTIL I MET YOU I NEVER KNEW WHAT TRUE LOVE MEANT.

YOU ARE MY EVERYTHING.

THE ONLY WOMAN I WOULD WANT TO SPEND THE REST OF MY LIFE WITH.

I KNEW I WANTED TO MARRY YOU AFTER OUR VERY FIRST DATE (THAT WASN'T A DATE).

YOU KISSED ME IN THE BUTTERFLY HOUSE AND MY HEART SOARED HIGH WITH THEM SWEETHEART.

I FELL IN LOVE WITH YOU THE MOMENT I OFFICIALLY MET YOU AND YOU SASSED ME BACK WITH YOUR STUPID 'YOU SMELL LIKE GRASS' COMMENT.

YOU WILL ALWAYS BE MY WORLD, SWEETHEART AND NEVER WILL YOU FEEL UNLOVED OR WANT FOR ANYTHING.

MY HEART SWELLS THINKING ABOUT OUR FAMILY TO COME, OUR TWINS AND ANY OTHER BEAUTIFUL BABIES THAT MAY COME ALONG IN THE FUTURE.

MY FUTURE IS WITH YOU, ANNIKA ELIZABETH BROOKS.

IT WILL ALWAYS BE ONLY YOU.

FOREVER,

JAIRUS KINGSLEY BROOKS

YOUR HUSBAND.

I hold the letter to my chest, wiping my arm across my eyes.

"An, why are you crying? You'll mess up your makeup."

"He...he...Jai...here read it," I sob, handing Amanda the letter.

She reads over it, smiling so wide. "Oh Annika, that is so beautiful."

"I know, I...love him so much."

She hands the letter to Bella, who quickly reads it to, and says chuckling, "Damn Anni, it's a pity Blondie doesn't have a brother."

Standing up I playfully slap her arm, "Funny Bel. He does have a super hot best mate though, huh?" I wink at her.

"Yeah, that he does," she replies blushing.

"Something happen last night?"

"No," she snaps, blushing more which is so unlike her.

"I saw you together Bel before Dad asked everyone to sit down for dinner."

"Oh, um, yeah, nothing happened."

She looks down at the floor. "Bel?"

"Yeah?"

"Do you like him?"

"Yeah, but I need to steer clear of guys Anni. Especially guys like Travis. I can't get my heart broken again."

Amanda touches her arm lightly, "I'm sorry Bella. I kinda thought my little brother might have fallen for you at some point. But he hasn't and he's probably not the right guy for you."

Bella smiles weakly, "Thanks, Amanda. I wish I didn't fall in love with guys who don't want me."

"You can't help who you fall in love with. Maybe you should give Travis a chance," I suggest, but she shakes her head, turning to walk over to her dress which is hanging up over the window.

We don't say another word, just finish getting ready to head to the ceremony.

My heart aches for Bella. I want her to have her happy ever after too.

Forty | Absolutely Perfect Yes

Jairus

It's hard to believe our special day is finally here, that I'm standing under a wedding arch in the botanical gardens waiting for my beautiful Annika to arrive to marry me.

Glancing around at the guests I can't help but smile, but I'm so nervous as well, in a giddy excited kind of way.

In the front row of seats is Anni's mum, who gives me a wave, blowing a kiss to her husband, Anni's dad who is our officiant for the ceremony.

It's perfect that he's a semi-retired minister and could be such an important part of our day. Anni had insisted on walking down the aisle herself, not wanting her dad to give her away for just a fleeting moment, but rather be the one to help her express her love.

Shuffling on my feet I'm getting more anxious as people gather around the area, onlookers who have realised who I am.

Travis is standing next to me, and digs an elbow into my side, "You good man?"

"Yeah, yeah, I'm good. Just wanna see her."

"I know man, I'm sure she'll look stunning."

I look to Austin standing next to Travis, and he nods, "She looks beautiful, Jairus."

Smiling at him I rub my hands together, giddy to get started when the music starts, signalling the girls' arrival.

The black Chrysler limousine is pulling into the gardens, driving slowly and carefully down the footpath before stopping just before the aisle of white flowers we have set up with chairs for the guests on either side. The wedding arch I'm standing under has white roses and jasmine intertwined in it and the smell will forever be etched in my mind as a memory of this day.

Amanda is the first to step out of the car, beginning the short walk down the aisle to stand on the other side of the arch.

She gives her brother a sweet smile when Bella steps out of the limo.

I turn to look at Travis for a moment, and he's practically salivating seeing her in the flowing emerald green dress.

It shows off her body for sure, and I elbow him whispering in his ear, "Bella looks gorgeous huh?"

"Walking wet dream, man." He licks his lips and gives Bella a wink when she reaches the arch.

Anyone would think something had happened between them, and if it had Travis hadn't mentioned it to me.

My heart starts hammering in my chest, as my Annika steps out of the limo and starts walking down the aisle towards me.

I've never seen her look more beautiful than in that perfect moment. Her dress is lacy, long sleeved with a sweetheart neckline. It hugs her curves, her small baby bump and delectable arse.

Her veil is pinned to her hair, which is in ringlet curls, down and framing her heart-shaped face. It's plain to see she is barely wearing any makeup, but some mascara and lipgloss and still she is absolutely stunning, glowing.

Tentatively she walks on her ballet flats, closer to me with every step and her smile is wide, her eyes locked on me.

I can't help but grin.

When she reaches the arch, I take her hands in mine, leaning down to whisper in her ear, "Sweetheart, you look stunning. Absolutely, breathtakingly beautiful."

She giggles, and whispers back, "Baby, you look absolutely deliciously handsome."

The music has stopped and she looks to her dad, nodding that she's ready to start.

I nod as well, as he begins with the ceremony.

"Dearly beloved, we're gathered here today to share in the love of Jairus Kingsley Brooks and Annika Elizabeth Mathers, my beautiful daughter who has chosen this amazing young man to be her husband. They share a love that is once in a lifetime, and it is my pleasure to marry them. Jairus, do you take Annika to be your wife?"

"Fair Dinkum, bloody oath I do," I bellow, laughing a little.

"Annika, do you take Jairus to be your husband?"

Anni laughs and says sweetly, "Fair dinkum, I do."

The crowd laughs at our little joke and her Dad can't help but smile.

"Jairus please take Annika's hand as you exchange the vows you've prepared for each other."

He looks at me, smiling and nodding for me to begin.

Holding Anni's hands in mine, I take in a deep breath before I start to speak slowly, "Annika, sweetheart, from the moment I met you I knew you were meant to be mine and I honestly have no other words to say that could even begin to describe how I feel about you. My love for you is endless, you're my world, my everything and I will love you until my dying day."

She has tears in her eyes, but her sweet smile is still on her lips when she speaks her vows to me, "Jairus, from the moment I met you I knew you were special. I knew you'd cherish me, and make me feel things I never had before. I fell in love with you hard, all at once and didn't know what hit me, because it was and still is so consuming and intense that I feel it deep within my heart. My love for you is never ending, forever and it will always be only you, until my dying day."

Her words make my heart swell with love for her.

I want to kiss her to seal the deal but it's not time yet.

"Now that the couple has shared their vows with each other, they will now exchange rings to symbolise the commitment and promise they've made to one another today," Anni's dad says.

Travis hands me the rings from his pocket, a diamond encrusted band for Anni and a simple titanium band for me.

"Jairus, as you place this ring on Annika's finger, repeat these words after me, 'This ring symbolises my love for you and the promise we made today.' "

I repeat the words, sliding the ring onto Anni's finger, making her giggle when she looks down at it for a moment.

Thankfully it fits, even though her fingers have swollen a bit with her pregnancy.

"Annika, as you place this ring on Jairus's finger, repeat these words after me, 'This ring symbolises my love for you and the promise we made today'."

Anni repeats the words, sliding the band onto my finger and kissing my knuckles softly. It's a sweet gesture that makes me grin with happiness, but all I really want now is to seal the deal, to kiss her for our first kiss as husband and wife.

"Jairus and Annika, since you have declared your love together in marriage, and have pledged yourselves to each other by your vows and by the giving of rings, and have declared your promise of love before God and these people here present, I now pronounce you husband and wife in the name of the Father and the Son and the Holy Spirit. Jairus, you may kiss your Bride."

I give Anni a smirk, leaning forward to crash my lips to hers, snaking an arm around her waist as I dip her low in a sweet passionate kiss.

The small group of guests cheer, wolf whistle and clap when we break apart and Anni's dad announces, "Ladies and Gentlemen, it is my privilege to introduce to you for the very first time, Mr and Mrs Jairus and Annika Brooks."

Grabbing Anni's hand in mine, I raise it above our heads, calling out a 'whoop, yeah'!

Quickly we complete all the formalities of signing the register before we head down the aisle to be congratulated by our family and friends.

It's absolutely perfect.

Forty-One | Take Her Home

Inside the lavish ballroom of the RACV City club, Jai and Anni's reception is in full swing. I'd been barely able to have a moment alone with Bella, except for when we sat down for entrees to be served.

There is no set seats, even at the Bridal table, so I sneakily pull up my chair next to hers. She smiles at me, and I edge a hand onto her thigh. The thin silk fabric doesn't hide the fact that her skin heats with my touch.

She shifts in her chair, my hand rubbing her thigh, dipping between her legs when she opens them a little.

I don't dare look at her, even when I gather the fabric up from her knees so I can slide my hand into the lace of her knickers.

Slowly, teasingly I run a finger across her clit, making her let out a gasp.

Our food is bought to the table and I glance down at it, before glancing at Bella who has her lip between her teeth and is clearly enjoying the naughty little tease I'm giving her under the table.

It turns me on, and clearly her at how wet she is, that no one else knows what is happening.

Without giving her any warning I pull my finger out, so tempted to lick it clean, to taste her no doubt, delicious honey.

But it's not the time or place for that, and I know one taste will have me craving her like the meal that's in front of me.

She gives me a look, that is all lust, and I lean across to whisper in her ear, "You look and feel fucking incredible, Bella."

I put a forkful of Ravioli in my mouth, licking my lips as it tastes divine, but my eyes don't leave Bella's.

We eat in silence, sneaking looks at each other and smiling between mouthfuls. My stomach is in knots and I'll be damned if I'm not at least kissing her before this night is over.

After dinner and the speeches, which I'd nearly fucked up because I left my notes at home, I'm heading back from draining my snake in the bathroom when I see Bella and Jaxon fighting. He's holding her baby in his arms, rocking her and the poor child is wailing like a banshee. They're standing next to the room divider that leads to the toilets so I shuffle back, standing behind it to listen.

Bella screams, "Take her home then Jaxon. You clearly don't want to be here and I'm not ready to go home yet!"

"But Bella, I can't look after her all night. It's not fucking fair!"

Through the gap in the divider, I can see Bella ball her fists in anger, "Seriously Jaxon, you're her Dad. Grow the fuck up!"

"Fine! But if you come home drunk, you'll regret it."

He storms off, leaving Bella seething. I wait a moment and step out from behind the divider, stealthily like I didn't just hear their fight.

"Hey, sunshine, you good?"

"No, I'm so fucking angry with him. He's such a tool."

"Who? Ya baby daddy?"

"Yes, Jaxon. He seriously can't even have her for like a night. When I got home from the rehearsal dinner last night, she was crying in her cot because he hadn't even fed her and expected her to sleep with an empty belly."

Tears sting her eyes and I honestly have no idea what to say. "That's fucking wrong. Maybe you need to talk to him about it. About what he needs to do."

"Yeah," she says softly, brushing her arm across her cheeks to wipe her tears away, "but right now I just want to get tanked and forget for a while."

She heads back into the main part of the ballroom, grabbing a bottle of beer from the tub on the bridal table. Flicking the top off like a pro, she gulps it down, instantly looking for another drink. This time she grabs a glass of champers from a wandering waitress, and downs it like its water.

"Bella, sunshine, slow down woman. You'll be tanked in a minute."

"That's the plan Travis," she taunts, waving me away when she grabs another champagne.

Like a lost puppy dog I follow her towards the dance floor. She stops in the middle of the small crowd, turning to look at me with a sexy smirk on her face. My cock twitches in my slacks, hardening just from that look on her gorgeous face.

The song changes to a slower one, 'There's no way' by Lauv and giggling she beckons me to dance with her.

"Come on best man, show me your moves."

"Oh it's on, sunshine," I chuckle, grabbing her around the waist and pulling her body against mine.

My cock tents more, desperate to be free of the confines of my dress slacks.

"Mmm, seems like you like dancing with me," she teases, her tone seductive.

"You don't say. But I liked touching your clit under the table more," I taunt with a wink.

She wraps her arms around my neck, pulling me down so her forehead is against mine, her lips just a whisper away.

Our lower bodies are swaying together to the slow beat of the music and I'm all in.

"Bella," I murmur her name, loving how it sounds rolling off my tongue.

"Travis," she purrs back, making my cock throb.

There's no way I can hold back now.

I have to kiss her, have to know how her lips feel against mine.

I've thought of nothing else for months and its time I made a claim on her.

Licking my lips I crush them to hers in a hard kiss that makes her moan against my mouth. She fists my hair, pulling me closer.

I grab her arse cheeks in my palms wetting the silk with my clammy hands.

My whole fucking body is on fire, her kiss pulling me under when she licks my lips with her tongue to part them and deepen the kiss.

Her tongue laces with mine, we're locked in our own illicit moment and no one else in that room fucking matters.

If I don't break the kiss now, I'm sure to have an ugly sticky stain on the front of my slacks.

I'm feeling breathless too, and pull back from her kiss, biting her lip before I speak, "Fuck Bella, that was some kiss."

She doesn't reply, instead bites down on her lip, giving me a sexy lopsided smirk before taking my hand and pulling me away from the dance floor.

With her other hand, she grabs another champagne, downing it and another in quick succession.

"Take me home, Travis," she begs, stumbling a little in her heels, which shows me she's clearly gone past tipsy.

I don't want to take advantage of her, but fuck it if i don't want to kiss her again, somewhere more private like my bed.

Forty-Two | Morning Freak Out

Bella

Jolting awake I sit up, scanning the unfamiliar surroundings. Rubbing my eyes, I look down realising I'm only wearing my strapless bra. Lifting the sheet up, I'm thankfully still also wearing my white g-string. It feels a little damp in the crotch area, which concerns me.

Turning my gaze I look at the figure lying next to me. He's clearly dressed, in a white fitted t-shirt but I'm not sure if he has anything else on.

As though he knows I'm looking at him, his eyes flutter open and he stares at me a moment before he speaks. "Morning sunshine, last night was great huh?"

My tongue is stuck to the roof of my mouth, I don't remember anything from the night before. Not one thing other than knowing it was Anni's wedding day comes to mind.

Travis sits up in bed, still staring at me, but edging a little closer to me on the bed. He leans in, giving me a closed mouth kiss.

I should have turned away, but I feel like I've kissed him before and the simple closed mouth kiss has my lips tingling.

"Did we? Did we um?"

He chuckles, pulling his t-shirt over his head and handing it to me. "Put this on and I'll tell you."

I take his t-shirt from his grip, slipping it over my bra and inhaling the smell of him on it. I break out in goosebumps and again he chuckles, pulling me down to the bed, pinning me down with his body over mine.

"So, Bella, you wanna know if we fucked?"

"Yeah?"

He leans closer, his mouth at my ear when he whispers, "Yes, we fucked all night."

I hiss in shock, pushing my hands against his bare chest.

The moment I touch his bare skin I regret it, as warmth and desire rushes through me. If I did have sex with him, I'm pissed off I wasn't sober to remember it.

But I know I didn't because surely I wouldn't forget the way he makes me feel.

I'm sitting up now, making him fall back onto the bed, and he laughs at the obvious scowl on my face.

"Ok, we didn't fuck. But do you remember anything from last night?"

"Um, I...um," I bite down on my lip, trying hard to recall anything I can from the night before, "Did we kiss?"

"Yes, Bella, we kissed and if you didn't have morning breath from hell, I'd be kissing you right now."

"Oh, well, um...I...um."

He laughs. "Spit it out sunshine!"

"Why was I only in my underwear whilst you were half dressed?" I ask, gazing down at his y-front blue boxers that don't hide much at all.

"You chundered all over that pretty green dress of yours, so when you passed out on my bed I removed it and washed it."

"You did what? Washed it?"

"Yeah, it had spew on it, Bella."

"It's silk, Travis. It's probably ruined," I shriek, jumping off the bed in annoyance.

"I'm sorry, I didn't know. I...just wanted to do something nice for a change."

"Yeah? Well, you fucked up," I spit at him.

He tries to apologise again, but I'm not listening to his words, the anger racing through me. "Where is the dress now?"

"Hanging up in the ensuite," he replies, pointing across the room to an archway.

Running in I find my dress hung up on a coat-hanger on the glass wall of the rather nice looking shower.

His apartment is quite snazzy, but his furniture is old and rundown, which confuses me somewhat.

Taking the dress off the hanger, I'm surprised it seems to be okay and it smells like Imperial Leather soap, manly with a hint of musk.

Draping it over my arm I walk out, stopping at the door of his bedroom a moment.

"Well, I'm going home. Thanks for...um...the kiss...and taking care of me. But I...need to get home to Nora now."

He laughs at me again, looking me up and down licking his lips.

"You might want to ask me to borrow some pants?"

It dawns on me that he's right. I'm only wearing a skimpy g-string and his t-shirt.

"Oh, shit," I reply, lifting his t-shirt off, and throwing it back at him. I slip my dress back on, shivering when the cold fabric touches my skin. Travis' t-shirt wasn't much to be wearing on a spring morning either, but I'd felt warm and cosy wearing that.

"So, I'll see you around, maybe," I taunt him, turning to leave his bedroom and apartment without another word.

I don't know if he responds or not, but all I want is to get back to Jaxon's and see Nora.

It's stupid to be still living with Jax especially when all we seem to do is fight, but my only other option is to move back in with Austin and he seems to be getting cosy with Dana, so the likelihood of getting anything from him is well and truly gone.

I haven't slept with Jax for months, and I'm literally as horny as anything. He doesn't want to touch me, even though he continually tells me he loves me.

I know it's because I rejected his proposal, but I deserve more than that. I don't want to be in a loveless marriage, dealing with okay sex for the rest of my life just because he's my daughter's father.

Jaxon doesn't make me happy, and he most certainly doesn't make me feel like Travis does. All he needs to do is look at me, and my whole body hums with need. And just thinking about that feeling as I head back to Jaxon's is enough to make me freak out, because I know something else happened last night between us that has made me want Travis Banes even more than I did before and I need to stay away, or my heart is going to be trampled on.

Forty-Three | Not Fighting Fair

Bella

I'm dreading getting back to Jaxon's, knowing he's going to give me the third degree about where I've been all night.
I really don't want to hear his shit when I've done nothing wrong.
Ok yeah, I'd stayed out all night and left him with Nora, but he's a grown man and her father.

Opening the door, he's standing in the lounge room, holding Nora and rocking her whilst she screams at the top of her lungs.
He looks at me scowling, "Where the fuck have you been, Bella?"
He says my name slowly with a patronising tone.

"None of your damn business, Jaxon."
"It is my damn business, Bella. You didn't come home last night, leaving me with your kid all night. Who by the way, no matter what I do she screams the house down."
He shoves Nora into my arms, and her crying stops when she looks up me.
"Our kid, Jaxon," I remind him, still rocking Nora as I head down the hallway to change her nappy that is clearly soiled. "And don't you know how to change a damn nappy."
I hear him following me, "I just changed her."

"Yeah? When? Last night before you put her to bed without her bottle?"

I put Nora down on the change table, grabbing a nappy whilst I hold her with my other hand. I press a kiss against her belly and she giggles. Taking off the dirty nappy I throw it in the rubbish next to me, putting the new one on her quickly.
She's so chaffed so I shake a bit of baby powder on before closing the nappy and blowing a raspberry on her belly.
Again she giggles.
Her sweet little laugh is the best sound in the world, making me forget for a moment that Jaxon had followed me.
Turning around, after picking Nora up and holding her against my hips I find him standing against the door jamb, pouting.
"She's so good for you. I can't do anything right."
"You just have to try Jaxon. I can't be with her all the time, and last night I had every intention of coming home."
"Then why didn't you?"
"I um…I had to much to drink and I went to stay with Amanda in her room."
I hate that I'm lying to him, but he's not going to dig for more.
"Oh ok, but don't you think you could have sent me a message. Leaving me home alone wasn't exactly fair Bella."
Walking out to the kitchen, I brush past him, scoffing.
"If you had any brains Jaxon, you'd have realised you had my damn phone in the car."
"You could have used someone else's phone," he says to me like it's the most obvious thing in the world.
I don't remember much from the night before as it is, and his phone number certainly isn't stored in my memory.

I've always been useless at remembering things like that.

"Right, so I'm supposed to have your number memorised and know it when I'm drunk?"

He doesn't reply, just stares at me when I flick the kettle on to make a coffee. I try to hand Nora back to him, but he leaves the room, grabbing his keys and slamming the door.

"Well, looks like it's just you and me today, Nor Nor."

She giggles when I tickle her. Whilst the kettle boils, I take her into the lounge room and lie her down under her play gym on the floor.

Quickly running back to the kitchen I make a coffee and head straight back in to watch her play. I'm so angry at Jaxon for again not fighting fair, but I don't regret not coming home at all. Something happened between Travis and me, a kiss he tells me and I'm annoyed at myself that I got so drunk I can't remember it.

Forty-Four | Wanting Her Bad

After training I pull Jai aside in the change rooms, giving him a slap on the back when he's getting changed from his footy gear.

"So, bro, how's married life treating you?"

He laughs, "Same as before, except I can call her Mrs Brooks now."

"Yeah, I bet you're a dirty boy, calling that out whilst you fuck her."

He gives me a playful slap, blushing. "Yeah, but you can't talk. You're as dirty as they come when it comes to sex Travis."

"Yeah I know, and speaking of...." I let my words trail off.

I want to talk to him about what happened with Bella and I, but I'm unsure if he's still going to warn me away.

His eyes boggle at me. "You didn't?"

"Didn't what bro?"

"You did! You fucking slept with Bella!"

I sit down on the bench seat in the middle of the room. "Nah, I didn't but I fucking want to."

"So, you just pashed?"

I feel a stab of guilt hit me, wondering if he saw our hot kiss on the dance floor that just won't leave my mind.

"Yeah, on the dance floor, and then at mine when she came home with me."

"So after that hot dance floor pash, you took her home, but didn't fuck her?"

"No, she was tanked, and I couldn't go through with it. Plus she chundered all over her dress and passed out."

"Oh shit, well maybe it was a good thing. She doesn't need to be fucked and dumped right now."

"Who said I was going to do that?"

"No one, but you're not exactly the relationship type Trav, and Bella has a little girl now. She needs a bit of stability I'm guessing."

"Yeah I know that, but it doesn't stop me from wanting her."

"Yeah, I get that, but I don't know. I still think you should keep your distance."

"Oh come on man. You honestly think I can stay away after I've kissed her."

He doesn't reply, just makes some odd groaning noise as he continues getting dressed.

I finish getting dressed myself and grab my bag to head out, "I'm gonna head out man. But don't think you going quiet on me means I'm going to back down on the Bella front."

He laughs, following me out of the change rooms. "I get it Travis," he says suddenly making me jump.

"Yeah, pull the other one."

"No mate, I do. You know how bad I wanted Anni when I met her."

"Yeah, you were pussy whipped from the start."

"Exactly. So let it be. If Bella is meant to be your woman she will be."

"Yeah, I guess you're right, mate. See ya before the game."

"Yeah, catch ya then," he replies sliding into his Stinger and reversing out with a wave.

Getting in the Jag I think about his words, that if Bella is meant to be mine it will happen.

And damn do I want her to be mine.

Forty-Five | All He Wants

The nursing home is decorated like someone threw up Christmas decor. Every surface has some kind of decoration, tinsel hanging along the walls and across the hallways.

In the dining hall, that I pass as I head to Dad's room, is a floor to ceiling Christmas tree that has ornaments covering every possible branch.

My stomach lurches looking at it, the memories of Christmas as a kid surfacing.

Mum loved Christmas, always spoiling Tessa and me with a mountain of presents I knew they couldn't really afford. Tessa had no idea of our parents' financial struggles when we were young, but I heard all the arguments about money, being too inquisitive for my own good and sneaking into Dad's office to watch the footy on the tv in there while Tessa was watching Disney movies on repeat in the lounge room.

Getting into footy as my career, I'd spent most of my first couple of years earnings on helping my parents out of debt and then Mum's medical bills from years before that Dad hadn't be able to pay. Tessa had escaped it all, as soon as she was old enough, packing up, selling all her belongings and heading off overseas for a working holiday. Sometimes I envied my little sister for getting away, but I also love playing footy more than anything. But it's not all I want now.

Reaching Dad's room, I wrap my knuckles on the door before opening it when I hear him trying to speak.

Stepping into the room, I hold back my groan at how much Christmas decor surrounds him.

Kissing his cheek I say as happily as I can, "Merry Christmas Dad."

He smiles wide at me, wrapping his arms around my back to pull into a tight hug.

"Hhapp...y...Chrrissmas son," he stutters softly into my ear.

I pull back from the hug to sit down in the chair beside his bed.

I can't help but let out a deep sigh. Being in my Dad's presence I've never been able to hide my emotions from him.

"Something up, son?" he manages to ask, getting the words out perfectly, lightly touching my thigh that I'm bouncing up and down in nervousness.

"I've met someone, Dad."

He smiles so wide, I think his face is going to break. "Issn't ththat good?"

"Well, yeah, but she can't be mine and I don't want to break her heart."

He gives me a puzzled look, simply asking, "Why?"

"Because she has a kid, and i'm a basket case when it comes to relationships."

Dad chuckles softly, "Haass annytthing hhappenned wwwith yyou gguyys?" he stammers, breaking my heart at how much he's struggling to get the words out.

I feel myself blush, "We've kissed, but nothing else."

"Annd hhoow ddid yyoou fffeel?"

"I can't explain it Dad, but I just want her more. Bella is all I want for Christmas."

"Ttthen mmmake hhher yyyours."

222

"Yeah," I laugh, taking his hand when the door opens and a nurse announces it's time to head to the dining hall for Christmas lunch. After she turns down the hall, leaving the door open, I help Dad out of bed and into his wheelchair.

I push him out of the room, down the hallway and the sound of Christmas carols assaults my eardrums the closer we get to the dining hall.

Pushing him up to the table, I kiss his forehead before heading towards the buffet to fill a plate with food for him.

I'm only halfway through the selection of food, and the plate is already loaded with meat and potatoes. Piling on some veggies I pour on some gravy before heading back to the table.

Dad licks his lips when I put the plate in front of him.

Quickly I race back, grabbing some cutlery and a small plate of food for myself. We eat in silence, and I help Dad cut his food into small pieces, feeding him a little when he struggles with his fork. Seeing him like this breaks my heart, and I dread the day his condition worsens and hope like hell he doesn't have another stroke.

I'm spooning my own food into my mouth when I feel someone step up behind my chair. The person doesn't say anything at first, instead puts two small warm hands over my eyes and softly says, "Guess who, Travy?"

I know her voice instantly, and her use of my childhood nickname. Screeching her name, I stand up, stepping aside to pull her into a hug.

"Don't break me Travy," she laughs.

Breaking the hug, I apologise, "Sorry Tessa. I just can't believe you're here. Why didn't you tell me?"

"I wanted to surprise you for Christmas. And…" She cuts her words off, looking down at the floor.

"Tess, what's wrong? Didn't you bring Ryan?"

She looks up at me, on the verge of tears, "He dumped me. Right after he cheated on me with some skank."

"Oh Tessa, I'm so sorry. Sounds like he didn't deserve my little sister."

"Yeah," she says softly, turning to Dad and bending down to kiss him on the cheek.

"Merry Christmas Dad. Thanks for keeping my secret."

He smiles at her, and she hugs him. "Haapppy Chrismmass Ttessa."

I look at Dad, "You knew?"

He nods and I poke Tessa playfully in the ribs, "That was sneaky, little sis."

"I know," she laughs.

"How long you staying for? Want to crash at mine?"

"Um yeah, I hired a car, but I honestly don't know. I wouldn't want to put you out."

"Don't be a silly billy Tessa," I tease, "I've fucking missed you, so I won't take no for an answer."

"Ok, great," she says excitedly, before asking, "how's the spread?"

"Pretty damn good actually. Catch up with Dad, I'll go grab you a plate of grub."

"Thanks, Travis," she says sitting down on the other side of Dad at the table.

After grabbing her food, I sit back at the table and she devours it like she hasn't eaten for days.

"Hungry huh Tessa?"

"Um yeah. I…um…"

I know exactly what she's going to say and I'm excited for her, but upset for her at the same time.

"You're pregnant? With Ryan's kid?"

"Yeah, pretty shit huh?"

Dad smiles at her, seeming a little excited, but he doesn't speak.

"I'm so sorry Tessa, but I'm here for you. I don't know shit about kids really, but anything you need its big bro duty for me."

"Thanks, Travis, that means the world."

She kisses my cheek and finishes her food in silence.

Once lunch is over, we both wheel Dad back to his room, tucking him into bed and giving him a kiss goodbye before we leave.

He's asleep before we leave the room. Tessa follows me out and has conveniently parked right next to me, so I tell her to follow me back to mine.

Driving home I can't help but think about what I really want for Christmas. Having Tessa home and the impending uncle status are pretty fucking huge, but still, all I really want for Christmas is to have Bella in my arms.

Maybe it's because it's Christmas or maybe the excitement of having my little sister home, but I'm feeling super sappy.

Flicking the radio on I don't even change the station when Christmas songs come on the radio and I find myself singing along.

Forty-Six | Making Christmas Memories

Annika

It feels a little surreal being back at the Belvinz's for Christmas, a year down the track with Jairus again, this time as my husband. So much has changed in the past twelve months in our lives and I'm beyond happy that we've all grown up so much.

We are all seated around the dining table, my parents, Austin's parents, Austin with Dana by his side, Amanda, Lillie, Jairus and me. It feels so special that we can all be together again, and this time there's no awkward tension between the guys like last Christmas when they were both in love with me.

I was already in love with Jairus months before Christmas, it just took my head a little longer to catch up with my heart.
Austin's mum smiles at me between a bite of food, "You're glowing Annika," she says sweetly.
Gulping down my mouthful of food I reply, "Thanks Mrs Belvinz, I feel like an elephant. I can't believe the twins aren't due until July."
She laughs softly, "Are you going to continue your nursing degree once they're here?"
At her words, a knot twists in my stomach. What to do about my career has been on my mind ever since I found out I was pregnant.

I'm struggling now and things are going to be even harder when the twins arrive with Jairus in the middle of the footy season.

I gulp, returning her smile, "I'm not sure. I'll probably put it on hold for a bit while they're young and go back to it."

"Yeah, you don't want to miss out on being with them when they're babies."

She looks towards Austin like she's wondering when Dana and him will be having a baby. Biting my lip I nod at her, "Exactly. By the way, this food is delicious."

"Thank you, dear," she replies looking around at everyone nodding in agreement.

We continue eating then, everyone occasionally making idle chit chat between themselves.

Jairus has a hand on my thigh, and he's looking at me out of the corner of his eye. I lean into him, whispering in his ear. "What baby?"

He leans in, cupping my cheek when he whispers back, "I want this lunch over so I can unwrap my Christmas present."

I giggle softly, "What present?"

His hand edges under the hem of my dress, higher up my thigh. "You sweetheart," he taunts with a cocky grin.

My whole body tingles with the thought of getting up to some naughtiness with my sexy husband. I don't reply, but feel myself blush. Excusing myself from the table I take my plate to the kitchen, bending down to put it in the dishwasher.

I'm startled when someone else enters the kitchen, stepping up behind me.

"Anni, are you ok? You rushed off pretty quick."

"Shit, Aust, you scared the shit out of me."

"Sorry, I just wanted to see if you were ok."

"I'm fine. Just needed a moment."

"Ok, everything good with you and Jai?"

"Of course Aust. He kinda got me a little excited, that's all," I say blushing and giggling.

"I don't want to know that babe," Austin laughs.

"Sorry," I reply, "are you sure that's honestly why you followed me? You seem a little anxious."

"Well, um, I wanted to ask a favour."

He looks down, shuffling his feet on the floor. He leans against the bench next to me, and I touch his arm lightly to get him to look at me.

"Sure Aust. You're my bestie."

"I'm planning on proposing to Dan, and I was hoping you'd help me organise it."

I can't hide my excitement, smiling and shrieking with excitement. "Oh my god, Aust! That's so exciting! What do you want me to do?"

"I've just rented a new place in Hawthorn, and I want to have it all set up with roses and a banner or something."

"Aww Aust, that sounds sweet. So how do I fit in?"

"We're not heading back until New Year's Eve before your party, so I was thinking I could give you the key to set it up for me, and then I'm going to take Dan there instead of our Richmond place to surprise her."

"That sounds amazing Aust. I'm happy to help. I'm so excited for you."

"Thanks, I hope she says yes. I know we haven't been together that long but I've fallen for her and I know she's the right girl for me."

"That's great Austin. I'm so glad you found someone. And she will say yes; she really loves you."

He smiles, "I know. Thanks, babe." He pulls me close for a hug. "I'll give you the key and the address before you head home today. You can just leave it under the doormat at the new place."

"No worries," I reply giddy with excitement.

~~

The rest of the day passes quickly, thank god, as my whole body is tingling in anticipation of Jairus having his way with me.

Austin hugs me goodbye, handing me the keys for his new place. He whispers in my ear that he'll text me the address and I nod taking Jai's hand as we walk out.

We follow Mum and Dad, walking down the road towards my childhood home. I'm still holding Jai's hand, and I let out a giggle.

"What's so funny, sweetheart?"

"Nothing, it's just so amazing to be back home, and sharing another Christmas with you, now as my husband."

He smiles wide at me, that sexy cocky grin that makes me melt, "We'll have plenty more Christmases together, sweetheart."

He winks at me, his eyes lighting up with desire. It makes butterflies of longing flutter in my belly.

Reaching my parents' house, we follow them inside, bidding them goodnight the moment we step inside the front door.

Jairus still has the cocky grin on his face as he drags me down the hallway to my bedroom. Pushing me inside the door, he closes it behind him with a kick when he grabs me around the waist.

His lips quickly find mine in a heated kiss, making me moan against his lips. My knickers are soaked, I'm so damn wet for him. I can feel his dick pressing against the bottom of my baby bump and laugh when he breaks the kiss, groaning.

"Fuck Anni, I've been dying to kiss you all day."

His gaze is locked on mine. I take a step back pulling my sundress over my head and giving him a smirk as I beckon him closer to my bed. He yanks his T-shirt over his head, and I lick my lips gazing over his hot as sin body.

Sometimes I still can't believe he's mine, that I get to be the lucky woman that gets to make love to the delectable Jairus Brooks.

My knees hit the edge of my bed and I gasp when Jai enters my personal space, grabbing me around the waist again and kissing up my neck towards my ear.

I can't help but arch my neck back, pleasure pulsing through me, and moans escaping my lips.

His breath is in my ear when he whispers, "I'm going to fuck you so hard, sweetheart."

It sends tingles rushing through my body, making my clit throb with want. Fisting his hair I pull his face to mine, crushing my lips with his in a demanding kiss. His hands drop from my waist to cup my arse cheeks inside my knickers, and still kissing me he pushes them down so they fall to the floor.

Our kiss is frantic, so hot and fuelling the throb of my clit even more. He moans when I grab his dick in my grasp through his jeans. Biting my lip, he curses a loud husky 'fuck' breaking our kiss.

I look at him, batting my eyelashes, "Can I take off your jeans, baby?"

He doesn't reply but smirks as he yanks open his belt and drops his jeans to the floor so quickly I'm baffled.

"Someone's eager," I taunt, running my hands over the bulge in his boxers.

"I'm always eager to fuck you, sweetheart," he teases me back, his lustful gaze sweeping over my nearly naked body.

"Take off that pretty bralette, Anni. I want you completely naked for me."

I comply with his request, slipping the straps of my bralette down my arms before sliding it down my torso and over my baby bump. Our eyes are locked on each other, and he removes his boxers at the same time.

"Mmm, Jai, your dick looks delicious."

"Oh really?" He laughs smirking.

I drop to my knees, taking his dick into my mouth to suck him deep. Grabbing my hair, he makes me rock back and forth on his length before pulling me up.

Brushing the hair out of my face, he kisses me again, softly at first then harder when I feel his fingers slide inside me.

A hot moan escapes his lips against mine.

"Fuck, Annika, you're so wet. God, I want to fuck you so bad."

He puts the fingers into his mouth, closing his eyes a moment and letting out a groan of pleasure as he licks them clean.

When he opens his eyes, I've turned around, my arse facing him and in the air. Leaning on my elbows, I turn my head back to look at him.

"Fuck me from behind, baby."

He groans again, grabbing my hips as he enters me.

"God, Annika, fuck!" He bellows, slowly thrusting in and out, his groin slapping against my arse as he increases the pace.

"Touch me, Jai, please," I beg, lacing my tongue with lust.

He stretches over my back, still pounding into my sex and reaches around to flick my clit. My whole body quivers at the sensation.

"Mmm, baby, so good," I cry out stretching up a little to kiss him. I part his lips with my tongue, lacing them together as our bodies rock together. I can't think, can't take it anymore, the sheer pleasure rushing through my body.

Breaking the kiss panting, I hiss my words, "Jai, I'm gonna come." He takes his hand from my clit, putting his fingers in his between his lips again, and huskily he says, "Hold on for me, sweetheart."

"Ok," I reply biting down on my lip when he thrusts balls deep inside me, his warm release starting to spill into my walls.

"Fuck!" He screams out as he fills me and my climax rocks my body into a trembling mess.

He pulls out, falling against the bed next to me and grabbing me around the waist to pull me down next to him.

"That was phenomenal," he says softly, kissing my hair and pulling me closer.

"I know," I reply, turning my head to face him and placing a soft kiss against his lips.

"I love you Jairus Brooks."

He smiles at me, "I love you too, Annika Brooks."

His eyes look over to the digital clock on the bedside table that just flicks over to midnight.

"I hope you had a Merry Christmas, sweetheart."

"I definitely did, baby."

"Good, snuggle into me. I want to hold you and my babies close."

Smiling I pull the sheet up over us and drift off to sleep wrapped in husbands arms thinking of all the memories we'd made this year.

Forty-Seven | Trust Your Heart
Bella

Christmas was again over for another year. It was weird being back at Mum's, without Nora. It hurt like hell leaving her with Jaxon and his family, but I needed the break and he needed some time with his daughter.

Rubbing my eyes I wander into the kitchen to find Mum at the stove cooking up a big breakfast of bacon, eggs, tomatoes and hash browns. It smells divine, and I inhale it sitting down on the stool at the breakfast bar.

"Morning, Mum. Smells great," I say when she turns around to smile at me.

"Good morning, Bella. I hope you're hungry."

"For your cooking, I'm always hungry Mum."

She plates it up, sliding a plate across the bench to me.

Leaning over it, she looks at me questioningly as I start eating.

"What Mum? Why are you looking at me like that?"

"Like what?"

"Like you know something I don't," I laugh softly.

"I can tell something is bothering you, Bella."

Taking a big mouthful of food, I swallow it hard and sigh.

"Ok fine, Mum. I'm confused that's all."

"About what? Man troubles?"

"Yeah, I'm still in love with Austin, but now he's with Dana and..."
I take another mouthful of food, wondering how I can tell her about what's happened between Travis and me.

Yes, we've only just kissed, but just being in the same room as him makes me want to give in to any temptation he asks of me.

"And what Bella?" Mum snaps like she's angry at me.

"I kissed someone else. Travis, he's Anni's husbands best mate."

"And is that a bad thing?"

"Yeah, he's a bit of a douche, but um...I don't know."

Mum smiles at me then, "You need to trust your heart and your body."

"What do you mean?" I ask confused.

My heart and body are telling me two different things.

My heart wants Austin, even though I know I can't have him, but my body wants Travis, even though I know I shouldn't want him.

"How does your body feel around them?" Mum asks.

"Mum, seriously," I scoff.

"No Bella beautiful listen to it," she snaps again, "you may be in love with Austin, but if you don't feel a physical connection with him he's not the right man for you."

"Yeah, I guess," I reply finishing my food and jumping off the stool to put my plate in the dishwasher.

Mum is giving me knowing glances, and a part of me wishes she'd just tell me what to do, but I know I have to make the choice for myself. I need to trust my heart but listen to my body.

I give Mum a hug, "Thanks for the advice, Mum."

"What are Mum's for Bella beautiful. When are you heading off?"

"Around lunch, just going to have a shower and head off after."

"Ok," she says, kissing my forehead.

I head down the hallway to the bathroom, stripping my clothes off the moment I shut the door.

I survey my body in the mirror, tapping the tiny pooch still left over from carrying Nora. My breasts feel so full from not having pumped the last few days whilst I've been away from her.

I admired my body before, loving showing it off, but now I admired it for different reasons.

Getting into the shower, my thoughts wander to whether Travis would appreciate and love my simple curves and be able to appreciate my baby body or whether he'd be repulsed like Jaxon seemed to be of late.

Just thinking of Travis is making my clit throb and a memory crashes into my mind that I'd forgotten about in my drunken state at Anni's wedding.

I can feel his fingers on my clit, as I shut my eyes and slowly touch myself. I'm so aroused with the thoughts of him touching me and kissing me I come apart in barely a minute.

Leaning against the wall, I curse myself for masturbating thinking of him, but Mum's words ring in my head as I get out.

'Trust your body, Bella beautiful.'

If I was going to trust my body, I knew the answer already.

My body belongs to Travis Banes.

But my heart hasn't gotten that memo.

Forty-Eight | New Year Celebrations
Dana

Walking into Jai and Anni's penthouse, I'm clutching Austin's hand giddy with excitement at telling them our exciting news.

I can't stop staring at the diamond ring on my finger. The way it catches the light, sparkling, sends a rush of electricity rushing through my body.

Hearing Austin tell me he loves me was beyond amazing, those words from his lips I'd been waiting months to hear.

The moment we step in the door, Austin drags me over to Anni and they share an unspoken conversation that ends with him dropping my hand and hugging her. She walks off a moment to go and grab us some drinks and I look at Austin incredulously.

I'm kinda worried, even though it's stupid to even entertain the thought that something would be going on between them.

Having been cheated on, the fear of it happening again still plagues me.

Sensing the fear that's pulsating through me Austin takes my hand, "You ok, Dan?" he asks and I can't help but panic that he didn't call me gorgeous.

Sheepishly I look him in the eyes, "Um...is there something going on with you and Anni?"

He laughs, loud, slapping a hand against his stomach.

"Seriously, gorgeous, you're kidding?"

"No," I stammer, biting on my lip a moment before I continue, "you just kinda spoke to her without words, and then hugged her."

He shakes his head, rubbing a hand up and down my bare arm.

"Dana, I love you. And Anni is my best friend. We have a past together yes, but she's not the woman I'm in love with."

"Ok, but..." I reply, not really sure what I want to say as all I really heard was 'Dana, I love you'.

"She actually helped me organise everything for proposing to you."

My eyes boggle at him, and I laugh, "Really?"

"Yeah, she set up everything at the house so I could surprise you."

"Oh, I feel like a dufus."

He doesn't reply at first, just pulls me close for a sweet hug before whispering in my ear, "I love you, Dana."

I pull back from his hug, giving him a soft kiss when Anni returns with drinks for us. She waves Bella over from the other side of the room and they both congratulate us, gawking at my sparkling ring.

"It's stunning Dana," Anni says, elbowing Austin in the side, "this dufus actually did something right for once."

"Hey babe, that's mean," he shrieks sticking his tongue out at her.

"Just teasing you, bestie. I really am so happy for you both."

"Yeah, congrats Austin. And you to Dana," Bella says without a smile on her face.

I get the sense she's not happy for me, but I shrug it off when I feel someone else step up to us.

It's Travis.

He meekly congratulates me, giving me a peck on the cheek and nods at Austin, "Congrats to you to man for snagging this one."

"Thanks, mate," Austin replies, returning the nod before gulping down his beer.

I see Travis looking at Bella, and I wonder if there's something going on between them.

I'd seen that lustful look in his blue eyes before and I knew it could charm any girl out of her knickers.

He doesn't say anything to her though, just turns away and heads out without a backwards glance. I make a mental note to speak to him after a game soon and then I turn to Anni.

"Anni, I think we need to dance for old times sake. What was that song you danced on the table top to that night at your party?"

"Oh, yeah. Turn the music up!" she shrieks in delight, grabbing my hand and Bella's and dragging us both into the middle of the room where the sound system is set up and connected to her iPad and Spotify. Stopping the music that's playing, she quickly finds the song and we all start dancing together. The boys all turn to stare at us and our laughter fills the room.

It is certainly a New Year's Eve worthy of celebration. I've never been happier and when my fiancé steps up behind me grabbing me around the waist and grinding against my arse I know the new year is only going to get better.

Turning around in his arms, I kiss him hard, and my heart pounds when he says, "Happy new year, my gorgeous fiancé."

No words have ever been sweeter.

Forty-Nine | Fist It Hard

Rushing home, I'm practically panting when I open my front door. It's just before Midnight and all I want to do is crash into bed and jack off to calm my aching cock from seeing Bella again. Knowing I can't have her and didn't have her when I could've has been on my mind since the day after Jai's wedding.

Images of her in my t-shirt that morning surface in my mind frequently and make my cock spring to attention in an instant. And seeing her tonight, her curves not hidden by her midriff-baring white tank top and her arse peeking out of the skimpy denim shorts had my cock begging for release.
Plus the tank top brushed the edge of her perky tits, showing enough to tell me she wasn't wearing a bra and fuck was that side boob view glorious.

The whole way home in the taxi, I'd been undressing her in my mind and now inside I'm about to yank my cock out of my pants and jack off in the middle of my living room when I hear a murmur coming from the couch, "Travy? Is that you?"

Shit! Fuck! Tessa is asleep on my fucking couch.

Shuffling towards my bedroom, I call out, "Yeah Tessa, it's me. Go back to sleep yeah?"

Closing my bedroom door behind me, I hear her mutter an 'ok'. Waiting a few minutes until I'm sure she's gone back to sleep I flop down on my unmade bed, fumbling with the fly of my jeans and yanking them down over my painfully hard cock.

Kicking my jeans off, I sit up and pull my t-shirt off throwing it on the floor as well.

Through the opening in my boxers my cock is peeking out and grabbing it in my fist I stroke it, pulling the skin back to expose the tip that is already gathering drops of pre cum.

After a couple of minutes I pull my boxers off too, and slide back further on my bed spreading my legs wide.

Grabbing my cock with one hand again, I sit back against the headboard with the other hand behind my head.

Closing my eyes I again start to pump my hand up and down on my cock, picturing Bella stripping for me.

She firstly pulls her tank top over her head, throwing it on the floor, locking her eyes on me as she shakes her dark chestnut locks back. Her nipples are hard, and her tits are fucking perfection, exactly the right size to cup in my fists and take in my mouth.
I beckon her towards me, wanting to suck them into my mouth, but she shakes her head at me smirking like a damn she-devil. Instead, she undoes the fly of her skimpy denim shorts, hooking her fingers in the sides as she shimmies them down her lightly tanned thighs. I let out a moan, still pumping my cock hard.
Now she's standing in front of me in only a lacy black g-string that clearly shows her pussy is bare.
I curse, 'god, Bella, let me lick your fucking pussy now.'

She lets out a giggle, and a moan rolled into one as she slips her g-string off. Stepping out of it she licks her lips as she climbs onto the bed, crawling towards me on all fours.

"Mmm, fuck," I moan, still fisting my cock so hard.

I fucking want her, I want her here so I can touch her clit again and taste her before slamming my cock in her so hard she comes apart beneath me over and over again.

Just thinking about her stripping for me, I'm so close to blowing my load. I've got droplets of pre-cum pearling on my tip and I slide a finger across the creamy liquid bringing it up to my lips and licking it before I pump my cock hard again.

Cupping my balls I shoot my warm load over my stomach, sighing and screaming out her name.

Wiping my stomach with the black satin sheet, I crawl underneath them and tell myself to stop thinking about her.

No sheila has ever gotten to me so bad.

My body wants Bella Mishal. But I'm pretty sure that she wants a relationship, somebody to love and I'm not down for that.

Fifty | Sisters Relocate Together
Bella

It's hard to believe another year has gone by, and even harder to believe that my little sister is all grown up and about to knock on my front door any moment to move in with me.

I'd moved back into the Richmond apartment just after the new year when Austin had moved into his new place with Dana.

Stupid me was still pining after him, and I slept in his old room sometimes in his bed that he'd left behind because his new place was furnished.

It still smelt like him and his Tommy Hilfiger cologne.

I'd think of him, and the times we fucked in this bed and mine, but now it only made my heart ache and not my body.

I'm pottering around the apartment, making sure it's spotless so Elyse feels at home.

I'm startled by a knock on the door. Running to it I open it wide and scoff when it's not Elyse standing on the doorstep, but Jaxon.

"Hey Bel," he says a little sheepishly, not able to look at me.

I'm only wearing a tank top and cheeky knickers, and I curse myself for not putting on some leggings when answering the door. I make a mental note to always answer the door wearing daks in the future.

"Jaxon, what are you doing here?"

"Um...coming to pick up Nora. It's my weekend, isn't it?"

I calculate the dates in my head, knowing he's right but it completely slipped my mind with Christmas in the mix.

"Right, um, yeah. Come in, I'll get her up and grab her stuff."
He follows me in, towards my bedroom where I have a corner set up as a mini nursery for Nora.
She's awake in her cot and picking her up I coo at her, "Hey baby girl, Daddy's here."
She giggles at me, turning her head to look at Jaxon when he walks in. He glances around the room, scoffing. "Bel, our little girl should have her own space. Come back and live with me." He says the words like a statement, rather than a question and it makes me want to chunder.
I can't stand being a metre away from him anymore, let alone living in the same house and sleeping in the same bed. His touch makes me repulsed now, and I know I only have one person to blame for that, but I can't think about him right now.
I need to collect my thoughts.

"You know that's not going to happen Jaxon. We're never getting back together, so please just let it be."
I hand Nora to him, and he rocks her in his arms, looking down at her and then up at me as I organise the nappy bag with some clothes for her.
"Do you have any nappies at yours?" I ask him, my fingers brushing against the disposable nappies on top of my drawers.
"Yes, Bella, I have everything, but some clothes. Can you hurry up? I've gotta go meet up with Jace and his new girl."
A knot twists in my stomach, hearing my ex's name on his twin brother's lips. I'm seriously disgusted with myself for fucking them

both, and even though I love Nora to pieces I'm even more disgusted with myself that she's connected to the McMasters by blood. My poor baby girl doesn't have a hope with us both as her parents.

"I didn't need to know that Jaxon, but thanks and here," I spit, shoving Nora's nappy bag at him.

He grabs it awkwardly, still holding Nora in a cradle position when I walk him out to the door.

Opening it, he tries to bend down and kiss me on the cheek, but I step back and he stumbles a little bumping straight into Elyse who is about to knock on my door when I open it for Jaxon.

"Oh, um...shit...Jaxon, sorry," she apologises.

"No, worries Elyse. I'm heading out," he says walking out, "see you on Sunday, Bella," he calls back to me.

Elyse shoves me inside, dropping her bag at her feet.

"What the hell was going on there, Bel-bear?"

"Well, hello to you to Ely-bug, and nothing is going on there. We aren't together."

"Sorry, Bel-bear," my little sister replies, hugging me and squeezing me tight.

"Let me breathe, Ely-bug, yeah?"

"Eeek, I'm just excited to be here."

"I know, Elyse. I'm glad you're here too. Time for a girls weekend, now that Jaxon has Nora."

"Yeah, talk about good timing. But are you sure nothing is going on between you? He was about to kiss you."

I laugh, slapping her arm, "Trust me, Ely-bug, that ship has sailed. I don't think I was ever onboard the Jaxon ship to begin with."

She gives me a confused look. "But isn't Nora his? You must have fucked him to have a kid with him?"

Again I laugh, "Yes Elyse, I fucked him. One too many times."

"So, it was just about the sex?" she asks like I'm going to give her the answers to the mysteries of the universe.

"Yeah, it was. And a way to block out my feelings for Austin."

"Yeah," she says softly, picking up her bag and shrieking, "So big sis, show me around my new digs?"

"Someone's keen," I laugh leading her towards Austin's old room. She flops down on the bed and pretends to do a snow angel on the mattress. The smell of Austin's Tommy Hilfiger cologne wafts back into the air.

"Smells like hot guy in here," Elyse laughs sitting up.

"Yeah, this was Austin and Jairus's old room."

"Oh, well I better make it smell like girl then," she laughs, jumping up and hugging me again.

"I love you Bel-bear. I'm so excited that we get to live together."

"Me too, Ely-bug. Get settled in, bathroom's down the hall and when you're good we'll order pizza and have a girly night in watching 'The Bachelor'."

"Sounds great," she replies, giggling when I walk out.

It felt good to share my feelings with her, and I'm definitely sure I've made the right decision having her move in with me so she could go to Uni. The only thing I'm not sure about is whether moving back into the old apartment is the right thing, but it's time to make new memories with my little sister to block out the old ones and heal my heart.

Fifty-One | Party Night Pashing

After showering, I'm gawking at myself in the bathroom contemplating if I should shave or not.

Fingering the stubble I decide I can't be bothered, plus I kinda like the look of my face with a beginning goatee.

Back in the bedroom, in the walk-in wardrobe, I pull on some light denim jeans and shrug my arms into a pale pink long-sleeved shirt. Pushing the sleeves up to my elbows I button it up before slipping my feet into some brown dress shoes.

I feel like a pansy sometimes, as I definitely like to look good, always taking pride in what I'm wearing but it suits me well.

My look always had sheila's falling at my feet, so why not rock the metrosexual vibe?

Heading out, I glance in the mirror one more time, quickly trying to decide if I should tuck the shirt in or let it hang out.

I go for the latter and grab my keys, phone and the card with a couple hundy tucked inside before heading out to the Jag.

Driving through the city streets, towards Hawthorn I'm pushing the Jag to her limit, shifting gears only when the hum of the engine demands it. It feels kinda bittersweet going to Dana's engagement party, like this is truly the end of there being an us. It's not that I want a relationship with her, and I definitely don't want to be engaged to anyone.

God, Meaghan fucked you up man. You're damaged goods, who the fuck would want to marry you anyway?

My fucking subconscious is right and turning into the carpark behind Night Owls bar, I smash my fist against the steering wheel in frustration. The horn sounds, but luckily no one is around to witness my stupid meltdown.

Getting out of the Jag, I head inside, mentally giving myself a kick up the arse to stop being such a pansy and also preparing myself for seeing Bella. The afternoon cocktail shindig is in full swing when I saunter in. I spot Dana first, heading over to congratulate her I grab a glass of champers from the wandering waitress and gulp it down in a couple of mouthfuls.

I know I shouldn't drink much, but a few will help me loosen up a little and not feel like a carp out of the river at a fucking engagement party.

I don't see the point of them, and it has been forever since I've been to one, considering my best mate didn't even have one.

Reaching Dana, I give her a quick hug. "Congratulations again, Dan. You look ripper," I say, looking my ex fuck buddy up and down. Her figure-hugging little red dress screams sex kitten, and in times gone by I would have loved to rip it off her and pound my cock into her, but she wasn't mine now and I didn't want her to be anymore.

She smiles at me, "Thanks, Travis. You scrub up all right too."

I laugh, "I know, I rock the pink shirt look."

She scoffs at me, laughing.

"Yeah, so where's ya man?" I ask, glancing around the bar.

"Probably somewhere with your best mate, since he's attached at the hip to her bestie."

"Yeah, you ok with them being best mates?"

"Yeah, Anni's a sweetie and so in love with Jairus. I don't have anything to worry about."

"Yeah, true," I reply a little sheepishly.

"You ok?" she asks me, sensing my unease.

"Yeah, ripper," I reply half-heartedly and of course Dana sees right through my bullshit.

Shaking her head at me, she says, "Don't lie to me, Travis."

"Fine, I'll tell you, but keep ya pretty lips zipped."

She pretends to zip them before I speak, "I kissed Bella after Jai and Anni's wedding."

"What? Seriously?"

"Yeah, it was fucking hot Dan and I can't stop thinking about her."

She looks at me dumbfounded. "I don't know what to say, Travis. But I guess if you want her that bad you should do something about it. Follow your heart."

I laugh, "My heart has nothing to do with it Dana. You of all people should know that."

"Yeah, but I don't think Bella is as much of a skank as you seem to think."

I cringe at her words, feeling a pang of guilt hearing a word coming out of her mouth that I called her once in anger.

"I'm sorry Dan. I never should've called you a skank. You're probably right about Bella."

"Don't worry about it. It's in the past." She's about to say something else when a friend calls her over to the small dance floor.

I watch her walk away, smiling at me, before heading to the bar to grab a beer.

Jairus is sitting on a barstool, sipping a beer.

Slapping a hand on his back, I sit down next to him. "Hey man, where's ya wife at?"

"Went to the dunny with Bella," he replies with a hint of a laugh, looking across at me when he says 'Bella'.

"Right, whats with sheila's going to the dunny together?"

I signal the barman for a beer, and he quickly slides one down to me.

"Stuffed if I know, man."

"Are you good? You seem in the dumps?"

"I'm fine. Just buggered getting back into training and don't really want to be here."

I laugh at him, feeling the same, "You and me both brother. I'm only here because Dana asked me."

He scoffs, nearly spitting out his mouthful of beer, "Yeah right, man."

"What? Can't a brother be friends with his ex hookup?"

"Not saying that at all."

"Then what are you saying?"

"Don't fuck with me man. You're here so you can hook up with Bella again."

My cock twitches in my daks at the thought of hooking up with her again, I can't deny I'm attracted to her.

She's a dark-haired goddess.

"Um, yeah, but..."

"But what Travis?"

"I have to stay away from her. I'm not the guy for her."

He mutters a simple 'mmm' before taking another sip of beer.

I gulp some of mine down, wiping my bare arm across my chin to collect the foam. And that's when I feel her near.

Anni and Bella are walking across the room, giggling as they chat with each other.

Fuck me, does she look as hot as sin.

Her dress is a dark grey halter neck figure-hugging number showing off her hips, tits and arse, with a split in the front on one side that stops halfway up her toned thigh.

My cock again twitches in my daks, and I lick my lips as they approach.

Anni steps up behind Jai, wrapping her arms around him and kissing his cheek.

"Miss me, baby?" she asks him. He gives her a devious smirk and turns to kiss her.

Watching my best mate kiss his sheila is kinda repulsive but a turn on at the same time, especially with Bella leaning over the bar next to me. Grabbing my beer again I turn to face her and run my fingers over the bare skin of her arm, leaning close to whisper, to her, "You look fucking gorgeous, sunshine."

I feel her shiver at the touch, and when she turns to look at me with lust in her eyes, I nearly cream my daks on the spot.

I want to pull her close and fuck her mouth right here, but don't want to give my best mate a show, instead, I clutch her hand, leaning close and kissing below her ear.

"Follow me sunshine."

Giving me a smile, I'm delighted that she doesn't resist me leading her away, down the narrow hallway that leads to the stairs and upper decking area.

It's surprisingly deserted for a warm summer evening, but I'm kinda glad at the same time.

Without giving her any warning I pin her against the wall, grabbing her hands and holding them above her head whilst leaning in, my forehead against hers. Her breath is laboured, she's panting and it's turning me on so bad. Shifting back a little, but not moving my hands I ask her, "Bella, do you remember our first kiss? How hot it was?"

She nods her head at me, licking her delectable plump lips before taking the bottom one between her teeth.

"Fuck, Bella. You turn me on!" I groan, sliding my other hand down to the split in her dress.

She's still panting, and it's delicious torture.

Leaning in I kiss under her ear, down her neck and she whimpers in pleasure, arching it back. Her mouth opens, and in a raspy voice she moans the words, "Kiss me, Travis."

Fuck me, if those aren't the sexiest words ever.

"Fuck, Bella," I moan looking down at her again.

I trace her lips with a finger, and her tongue darts out to lick it, making my cock scream in my daks.

Her eyes are locked on mine, burning into me. And she's doing the raspy panting breathing again, her mouth slightly open.

I can't fucking take it anymore. I need to kiss her again.

Taking my hand from holding hers above her head, I stroke her cheek, "You're fucking beautiful, Bella."

Her breath hitches when I say her name, but I don't give her another moment to think, to take another breath in before I crash my lips against hers. She gives me entrance straight away, teasing me by slipping her tongue between my lips.

Teasing her back with our tongues dancing, I bite her lip, pulling it back in my teeth before pressing my lips back to hers to soothe the sting. The little gesture elicits a moan from her, and she moves her hands from above her head, grabbing my hair to push me closer against her.

I can feel my cock pressing against her belly, desperate to be free of the confines of denim.

Breathless I break the kiss, cupping her cheeks in my palms. "God, sunshine. You know how to kiss a guy senseless."

She doesn't say anything, just smirks at me and pulls my lips back to hers for a fierce kiss that sends the blood racing through my body. Her hands slide from my hair down my back and under my shirt. Her hands on my skin are setting my body on fire and it makes me grind into her, kissing her harder.

With our lips still locked, her hands roaming my body, I slide my hand further up her thigh, reaching the flimsy lace g-string she has on. I'm about to rip it to touch her clit, to really touch her as I started to months ago at Jai's wedding, but she whimpers against my lips and pulls back. Her cheeks are flushed and she's clearly got pash rash.

"Not here," she mewls at me.

"Come back to mine then?" I suggest, running a hand down her side.

"I shouldn't."

"The night's not over sunshine. I want to kiss you all over."

Again she lets out a little whimper, and I'm not sure if she's scared of how much she wants me or if she's turned on.

"Ok, take me to yours."

Inwardly, I let out a squeak of glee and my cock jolts in my daks. She's not going to know what's hit her when I have my way with her.

It's no lie that I want to kiss every inch of her skin, and want to sink my cock inside her pussy, but as she follows me out holding my hand with a smile on her face I know for once I might need to take it slow, to get her to trust me.

How she makes me feel is different to how I've felt for any other sheila and it's got me damn scared.

Fifty-Two Kiss Me Sunshine

Driving back towards Prahran to my apartment, I can't stop staring at Bella sitting in the passenger seat of the Jag.

The tension between us is thick, but neither of us dares to speak.

I try to open my mouth, to make small talk, but nothing comes out and I find myself licking my lips thinking about kissing her again and again. Her kisses are like none I've ever had.

I can't think about anything else, but the feel of her lips on mine, and the way she tastes, it's like fairy floss, sweet and addictive.

Stopping outside my apartment, I'm sure I've broken the speed limit fifty times over in an effort to get back as quick as possible.

Getting out of the Jag, I saunter around to the passenger side, opening the door for her like a gentleman.

What I want to do to her is far from gentlemanly though.

She gives me a sexy as fuck smirk, taking my hand in hers.

A tingle rushes up my arm and all through my body, straight lightning to my cock. I groan, pushing her against the side of the Jag. Cupping her cheeks I smash my lips to hers again, a kiss so hard it makes her moan and push her pelvis against mine.

Panting she breaks the kiss, looking at me with hooded eyes, full of lust.

God, I fucking want her

Taking her hand again, I lead into my apartment nearly tripping up the stairs and fumbling with the keys when we reach my front door. Quickly opening it, Bella follows me inside.

I give her a moment to scan the surroundings again, and she smiles, "Your apartment is beautiful."

Her words strike me as a little odd, and I chuckle a little grabbing her around the waist, "No, sunshine, you're beautiful."

She lets out a whimper, biting down on her lip and locks her eyes on mine. My cock twitches and some strange fluttery feeling stirs in my stomach. She's got me in knots, and it feels shit but insanely fucking good at the same time. I've never wanted a sheila as much as I want Bella.

Brushing the stray hairs from her flushed cheeks, leaning in I kiss her softly. She moans, kissing me back harder, melting into my arms and climbing me, wrapping her legs around my arse.

Holding her tighter, I walk backwards towards the couch. When my legs hit the edge of it, I slowly sit down, still kissing her and pulling her down onto my lap. She breaks the kiss, panting. "Fuck, Travis, you know how to kiss."

I laugh, "So do you. So shut up, and kiss me again."

My tone is demanding and lustful, making her smirk before crashing her lips to mine and licking my lips to deepen the kiss. She tastes fucking incredible, sugary sweet and absolutely fucking addictive. My cock is lined up with her pussy, her dress hitched up her thighs. Moaning, she starts rocking her pussy over my bulging cock, "Mmm, fuck sunshine," I say against her lips before she pulls back panting again.

Giggling with her eyes locked on mine, she stands up, reaching under her dress to slide the scrap of nude lace underwear down her legs.

Before climbing back onto my lap, she leans over me to undo my jeans and I yank them down my legs to my feet.

I want to tear all our clothes off, to touch, lick and kiss every inch of her skin but I also want her mouth on mine again.

Taking her hand I pull her back down onto my lap, again hitching her tight dress up, this time to a pool at her pelvis.

Cupping her cheeks I bring her lips back down to mine. This kiss is intense, as she starts to rock her bare pussy against my cock again, teasing the beast and teasing my mouth with her tongue lacing with mine.

Our bodies are so close, the only barrier between us is the cotton of my boxers. Breaking the kiss, about to pull them down and ask her for permission to take her pussy as mine I'm shaken from the lust haze by a voice from down the hallway.

"What the fuck Travy! Seriously!"

Fuck!

My sister is crossing the room, in pyjamas whilst rubbing her wet hair with a towel. Bella jumps off my lap in shock, looking at Tessa and then back at me, with a questioning look in her eyes.

Standing up I put an arm around her waist, but she brushes me off and gives me dagger eyes.

"Um, sorry Tessie, this is Bella, my...um...shit."

What the fuck do I call her? Fuck buddy? No. Hook up? Fuck no. Girlfriend? No fucking way.

Bella is still at a loss for words, glaring at Tessa. "And Bella, this is my sister Tessa."

The look Bella gives me hits me right in the chest.

"Right, your sister. You're an arsehole, Travis!"

I try to take her hand, words on the tip of my tongue, but she pulls away rushing to the door.

She's gone, straight from my arms and out my front door, like she was never here.

Cursing under my breath, I pick up my discarded jeans, and Bella's g-string before heading to my bedroom.

"Thanks a lot, Tessa."

My little sister has the gall to laugh.

"For what?" You were the one hooking up on the couch I'm sleeping on at the moment."

"Yeah, so. You could've...fuck, I don't know..." I curse, throwing my arm up in frustration.

"I could've what? Slept in your dirty as fuck bed?"

"Yeah, that and...not interrupted, or fuck I don't know...maybe actually confirmed you are my fucking sister."

Again she laughs, which is really pissing me off.

"Aww, I'm sorry big bro. Why are you so pissed that I interrupted a hook up anyway? You'll have another chick tomorrow."

Shaking my head I reply, "Yeah, but Bella is not just some chick. She's...she's...fuck I don't know."

"Ooo, is Travy in love?"

"No, fuck off! I don't do love, Tessa."

"Whatever you say, Travis. I saw the way you looked at her."

"Yeah, yeah, whatever," I reply, brushing her off and slapping her playfully with my jeans I'm holding. She laughs again, heading to the couch whilst I head to my bedroom.

There's no way I'm in love with Bella, I don't do love, and I barely know her.

Yes, I know she has a kid and the father proposed, but I really don't know anything else about her.

All I really know is I want her, the lust between us is on fire.

But I'm scared too because I know that being with her once is never going to be enough. I will crave all of her, just like I crave her kiss now that I've had more than one taste of her.

Fifty-Three | Stranger Comes Knocking
Elyse

Even above the sound of the horror movie I shouldn't be watching on tv whilst home alone I hear the rap of knuckles on the door and yeah I fucking panic. It's like the horror movie has shifted into my own damn reality.

Muting the tv I wait a minute to make sure I'm not hearing things, but the knocking continues, becoming louder and more insistent. I want to leave it, but also don't want the noise to wake up Nora who I finally got to take her nap only twenty damn minutes ago.

Standing up from the couch, I tiptoe to the door, my heart pounding in my chest. It makes me feel like a wuss, but I've heard stories of strangers kicking people's doors in to rob them when they answer so yes I'm panicking.

Damn Bella for not being home tonight.

It's not even dark outside yet and I'm scaring myself shitless.

Opening the door slowly, I peer out between the gap to find a fucking gorgeous ashen haired, hot as sin guy standing on the doorstep. I'm sure he's at the wrong house, and also sure he's not a robber, but even if he is I'd be happy to invite him in to take everything so I could just stare at him and watch his muscles ripple as he moves through my space.

Opening the door wider, I stand against the door frame trying to act sexy, but I probably look like a right idiot in my pyjama shorts and tank. Being a tomboy, I never could look girly, even if I was trying to.

He looks me up and down, appearing a little shocked and taken aback. I'm hoping that means I succeeded in looking sexy.

"Um, hi," he says in a husky voice that makes me feel like my damn knickers are on fire, "I was just wondering if Austin was home?"

Right. He's here for Austin. Damnit!

I gulp, trying to find the words to answer him when he's standing there just staring at me with his mesmerising hazel brownish eyes.

He speaks again, "Is he here?"

I shake my head. "Um, no. He moved out months ago."

I rush the words out quickly, partly wanting the conversation to be over so he'll leave and I can go take care of myself, of the ache in my knickers.

He gives me a dumbfounded look, running a hand through his thick ashen locks. I'm still watching him, practically salivating at his every move.

"Oh shit, um...are you sure?"

"Yeah, Didn't he tell you?" I ask, trying to rack my brain for any thoughts of who this sexy stranger that knows Austin is.

I feel like I know him but I can't place him.

"Nah I haven't seen him for a couple of months. He's skipped out on everything lately."

His words seem really melancholic and my heart feels sad for him.

"Well, I can let Bel know you dropped by and to let Austin know."

His mouth drops open at my words and he asks, "Sorry, do you mean Bella?"

"Yeah, Bella, she's my sister. I'm living here now with her and her daughter Nora. I started uni a month or so ago." I again rush out my words in a crazed panic.

He looks me up and down again, this time biting down on his lip before he speaks in the husky, sexy voice again. "Oh, shit...fuck no..um...you're...fuck!"

The recollection hits us both at the same time, and I feel a little stir of lust in my knickers again. I'd thought about him in the past months, wondering what it would've been like to be the one kissing him and now he's on my doorstep.

Holy shit!

"No way! You're the guy Austin was pashing last year when I came to stay with Bella?"

He blushes, and it's so damn hot. I want to drag him inside and reenact that kiss but with myself under his rippled muscular body.

"Yeah...names Kaden," he says stretching out his hand to me.

"Elyse," I reply.

I know I'm blushing when I take his hand and shake it.

A tingle rushes up my arm, and also to my damn knickers again.

"Nice to meet you Elyse," he says in that husky voice, my name on his lips like honey. "I should probably head to boxing but I'll catch ya later."

I nod, "Um, yep, later."

He turns to walk away, waving at me before I step back inside and close the door behind me.

Sinking to my butt with my back against the door I sigh deeply.

I never thought I'd see him again and now that I have it's sending all sorts of strange feelings through my body.

I think I have a crush on Kaden, but he'll probably never go for me for the one obvious reason, I'm a girl and he's clearly gay.

Fifty-Four | Remembering Naughty Times

Bella

Rushing home from Travis's I feel naked, vulnerable and exposed. Not wearing underwear is a contributing factor to the naked feeling but it's more than that.

Kissing him sets my whole body on fire, and I'm cursing myself for nearly letting my body take over.

I nearly fucked him, and I barely know the guy. I actually don't know him at all, except for the fact that he's Blondie's best mate and a major player.

From what Anni has told me, he had a thing going with Dana for a while, but considering she's engaged to Austin it's clear that Travis is not the relationship type.

Granted I didn't think Austin was either, but it was obviously just me. With everything that's happened of late, I wonder myself if I'm the relationship type either.

Finally home, opening the front door which I'm surprised is unlocked I find Elyse in the kitchen making a coffee.

"Hey, Ely-bug."

She turns to look at me smiling, "Oh hey Bel-bear. How was the party?"

I cross the room to the kitchen, sitting up on one of the stools, "It was ok. Austin seems really happy."

"That's good. There was a guy here looking for Austin, actually."
She takes a sip of her coffee, nodding at me.
"Yeah, who?" I ask, watching her cheeks flush.
"Kaden," she replies meekly, taking another sip of coffee to hide her red cheeks.
"Oh shit! Really?"
"Yeah, he seemed really upset that Austin hasn't spoken to him for a bit."
"Yeah, I um...think he pushed him away a bit when he got with Dana and now they're engaged so um yeah..."

My heart hurts, not only because saying Austin is engaged to someone out loud hurts like a bitch, but also because he pushed a friend like Kaden away.
I get it completely.
It's hard to be around someone you're in love with who doesn't love you back.

"So he was the guy pashing Austin last year? I was right."
"Yeah," I reply blushing myself, thinking back to our threesome.
"What Bel-bear? Did something happen with him and you?" She says a little too excitedly.
I feel myself blush deeper, not sure if I should be sharing such intimate and dirty things with my eighteen-year-old sister.
"I can't tell you Ely-bug."
She huffs, "Why? I'm not a prude, Bella!"
I know I probably shouldn't but find myself saying, "Fine, but you can't tell anyone?"
Giggling she says, "Ok my lips are sealed."

After she pretends to zip them shut, I let the words fall out of my mouth, "I had a threesome with him and Austin."

"Oh my god Bel-bear," she shrieks, "that's so dirty but hot at the same time."

"Yeah...it was," I reply laughing. She laughs with me for a moment before asking casually, "So why you home so late?"

"I um..I."

"Bel-bear, tell me. You left me home alone with Nora, even though the engagement party ended hours ago."

"I'm sorry, I uh was just...um...with a...um...friend." I stammer the words, friend sounding weird on my lips, especially in regard to Travis and the confusion of how I feel about him.

I don't hate him, I'm not even sure if I like him, but my body sure as hell loves being around him.

Elyse gulps down the last few sips of her coffee before taunting me, "A friend huh?"

"Ok...a guy...not really a friend...I don't know what to call him." She laughs at my indecisiveness. "A fuck buddy?"

"Elyse!" I bellow, trying not to laugh, "But yeah I guess but we haven't actually slept together unless actually sleeping counts. It's complicated."

"Do you like him?"

"Yeah kinda...he's fucking gorgeous but also a complete douche." I want to tell her more, but the feelings of anger after tonight are still too raw.

"Tell me more sis...who is this hottie?"

"Travis...the best man in Anni's wedding."

"Oh my god, Bel, he's so fucking gorgeous!"

"I know...literally sex on legs, but enough about that, how was my baby girl?"

"Perfect as always."

She smiles at me and I jump down off the stool to hug her, "What would I do without you Ely-bug? I love you."

"Love you too, Bel-bear."

As though on cue, Nora starts crying so I head to my bedroom to check on her. Picking her up I rock her gently, her crying not stopping. Putting her back down in the cot a moment, I peel off my dress, feeling so much better to be free of the constricting fabric. I'm completely naked, as I wasn't wearing a bra under the halter neck dress. I pick Nora back up and she instantly takes to my breast.

My thoughts wander to Travis, and the look in his eyes when I called him an arsehole before I rushed out.

It seemed as though my words hurt, and I can't help but wonder if the woman really was his sister.

Again, as usual, feelings have me thoroughly confused and even though right now I'm completely stark naked I felt more naked when I was in his arms, kissing him.

And that is fucking scary as hell.

Fifty-Five | She's Not Mine
Bella

A COUPLE OF MONTHS LATER

For the past couple of months, all I've done is work in my shitty
job at Lush and come home to Nora.

My emotions have been all over the place, and I can't stop
thinking about Travis, but have been avoiding all contact with him
which also means all contact with Anni.

I miss my friend so much, but it's for the best at the moment, so I
can hopefully forget about the gorgeous as fuck Travis Banes.

Nora has had some nights where she's slept through, last night
being one of them, which meant this morning I'm now rushing
around trying to get everything ready for her to head to Jaxon's.

I'm only wearing a t-shirt and cheeky knickers when I hear the
unmistakable stupid morse code knock he does on the front door.

"Fuck, fuck, shit," I mutter under my breath, scanning my room for
some daks to put on.

Finding my discarded leggings by the laundry basket, I shimmy
them on, grabbing Nora out of her cot and holding her against my
hip, heading to the door.

Opening it, Jaxon barges in, knocking me aside.

He doesn't even say hello and refuses to take Nora from me.

"Bella, we need to talk."

I'm confused already and have no idea what he'd want to talk about so urgently.

"What about? Can't you take Nor this weekend?"

"Um, no, but it's not that."

"What then? Tell me Jaxon."

"I don't think she's mine, Bella."

"What? What the fuck do you mean?"

"Come on Bella! Look at her hair for fuck's sake. It's practically red!"

"Whh...what are you saying?"

"I'm saying...I'm saying that Nora is not my kid Bella. Use your pretty brown eyes and have a look at her. I'm done being a dad to a kid who isn't mine and who quite frankly hates me."

"But Jax, please...you've...you've been her Dad since she was born. I..." I cut off my words, not sure what else there is to say.

I look at my daughter, smoothing back her hair, her dark strawberry blonde hair.

There's no way Jaxon is right, I don't want to believe him.

"Just wake up Bella! And fucking tell him she's his kid."

He doesn't give me a chance to reply, instead is gone out the open front door before I can even form another sentence.

Tears are stinging my eyes, dripping down my cheeks. Wiping them away, I sniff and jump when I hear Elyse walking into the kitchen, "Bel-bear, you ok? Was that Jaxon?"

"Yeah, he um...can't take Nora this weekend."

"Oh, sounded like he was pretty angry about something?"

"Yeah, it's nothing. Don't worry, but um...Ely-bug?"

"Yeah, what?" she asks, busily making herself some toast.

"I'm going to head to Mum's for the weekend. You wanna come or stay here?"

She contemplates my question for a moment and then shakes her head.

"I'll stay here, I have a tonne of assignments to do and could do without the distractions."

"Ok, no worries Ely-bug," I reply leaving her to finish her breakfast whilst I go and get ready.

I shove some clothes for myself in a gym bag and more stuff for Nora in her nappy bag. Awkwardly I sling both bags over my one shoulder and pick Nora to hold her against my hip again.

Shuffling out of my bedroom, I call out to Elyse that I'm leaving,

"Ok Bel-bear, travel safe."

"I will," I call back, opening the front door and walking slowly to the tram stop.

It's times like these I really wish I had a car, but money is tight enough as it is, without adding that expense.

Boarding the tram I put the bags down at my feet, and sit Nora on my lap. The thought of hiring a car crosses my mind to, but I know I can't afford that either. There is another option and I'm hoping she's home.

Realising I'm nearly at the stop closest to her house I pick up my bags again and disembark the tram.

A few minutes later I'm in the elevator and at her white doorstep. Knocking, my heart is pounding. I'm afraid she's going to be angry at me for skipping out on her the last few months.

The door swings open to a smiling Anni, and I can't help but smile back, especially taking a good look at her heavily pregnant belly.

"Hey Bel, long time no see, what's up?"

"Hey Anni, I'm sorry I haven't been around. I was wondering if I could ask a favour?"

"Sure, anything, come in for a minute? I just made a cuppa."

I kick my bags inside the door, and follow Anni inside, putting Nora down to crawl on the floor.

"Coffee or tea?"

"Coffee thanks," I reply following her across to the kitchen and taking a seat on the breakfast bar stool.

I watch Nora out of one eye, sighing.

"So what's this favour?"

I swallow the lump in my throat, hoping I'm not asking for too much.

"I was um...wondering if I could borrow your car for a few days. I'm heading home to Mum's for a breather, and I can't face taking the bus with Nora."

"Yeah, sure. Is everything ok, Bel?"

"Yeah, yeah, everything is fine. I just need to get away from the city for a few days."

"Ok, you'd tell me if anything was bugging you though yeah?"

"Of course."

My words are lies, but I'm not ready to tell anyone what really happened after Austin's engagement party, and not ready to face the fact that Austin is quite possibly Nora's father.

He's engaged, he's happy and probably wants a family of his own with Dana.

"Great, so how're things? Did Elyse get settled in ok?"

"Yeah, she's loving it. Enjoying her vet course so far."

"That's good."

"How're things with you and Jai?"

"Pretty good, the tigers aren't doing so well this year so he's a little down and I honestly feel like an elephant, but not long now and the twins will be here."

"Yeah, anyway, I should probably head off, thanks again for this Anni. I'm honestly sorry I've been so distant lately."

"It's fine Bel," she says sweetly, grabbing her car keys from the basket on the bench and heading to the door, whilst I grab Nora who has snuggled up on the sunken couch.

Anni picks up my bags and we head down to her car.

She gives me a quick hug after I've strapped Nora into her capsule in the back of Anni's Beemer.

"Drive safe. Text me when you get there."

"I will. Thanks again, Anni. You're such a great friend."

"Anytime Bella," she replies before I get in the car and drive out of the basement carpark, tooting the horn and waving at her as she goes inside.

~~

Thankfully Nora sleeps for the few hours drive to Mum's.

Pulling up the car in the street, I cut the engine, getting out before waking Nora to get her out of the car seat.

Leaving the bags, I cradle Nora against my shoulder, a hand under her butt as I head up the path to the front door.

It's weird knocking, but I know the doorbell never works.

Mum answers almost immediately.

"Hi Mum," I say when the door swings open.

"Bella, dear, what's wrong? Is everything ok? Where's Elyse?"

"She's still in the city, but I just needed to get away. I hope that's ok."

"Of course, darling," she replies with a slight smile, but worry in her eyes.

"Thanks, Mum, can you take Nor while I get the bags out of the car?"

"Car?"

"Yeah, I borrowed Anni's car for a few days."

"Ok," she replies, reaching out to take Nora from my arms.

She stirs and looks up at her grandma. Mum's smile is so wide, it's sweet and brings tears to my eyes when I follow her back in with the bags.

I follow Mum to the guest room, where she thankfully still has the port-a-cot set up. She puts Nora in, handing her a pink teddy bear. Nora giggles, holding it close as she settles down to sleep again. I give her a kiss on the forehead and follow Mum out to the kitchen.

Without asking she makes a coffee, handing it to me and sitting on the breakfast bar stool opposite me.

"So dear, what's bothering you?" she asks, taking a sip of her coffee before brushing a stray hair from my cheek.

"I honestly don't know where to start Mum."

She takes another long sip of coffee, looking at me over the rim of the cup as though she's wondering what to ask me.

"Did something else happen with that young man you told me about at Christmas?"

"Yes, we kissed again and I..." I start to say 'I nearly slept with him' but I'm not sure if I'm comfortable confessing that to my mother.

"Did you have sex with him, Bella?" she asks in that annoying motherly tone.

I gulp, before guzzling half my coffee, cursing when I burn my tongue.

"No, I didn't but only because we were interrupted by a woman who he claimed was his sister."

"Oh," Mum snaps, "are you sure she wasn't his sister?"

"How the hell would I know Mum. We've barely said two words to each other," I admit, feeling like a complete idiot for my actions regarding Travis.

It's my own fault I know nothing about the guy because I can't control myself around him.

"Well, like I said last time Bella beautiful, you need to trust your body and your heart. It seems as though your body knows what it wants but your heart isn't ready yet."

"Yeah, I guess," I reply sliding off the stool to put my cup in the sink, "would you mind if I go out tonight? I'd like to catch up with some old friends."

"Of course darling. I'd love some Nor Nor and granny time."

"Thanks, Mum, don't wait up, please. I'll take keys."

She comes around to the other side of the bench, kissing me on the forehead before I head back to the guest room to get changed.

~~

It feels surreal being back in Archie's, this time actually being legally allowed to be drinking. Sliding into a booth with old school friends and sipping on my Cosmopolitan is like times gone by.

"So Bella, fill us in girl? We've missed you so much."

I look to Juliet and then at Olive, smiling and taking a long sip of my drink.

"There's too much to tell."

"Bel, come on. How're things with Jace?"

I laugh hard, spitting out some of my drink.

"We split up."

"What? Serious? You guys were the Stawell high golden couple," Olive says completely gobsmacked.

Juliet is also looking at me wide-eyed.

"Yeah he cheated on me, and I ...um..."

I feel my cheeks heat. I know they won't judge my actions, but actually admitting my stupid actions out loud makes me feel overcome with guilt.

"Come on girl, tell us!" Juliet shrieks.

"Ok... I slept with Jaxon...and Austin."

"Oh my god, Bella! Austin Belvinz, really?"

"Yeah, really and I fell in love with the idiot."

"No, you didn't," Olive says trying not the smile.

"Yeah I know, and oh I have a five-month-old."

They both look at me, mouths agape, "A what now? You have a kid?" Juliet asks.

"Yeah, pretty sure she's Jaxon, but I seriously don't fucking know. I'm such an idiot because I was sleeping with two guys at the same time."

"Yeah," Olive says softly, "so you're in love with Austin? Is he still as hot as ever?"

I'm about to reply when Juliet also says, "Tell me, he's ripper in bed yeah?"

"Yes, Olly, he's still hot, and yes Jules he's ripper in bed, but he's also engaged."

They look at me confused, and I see Jules take in a deep breath, "No fucking way! Are you guys engaged? That's so awesome Bel!"

I take a big sip of my Cosmo, "Um, no. He's engaged to someone else."

"Oh shit, Bel, that sucks balls," Olive says sweetly.

I laugh at their expression and reply, "Yeah, but it's not all bad. I'm actually here to get away from someone."

"Ooo, another hottie you got your eye on?" Jules implies winking.

"I wouldn't say got my eye on. We've pashed a couple of times and I want him but he's a complete douche and a liar."

"Oh, that's shit, Bel. Do we know him?" Olive asks, looking at me first and then at Juliet who nods.

"Maybe. He's um...."

"What?" they both blurt out in unison.

"A footballer," I blurt out in response.

"Oh!" Juliet screeches, "Didn't Annika marry a footballer? It was in the Herald Sun last year."

"Yeah, she did. He was our roommate and he's gorgeous."

"Yeah, so your football hottie?"

"He's Anni's husbands best mate. Travis Banes, the captain of the Tigers."

They both look at me with mouths agape again. "No fucking way Bella! You've seriously pashed Travis 'hot as fuck' Banes?" Juliet again screeches excitedly.

I'm about to reply, feeling the heat rise up my cheeks thinking about how I've nearly done more than pash Travis.

"I can't believe how lucky you are Bel. He's like the most eligible bachelor in the AFL. Even more so now Jairus Brooks is off the market."

"Um, yeah, but...um...."

"Spill it, Bel, you're thinking something."

I give Olive a look and realising what I'm implying she laughs at herself.

"Oh my god! Annika married Jairus didn't she?"

"Yep, and they're having twins in July."

"God, I'm so jelly of you both," Juliet says shaking her head.

"Me too. So why come back to Ararat when you could be in Travis's bed, huh?"

"He's got a girlfriend."

"You're shitting me? He's such a player. I find that hard to believe Bella."

I explain what happened last time I was at his house, and just like Mum said they both tell me that maybe Tessa really is his sister. I still don't know what to believe and still feel too sober.
I want to forget Travis, and life in the city for a while.

Quickly I down the rest of the Cosmo in my glass, before sliding out of the booth. "I'm going to the bar to grab something stronger. You want anything?"

They both shake their heads, and Juliet drags Olive out onto the dance floor as I head up to the bar.

Standing against the bar, after I've ordered my drink I feel someone step up behind me. The way the person shadows over me, I know its a guy and its a little intimidating.

The barman slides my whiskey down the bar. I scull it before turning to the figure standing next to me. He looks me up and down with an appreciative glance.

"Well, well, look who it is, Bella 'Biatch' Mishal."

Laughing I find my voice to reply, berating him with his own high school moniker, "Well if it isn't Matt 'Rudi' Rudensteine."

"In the flesh, baby," he taunts, winking at me.

I scoff. He clearly hasn't gotten any personality upgrade since high school, but he's lost the boyish body and it's clear he spends a lot of time outside as his skin is glowing from a dark tan.

I can't stop staring at him.

"Like what you see huh?" he taunts again.

"Um, no, I…"

"Don't kid yourself biatch….you still want me"

I signal the barman for another whiskey. "You know I never really wanted you, Rudi," I jeer back.

He feigns hurt, clutching a hand to his chest. "You still got a thing for carrot tops?"

"Yeah, I do actually."

He gives me an odd look, before leaning on the bar and signalling for a beer when my whiskey is placed on the bar in front of me.

I take a sip, still staring at Matt. A dirty thought pops into my head, and I know I shouldn't be thinking it.

Taking his beer he sips it, licking the foam on his lips suggestively.

"So, did you finally fuck Red?"

Sipping my whiskey, I lock my eyes on his over the rim. Licking my lips I watch him gulp, his Adam's apple bobbing as he awaits my response.

"Yeah I fucked Austin," I tell him, leaning in to whisper against his lips, "more than once."

He lets out a grunt, and it sounds kinda sexy.

Before I can say another word or move back his lips crash against mine. His kiss is demanding and I can't help responding.

It's far from the awkward kisses we shared when we were sixteen, fooling around in his bedroom before we lost our virginity to each other.

I'd been thinking of having sex with him before he kissed me, and now I want to more than ever because Matt certainly has improved his kissing technique so he's probably a ripper fuck, no doubt with a few notches on the bedpost.

I want to forget about Travis, so getting underneath someone else is sure to take him off my mind.

Breaking the kiss, I look up at Matt, "So Rudi, I take it you're single?"

He nods, "You bet Biatch. Don't tell me you're with Red?"

"No, he's engaged to someone else."

"Oh, and you're here tending to your broken heart. Poor Bella."

He pouts at me before laughing. I don't reply so he continues, "Want me to fuck away the pain?"

"I don't know. You were a lousy fuck if I'm remembering that night right."

"Come on Biatch, we were sixteen. I've got a few notches on the bedpost now, and no complaints. What ya reckon? Come knock boots at mine?"

"By mine, you mean your parents?"

"No biatch, I have my own place now. Moved out of the parentals just last week actually," he says with a laugh.

"Of course you did."

"So you gonna help christen my new bed?"

I don't reply, instead pull him down to kiss him again. He breaks the kiss, breathless a few moments later and takes my hand to lead me out of the pub.

I'm probably going to regret this, but right now, a little tipsy from the whiskey I couldn't care less that I'm about to have sex with the guy I lost my virginity to.

As he said, it's just fucking away the pain of not being able to be with the guy I'm in love with and trying to not to think about the guy I want so badly I might just fall apart.

Fifty-Six | Confide In Me

Pounding on the door wakes me from a blissful nap, in which thoughts of Bella had been filling my dreams. After she rushed out when Tessa caught us pashing on the couch, I've not been able to get her off my fucking mind.

Literally every second, whether I'm awake or asleep I'm thinking of her.

I want to talk to Jai about it, but I still get the feeling he's going to warn me away and keeping away from her the last couple of months has been pure torture.

Yeah, I'm a fucking idiot, because I should have made an effort to track her down and make her see that Tessa is my sister; but I feel so damn guilty for the way I treated her and thought it was best to leave her be, even if its the worse kinda torture known to man.

Getting out of bed when the pounding increases, I stretch on the shirt I'd thrown on the floor when I got home from training yesterday and slide down the hallway to the front door, my socks helping me glide across the floor.

Opening the door, I think about whether I should have put on some daks as well considering my y-front boxers don't leave much to the imagination. But it's too late to consider that anymore when the front door is pushed open and I rub my eyes, not believing who is now sauntering into my apartment.

"Seriously, Travis, could you take any longer to open the damn door?"

She's pissed off with me, but she's also trying to hide the tears that are streaming down her cheeks. Seeing her again is making so many emotions course through me, my cock aching from wanting to have her right fucking now as well.

"Well, hey to you too sunshine. What's got you so riled that you're turning up unannounced?" I raise my eyebrows at her.

Scoffing at me, whilst her eyes betray her scanning over my body she pushes her hands into my chest.

Instantly, even though she's not even touching my skin my body heats with her touch. Our eyes are locked on each other, daring each other to speak next, to cut the tension that radiates between us whenever we're in the same room.

Kicking the door closed, she steps closer to me and damn do I want to pull her against my aching cock, slamming her against the wall whilst our lips crash together in a kiss.

She seems stunned, starting to open and close her mouth like she wants to say something but doesn't have the words.

All I can think of is, *Fuck words,* I just want to kiss her senseless like I've been dreaming of doing again for months.

Biting on her lip, her gaze wanders over my body again, lingering on my semi-hard cock and she lets out the hottest little whimper before her pretty brown eyes are back locked with mine.

And I can't fucking take it a second longer, if I don't pash her now I'm going to self combust.

Stepping closer to her again, she lets out another whimper, which is by far one of my new favourite sounds.

Cupping her cheeks I crash my lips to hers, moaning against her soft mouth as she deepens the kiss, licking my lips with her tongue.

Fuck, it's the best, most sweetest torture ever, the unmistakable taste of her, fairy floss assaulting my senses and awakening my cock even more when her hands grab my hair to pull my mouth even closer to hers.

Kissing Bella is my drug.

Breathless, mere moments later she pulls back shaking her head, "No, no. I...we..." she stammers, turning away and walking over to the couch.

I follow, heart racing with worry that I've fucked up again, and she's going to go running like always.

Sinking down on the couch, she looks up at me standing next to the coffee table, to damn afraid to sit next to her for fear she'll push me away. Her eyes are blinking furiously, tears slipping from them and down her flushed cheeks.

Taking a deep breath, I sit down on the opposite end of the couch. "Bella?" I say her name softly, a whisper escaping my lips as I don't know what else to say.

She looks across at me, edging a little closer to me so our thighs are touching.

"Yeah?"

"What's wrong? Somethings got you crying?"

"I...I went home to Mum's to clear my head, to forget about you."

I gulp, feeling a pang of hurt hit me in the chest that she'd want to forget about me.

"And I wanted to get the image of her out of my head. But I..." she cuts her words off.

Reaching over to touch her thigh I ask, "But what sunshine?"

A smile curves at the corner of her lips, "I haven't stopped thinking about you even when I slept with someone else."

"Well, I haven't stopped thinking about you either sunshine," I tell her smirking.

"But that woman that caught us kissing."

Her words come out as a question more than a statement and I chuckle, "That woman was my sister Tessa. I'm not shitting you Bella."

"She seemed really pissed seeing us together though? And she didn't exactly say otherwise."

"Believe me, sunshine. Tessa is my annoyingly sweet kid sister and she needed a place to crash for a bit. I've got no reason to lie to you."

She appears to contemplate my words but doesn't reply, instead bites down on her lip and lets out her sexy whimper from between her plump lips.

"I let Tessa stay after Christmas because she's four months pregnant and her ex back in London cheated on her. She had nowhere else to go."

"I want to believe you, I really do, but how do I know you're not playing me?"

"Trust me sunshine, you'd know if I was playing you."

"Yeah? How?" she taunts me.

I lean in closer to her, resting my forehead against hers.

"Have I fucked you? And pushed you out the door?"

Again she whimpers, and squeaks out a, "No," sitting back against the couch so we're not so close again.

"Exactly, sunshine. If I was playing you I'd have already fucked you and sent you on your way."

"I guess," she replies meekly."So where is Tessa now?"

"I put down some dough for her to say in a serviced apartment. She gave me a grilling when she caught us pashing. Told me she didn't want to stay in my fuck pad anymore."

"Oh, um...shit."

"Bella, look at me."

Her eyes lock on mine. "Since I kissed you that first time, I've barely thought of, let alone actually been with another sheila. I want you, sunshine."

"I...I...but....I fucked my ex and I...went home to find out more about my Dad too and I got distracted and I..."

Tears are stinging her eyes again, and she's clearly trying to say something else but the words aren't coming out audible.

"Shh, come here," I muse softly, opening my arms for her.

She hesitates for a moment before moving across the couch and into my arms. Holding her close is making my heart beat a hundred kilometres a fucking hour, making my cock rise to attention and stirring up that odd feeling in my stomach.

Her back is against me, so she has to turn her head back to look at me when she speaks, "Thanks Travis."

"For what?"

"Making me feel better. I feel like such an idiot for sleeping with Matt. And for running away."

"You don't need to thank me. I can be a gentleman sometimes."

She laughs, her laugh is so sweet and sexy.

"Are you a gentleman in bed?" she asks, shocking me and awakening my cock as thoughts of taking her to bed crash into my mind.

"You telling me you want to find out?"

She nods before kissing me hard and teasingly pulling back before I have the chance to deepen the kiss.

"Oh, you didn't just do that sunshine," I taunt, grabbing her around the waist to sit her down next to me so I can stand up from the couch.

Giving her a wink I chuckle, grabbing her again and hoisting her over my shoulder. Her laughter fills the air as I plod down the hallway to my bedroom.

Throwing her down on the bed, her eyes are glued to mine and she's smirking at me like a damn she devil. My cock is throbbing in my daks, and fuck do I want to rip her clothes off to sink inside her pussy.

But I'm hesitating, standing at the foot of my bed staring at her. For some fucked up reason, I want to take things slow, to savour every inch of her body that I've been dreaming about touching, licking and kissing for months.

Kneeling on the bed, she giggles as she lifts the oversized t-shirt over her head.

She throws it on the floor, reaching behind her back to unclasp her bra.

I'm salivating with the anticipation of seeing her perfect bare breasts, and my whole body is humming with need.

She's going to be my fucking undoing.

Giggling again, she lets the bra fall to the bed and my mouth drops open staring at her, taking in the beautiful sight before my eyes.

Her tits are absolute fucking perfection, perky mounds with dark pink buds that stand at attention.

Her hands are now at the waistband of her leggings, about to pull them down.

I shake my head at her, diving towards her on the bed. "Let me do that, sunshine."

Leaning over her I push her down on the bed, smashing my lips to hers in a heated kiss. My hands find the perfect mounds and I palm her tits, kissing her deeper by taking her tongue with mine.

Her hips buck up to mine, and her sexy whimper breaks through the kiss.

Breaking the kiss, I taunt her, "That whimper you make is fucking hot."

She makes the whimper again, driving me crazy. "You tease me, sunshine," I taunt again, grabbing the elastic of her leggings and yanking them down her legs.

My eyes again boggle, taking in the fact that she was commando under the barely there fabric.

Her pussy is bare and just like her tits is absolute perfection.

"Fuck, Bella, your body is fucking perfection."

"Don't say that, Travis, please. I've had a kid."

"Yeah, well, still."

I'm completely lost for words, taking in every inch of her body and locking it into my memory. Her curves, her hips, every damn inch of her.

"Stop looking at me like that," she says softly, trying to grab the sheets to cover up.

"Like what?"

"Like you want to devour me."

I laugh, "I do want to devour you though, so don't you dare cover an inch of your glorious body, sunshine."

"I...I...I'm not ready...I...we...can't...fuck..." she hisses out the last word in a whisper and it hits me hard in the damn feels.

Seeing Bella vulnerable does something weird to my insides.

It makes me feel like I'm a good guy, which is so far from true. But with her sweet brown eyes looking up at me, and her lip between her teeth it's confirmed if I want all of Bella, I need to get her to open up more and take things between us slow.

Leaning over her again, I brush her dark hair from her cheeks.

"I'm not going to fuck you yet," I muse softly, kissing her lips quickly, "But I want to make you feel good."

She lets out her sexy whimper, before pulling me down for a fierce kiss that makes my cock and entire body throb.

Breathless I pull back, "Kissing you is my drug, Bella."

"Mmm," she moans grabbing the hem of my t-shirt and gathering it up. I help by yanking it off and my heart starts hammering in my chest as her eyes trail my body.

She reaches out, touching my recent tattoo of the birds flying down my torso. They only just cover the scar of Meaghan trying to slice me open. "What's this scar from?" she asks softly.

"Please don't Bella, ok. I don't want to talk about it."

"But? But you have scars all over your chest?" she says running her fingertips over each mark on my skin.

I've never felt so naked, so exposed. Her touch is searing, but also calming.

"Yes, I do," I hiss when she touches the one next to my belly button that's always been sensitive, "but please, I can't tell you yet. Let me make you feel good and forget about being made of scars."

"Mmm, ok," she replies cupping my cheeks to pull me down for another kiss. Taking her tongue with mine, I slide a finger inside her pussy and she whimpers against my lips, kissing me harder. She's so turned on, my finger makes a heavenly squelching sound as I thrust it in and out. She breaks the kiss, arching her back to push my finger deeper.

"More, fuck more please," she begs closing her eyes.

Sliding another two fingers inside her stretched pussy I press up on her g-spot before pulling my fingers out again.

"Touch yourself, sunshine. Touch yourself while I finger fuck you."

Obeying she reaches down between her legs, her finger flicking her clit. I watch a moment, loving how fucking beautiful she looks whilst pleasuring herself.

About to slide my fingers back in again, she shakes her head at me. "Take off your boxers, captain."

I chuckle at her calling me captain, it sounding sexy as fuck in her raspy voice. I don't reply, but follow her instruction, dakking myself swiftly and kicking my boxers to the floor.

Her eyes ogle my cock and if it's even possible it hardens more with her appreciative gaze.

Grabbing it in her hand, she starts stroking the length, slowly, then a little faster when I slip three fingers back inside her wet pussy.

Moans and whimpers escape her lips, as I thrust my fingers hard and fast inside her.

Her hands on my cock are driving me closer to the edge, no other touch has ever felt so fucking glorious.

Her touch is ecstasy.

"Mmm, fuck, captain," she calls out, my fingers teasing her g-spot and her clit at the same time.

"Fuck! Right back at you, sunshine," I chuckle when her other hand starts to fondle my balls whilst still stroking my cock.

Still pleasuring her I smash a kiss to her lips, biting down on her lip to tease her.

"Come for me, Bella," I hiss, "squirt all over my fucking sheets, sunshine."

As though on command her pussy trembles, her whole body shaking as her climax takes over. And the minute she lets go completely her orgasm pours out, squirting in a gush over my fingers and onto my sheets.

It's by far the hottest fucking sight I've ever seen and spurs my own release, my cum bursting out all over her hands and over my stomach.

"Fuck, sunshine. That was so fucking hot. Sexy as hell."

She scoots back on the bed a little, all of a sudden seeming super shy.

Biting on her lip, she pulls the sheets up and clutches them to her chest after wiping her hand on them.

"Why you shy now, huh?"

Her cheeks colour and she can't meet my gaze. "I...I...I've never...sq...squirted from a finger fuck."

I let out a chuckle, pinning her down on the bed, feeling a little frustrated that the sheet is between us as my cock is hardening again, ready for taking her as mine completely, but I can't.

Giving her a sweet kiss, I tell her, "Then whoever finger fucked you clearly had no idea, sunshine."

"Mmm, yeah, but it's embarrassing."

"Are you fucking shitting me?"

"No, I've soaked your sheets and I..."

"Never be embarrassed about being able to squirt, sunshine. It's seriously hot."

"Hmm, whatever you say, captain," she laughs.

"Oh I say, sunshine," I taunt, looking down at her underneath me.

Fuck, she's beautiful, and sexy as and mine.

"So, do you squirt when getting an Aussie?"

"Maybe, but you're not going to find out today."

I pout at her, "Why not sunshine? Can't I taste your pussy?"

"Nope, but you can shut up and kiss me again."

"Gladly," I muse, crushing my lips to hers for a kiss that makes my heart pound.

If I didn't know any better, I'd think I was falling for her because how she makes me feel is far beyond anything I've ever felt before.

Never have I felt content just lying together, entangled in the sheets kissing each other breathless, but right now that's all I want to do.

What the fuck is wrong with me?

Fifty-Seven | Mates Talk Trash

It's been a few weeks since I saw Bella and she came apart on my bed. I'm a dirty animal as I literally didn't change the sheets for a good two weeks after even though they were already rank, but the smell of her pussy on them was just intoxicating.

We're now in the thick of football season and most of the time the boys clear out quickly after a game.
I should have gone with them, but Jai is taking his sweet arse time and I'd rather get a drink with my best mate.
Getting changed he's glaring at me like he knows something is up.
And of course I can't hide much from him.

"Whats up with you bro?" he asks, slipping his t-shirt on.
I don't reply, so he asks another question, "How are you feeling about Dana getting married?"
"Doesn't bother me," I snap, a little harsher in tone than I mean.
"Don't give me that shit...you're pining after her."
"No, I'm not...i'm jacking off to thoughts of someone else."

Thoughts of Bella crash into my mind again, making my cock throb in my footy shorts.
"Oh really?" Jairus jeers at me mockingly as he elbows me.
"Yeah," I mutter.
"And?" He pokes me, "It's not Bella is it?"

There's no point denying it, so I nod, "You got me brother...I can't stop thinking about her...I haven't even fucked her but she's all I think about."

He gives me an incredulous look, a you can't be serious look.

"So what has happened between you guys then?"

"Pash sessions and I made her squirt all over my bed the other week...fuck it was so hot," I muse, reliving it in my mind and laughing when shock flashes in my best mates eyes.

"Fuck Trav, man,I don't know what to say."

"Me either... I feel like I'm cunt struck and I haven't even tasted her or fucked her," I tell him with a laugh.

"Seems like more than just your dick is talking this time mate."

And there he is, my wise beyond his fucking years best mate. Marriage has obviously messed with his damn brain.

"Don't talk shit," I snap at him, "feelings have nothing to do with it."

"If you say so...but feelings don't always play fair Trav. I know I've told you to keep your distance from her but I've seen you with her and there's definitely something between you guys."

Did I just hear him right? Is he finally giving me the all clear to make her mine?

Yeah, I don't need his permission but his approval means a lot nonetheless.

"Yeah but I don't do love and all that sappy shit. Meaghan fucked me over."

I slap a hand to my mouth the second I say the words, instantly regretting them.

Jai is glaring at me, giving me a literal what the fuck look. "Who's Meaghan? You've never mentioned her before."

"I don't want to tell you here. Can we go get a drink?"

"Sure, I'll text Anni." He nods grabbing his phone out of his bag and slinging it over his shoulder.

Grabbing my own bag, I start to walk out and he follows after pulling on some trackie daks over his footy shorts.

We head to the pub together and I hope like hell I can get the words out, as even though I'm scared I know its time to share my past with my best mate.

He's practically like a brother to me and I don't want to hide anything from him anymore.

It's time to get real, and stop talking trash.

Fifty-Eight | Touchdown Comes Hard

After spilling all to Jairus my head is in a complete tailspin.
I'm in no shape to drive home, my head also spinning from the
one to many whiskeys I downed to try and quell the nerves of
telling my best mate everything.
He was completely flabbergasted and rightly pissed off with me
for hiding something so important in my life from him.

Fucked if I know why I'm heading there, on the tram, but jumping
off on Bridge Road and down the laneway I'm on my way to her
house.
It's like some fucked up déjà vu going back there, and I think back
to the first day I saw her at the house party years ago.
I wanted her then and damn do I want her now, more than I've
ever wanted any sheila in my life.

Knocking on her door, my stomach is in knots, that odd feeling
deep within that scares the ever-loving shit out of me.
She opens the door, leaning against it and practically purrs her
words, "Hi, Travis. Are you ok?"
I don't greet her back. I'm too fucking mesmerised by her, how
gorgeous she is without even trying.
She's eye-fucking me and my gaze wanders over her body.

Her curves are only just hidden by the oversized t-shirt she's wearing, and it's clear all she's got underneath it is a barely there g-string.

Her perfect tits are showing through and they harden just looking at me. Knowing I'm having that effect on her makes my cock jolt in my footy shorts.

Shaking myself back to reality, I find my voice, "No Bella, I'm not ok. I fucking want you."

Her breath hitches, her tits rising and falling underneath the white t-shirt.

"I....I...can't," she says raspy, taking in another breath fighting her words, "We can't."

Chuckling I taunt her, "No honey, you meant to say we can."

She gives me an odd look, possibly from the endearing nickname I called her, which sounded foreign coming from my mouth, but I'm thinking about how she'll taste like the most luscious honey ever.

"We can't fuck."

Her words hit me first as a vice around my cock, hearing her say 'fuck' in reference to sex is orgasm on the spot shit, but the word can't and the look of worry in her bedroom eyes are making it pretty clear I'm not burying myself in her pussy right now.

But I desperately want to.

"Travis," she purrs my name again, stepping back from the door as an invitation to follow her inside.

Watching her as she closes the door, it's confirmed she's wearing a g-string and I don't hesitate in taking a good long look at her curvy arse.

Fuck! Every damn inch of her body is glorious.

Sighing she speaks again, "Anni and Jai will kill us if they find out we fucked."

Little does she know.

I laugh stepping a little closer to her, "Jai gave me his blessing…and damn right Bella honey I want to fuck you. Watching you cum and squirt all over my bed a few weeks ago was the hottest fucking sight I've ever seen."

Her hot as fuck whimper escapes her lips involuntarily, making my cock instantly hard.

"Your cock is the hottest fucking thing I've ever seen," she taunts with a laugh.

"Mmm, hearing you say cock and fucking is making me hard, Bella," I moan, her name drawn out on my tongue.

Lust flashes in her pretty brown eyes, her pupils dilating when she looks down at my tight footy shorts.

She licks her lips, moaning slightly.

I seriously can't take much more of this.

I fucking need her, all of her.

Starting with her mouth, her pretty pink lips, around my cock and it deep down her throat whilst she gives me a gobby.

"God Bella, you're such a fucking tease," I moan huskily, "please wrap those pretty pink lips around my cock."

No words leave her mouth, instead, she grabs my hand leading me down the short hallway.

Of course, I follow.

Tingles are running through my body and my cock is growing, painfully hard and tenting the front of my shorts.

Once in her bedroom, I take a quick glance around, noticing that there's a cot in the corner but her kid is not in it.

I look to Bella, standing in front of me.

She's smirking at me and I wonder for a moment if she's going to strip off the little clothes she's got on.

"Where's ya kid?" I ask.

"At her Dad's...and my sister is out too. We have the house to ourselves." Her tone is laced with lust and my cock throbs, ready for some loving from her.

Stepping towards me she laughs, dakking me and letting out an appreciative hum at seeing my cock hard again.

Giving her a devilish smirk, I pull my t-shirt over my head, throwing it on the floor whilst I step out of the shorts and jocks at my feet, kicking them away.

Bella sits down on the edge of her bed, and I step closer to stand between her legs. She looks up at me, lifting her t-shirt over her head to expose her perfect tits to my gaze.

Seeing her practically naked again makes my cock throb. Laughing she grabs it in a fist, stroking it fast, slow and faster again, with her other hand fondling my balls.

It feels fucking glorious, but I need more.

"Sunshine, please suck me," I beg huskily fisting her hair to guide her mouth towards my cock.

Her lips take in just the tip of my cock, puckering around it when she circles her tongue in the slit.

Fuck, she knows how to suck a cock, fuck me

"Fuck, sunshine," I moan, "take me deep."

She doesn't reply but eagerly obeys, whimpering as she slides my cock further into her mouth between her lips.

Her tongue taunts me, swirling over my length and in the slit when pre-cum pearls there.

Feeling her lap it up so urgently I'm close to letting go when she pulls back taking my cock all the way out of her mouth.

"You give damn good head, Bella. Can I come in that hot mouth of yours?"

She nods, letting out her whimper as she takes me into her mouth again.

Teasingly she takes my length in and out, and grabbing her by the back of the head I shove her against my pelvis to take me as deep as possible.

She gags but stays put and I shoot my load into her throat.

Still, with my cock spasming in her mouth, she swallows hard before she pulls off wiping her arm across her lips.

"Mmm," she sighs, falling back against the bed, sprawling out across the sheets.

She's sucked me to orgasm, but I could still take her, as seeing her sprawled out on her bed is making my cock throb again.

Kneeling on the edge of the bed I lean over her curvaceous body to kiss her. Her hands find my hair, kneading it her fingertips as she kisses me deeper.

Tasting my cum on her tongue is oddly arousing, not to mention Bella whimpering as she laces her tongue with mine.

That sound drives me absolutely wild.

Pulling back from the kiss, I lean over her, my forehead against hers.

"You drive me crazy, sunshine."

Her whimper escapes her lips, and she bites down on her bottom one, taking it between her teeth.

"That whimper drives me crazy, and I'm going to punish you for that, sunshine."

Lust flashes in her eyes.

I kiss her lips softly, then start to kiss over her neck, her collarbone and down towards her perfect tits.

Taking one pink bud into my mouth, I suck on it, palming her other tit in my hand. Her hips arch up, moans and her whimper escaping her lips.

My cock is already hard, pressing into her belly when I swap sides to give the other tit the same pleasurable torture.

"Please, captain, please," she begs, her new nickname for me sounding dirty as sin.

"What, sunshine? Please what?"

"Touch me, make me come."

I gaze at her for a moment, before kissing her softly. Her fairy floss taste hits me hard and I know I need to taste her pussy, wondering if it's going to taste just as sweet as her kisses.

Breaking the kiss, I chuckle, smirking at her as I trail kisses back down her body again, over her hips and belly.

Kissing her thighs I take the elastic of her g-string in my teeth, starting to slide it down her creamy skin, spreading her legs wide with my hands.

"Let me in, sunshine. I wanna take you to heaven."

She looks up at me, opening her legs wide when I throw the g-string on the floor.

Her pussy is bare, with her arousal dripping from the pink folds. Her gaze is still locked on me, so I plunge a finger inside her and her hips buck, a 'fuck' escaping her lips in a hiss.

Pulling the finger out of her body I smirk at her before slipping it between my lips, moaning as I lick it clean.

Fuck me, does she taste delicious, sweet as fucking honey.

"Tell me what you want, sunshine," I taunt her, kissing up her spread thighs, avoiding her pussy that smells so divine I'm desperate to kiss away every drop of her arousal.
"An Aussie kiss, please, Captain," she says raspy, throwing her head back down on the pillows when my mouth crashes against her pussy.
Teasingly I dart my tongue in and out, swirling it deep into her pussy walls to lap up the sweet honey.
"Mmm, you taste like honey. So fucking good!" I moan against her pussy lips, biting and flicking my tongue over her swollen clit.
She's writhing beneath me, her hips pushing up against my face and it's so hot, I could lose myself again without her even touching me.
The sounds she's making, moans and her whimper of pleasure are the hottest sounds i've ever heard.
Continuing the teasing licks and kisses over her pussy and clit, I sense she's close when she calls out, rather loudly, "Fuck, oh fuck...so good! Oh, fuck!"
To finish her off, I slip three fingers insider her pussy, biting down on her clit and she comes so hard, squirting her pussy juice all over the stubble of my chin.

Watching her come apart, her whole body trembling in release is so ridiculously hot.

I honestly have no words to describe how gorgeous she looks when she's pleasure drunk.

Afterwards, I crawl up the bed to lie next to her, pulling the sheet over our bodies.

Tugging her close, entangling our legs together and smoothing down her hair, I kiss her zealously.

Tasting herself on my lips, she whimpers, deepening the kiss by cupping my cheeks to pull me closer. Her kisses are intoxicating and make my heart race.

It both excites me and scares the fucking shit out of me but I can't get enough.

Breaking the kiss, I'm completely breathless, drunk on her.

"Bella, I...fuck...you make me feel," I blurt out.

"Sorry, feel what?"

She's clearly taken aback by my stupid words, that make no sense but complete sense at the same time.

"I don't do this...this cuddling afterwards...and I definitely don't feel satisfied without actually fucking a sheila but with you I...I don't know."

"Hmm yeah..." she mutters snuggling into me, "stay the night?"

Her words come out as rhetorical, so I don't say anything instead just pull her close for a lingering kiss.

Rolling over she snuggles against me again, pressing her curvy arse against my cock.

Holding her close feels right, yes damn scary but right.

Smelling her hair I inhale the vanilla scent, sighing as I drift to sleep, spooning her with an arm draped over her belly.

Yep, damn scary but it feels so damn good.

Fifty-Nine | Morning After Greetings

Jolting awake, I look across at the sleeping figure next to me. For a moment my heart races, thinking I've fucked up and have some blonde in my bed, but it skips a beat when I realise the sleeping figure beside me in the bed is Bella.

It's clear she's still naked, and even in her sleep she looks absolutely stunning, with her dark chocolate hair cascading over the pillow and the sheets taut over her hips.

Images of her giving me a gobby last night flash in my mind, but I push them aside to calm down my cock or I'll be sporting morning wood harder than steel.

Throwing the sheet back, I gaze over her glorious curves as I get out of the bed. Resisting the urge to touch her and have some morning fun I pull on my discarded jocks from the floor and head out to her kitchen to grab a drink of water. My throat feels parched like I've never drunk a drop of water in my life.

Walking out into the main area of the house, I stop dead in the middle of the room, seeing another chocolate haired sheila in the kitchen.

"Shit sorry...I forgot anyone else lived here," I blurt out, trying to remember the convo I had with Bella last night before her lips were around my cock and my tongue was buried in her sweet pussy.

This new sheila is tongue tied for a moment, swallowing hard as she looks me up and down. I know the effect I have on most women, so I'm not surprised by her reaction to my presence in her kitchen.

"So it was you making my sister moan last night?" she asks with an accusing tone.

"How do you know that anything happened between us?" I ask trying not to sound guilty.

"When I got home from my friends I heard Bella screaming oh fuck...oh fuck...that feels...oh fuck."

"Sorry...but I um..." I stammer like an idiot, the convo from last night clicking into place in my head.

This younger sheila is clearly Bella's sister. I can see the resemblance now.

"No biggie...i'm not innocent but don't break my sisters heart Travis," she warns.

I'm a little taken aback that she knows my name. It makes me wonder if Bella has talked about me.

"She's been through to much for another guy to fuck her over."

"I...um don't plan to fuck her over," I tell her, as wicked thoughts like fucking Bella over a chair crash into my mind.

"Sorry I didn't catch your name?"

"Elyse..." she replies with a gulp.

"Right...well um, nice to meet you Elyse. I'll...um...just grab the rest of my stuff and be out of your way."

I don't know why I'm such a blithering idiot, stammering out words. I have no reason to be feeling guilty about what's happened between Bella and I, but meeting her kid sister the morning after is making me feel like such a tool.

I don't want long term, I don't want a relationship but it's obviously what Bella wants.

I need to get out of her house, and her life.

Bella is still asleep when I go back to her bedroom so I quickly dress and leave, tiptoeing out in my footy boots to not wake her. Telling her I'm skipping out after last night, would make me feel even more guilt ridden.

Elyse is sitting on the couch with a mug in her hands.

"Tell Bella I'll text her later."

I have no intentions of doing anything of the sort, but I can't tell Elyse that after her warning to me.

"No worries Travis," she replies winking.

Opening the front door, I leave Bella's house without saying another word. Sprinting towards the tram stop, I try to shake the thoughts of Bella from my mind.

I know I need to keep away from her, but after tasting her sweet honeyed pussy last night and kissing her good night I crave her like my next damn breath of air that I cant seem to get enough of in my lungs right now.

My heart is racing and I know its not just from sprinting to the tram stop.

I crave Bella, and that is scary as fuck, because I'm afraid if I want my fill of her i'll fall for her. And love is to damn scary to think about for a second, let alone forever.

Sixty | Sisterly Chat Blushing
Elyse

The minute the hot as Travis leaves I'm rushing into Bella's room.
Climbing onto her bed on my knees, I check if she's awake.
Seeing she's not, standing up, I jump up and down on the bed like
a three-year-old to wake her.
Sitting up, she murmurs, pulling the sheet up around her neck.
She's giving me dagger eyes when I sit down cross-legged in front
of her.

"So tell me Bel bear, how was it?"
"How was what?" she mutters sleepily.
Bouncing on the spot on my arse, I taunt, "Come on Bel-bear, tell
me!"
"Tell you what Ely-bug," she replies rubbing her eyes and looking
at me questioningly.
Laughing I screech at her, "Don't play dumb Bel-bear, I know you
had sex with him...I heard you screaming!"

Bella blushes, shifting uncomfortably on the bed as though she's
thinking about him between her legs.
"You didn't hear anything Ely-bug," she defends, "nothing
happened."

Again I laugh, taunting my big sister, "Oh right, so you screaming out 'oh fuck' multiple times when I came home wasn't because of that gorgeous hunk?"

Again she blushes, not able to meet my eyes when she replies, "Ok it was but we didn't have sex...I'm not telling you anything else Ely-bug."

Her words make me a little excited and my own body feels on fire just thinking about what I'm thinking she's implying.

"Did he go down on you?"

Shock flashes in her eyes and she screams out, "Elyse! How do you even know what that is?"

"I'm not 12 Bella! I've had sex...you know that, but I've never had a guy go down on me...whats it feel like?"

"I can't describe it, but fuck Ely bug...last night with Travis...it's never been like that before."

Her cheeks colour again and she whimpers like she's reliving the pleasure.

Fuck I want Kaden to go down on me.

"Ooo...you love him!" I shriek out eagerly, "Are you together?"

"No and no Elyse...but he's definitely hotter than sin."

"Tell me about it...he came into the kitchen earlier in just jocks and his dick is huge even when it's not hard."

I lick my lips thinking about Kaden's hard dick too. I ponder telling Bella what's happened between us but it's probably not the right time yet.

Bella blushes again biting her lip, chuckling, "Oh yeah it's fucking glorious Ely-bug...but you shouldn't be looking."

Her words are chastising but said in jest and looking at each other we break into a fit of giggles.

"Don't worry," I say through a giggle, "I'm not going to steal ya man. Kinda got the hots for someone else."

"Oh really?" Bella teases.

"Yeah." I feel my cheeks heat with a blush thinking of Kaden.

"Tell me Ely bug," Bella pleads, "tell me who you're crushing on?"

I bite down on my lip and meekly reply, "Kaden."

"Oh Ely bug no..." Bella warns, shock on her face.

"I can't help it."

"I know Ely bug...just be careful."

I nod, heeding her words, 'be careful'.

They have a double meaning for sure. I push down the thoughts that have been plaguing my mind for the last week.

I definitely can't tell my big sister those.

"I know Bel bear...I will be," I promise, nodding again.

A knot is rising in my stomach, I swallow hard and reach out to hug Bella, but shrink back when I realise my sister is starkers.

"Put some clothes on you dirty bitch."

Laughing I stand up, jumping off the bed.

"I'm going to make pancakes," I call out as I leave her room.

I can't help but think that Bella isn't the only dirty bitch.

She hasn't slept with Travis, but...

No, Elyse don't think about him.

Don't think about how he makes your knickers wet.

Stop, just make the pancakes and forget about Kaden.

Easier said than done.

Sixty-One | All She Wanted

After a tough game, I'm as usual the last one in the change rooms. I'm about to head out, slinging my bag over my shoulder when Dana comes rushing in.

"Travis, hey, have you seen the pom-poms?"
"Yeah, some new sheila bought them down earlier."
She sighs, plopping down on the bench seat to calm herself.
"Thank fuck for that," she mutters when I sit down next to her.
Giving her a smile, I ask, "So how're things with you?"
Looking across at me she smiles sweetly, "Good, really good. How're things with you? You didn't play your best game today, so something must be up."

Taking my bottom lip between my teeth, I mutter, "I um...I've hooked up with Bella a couple of times."
"Hooked up, as in you've slept with her?"
"Nah, we've just kissed and shit, but Dan I think I'm fucking falling for her."
"And that's a bad thing, because?"
"Because she's got a kid and I'm not sure what to do. You know I don't do love."
"What you should do is take her out on a romantic date," she suggests with the sweet smile again, "show her you care about her. That's all I ever wanted from you Travis."

"Yeah I guess. I do care about her. It's just so new to me. How're you and what's his face?"

"Austin," she tells me, "and things are great. We've decided on a wedding date."

"Oh shit really?"

"Yeah," she smiles and blushes, "April next year."

"Awesome...I'm glad you found someone Dan. You deserve to be happy."

We both stand up at the same time, laughing.

"Thanks, Travis and so do you. If you want Bella, make her yours."

I give her a smile and reach out to hug her, squeezing her playfully.

"I will, thanks again, Dana. Don't be a stranger."

"I won't," she promises kissing my cheek before she walks off.

Even though I'm not one for romance, and all that sappy love shit, walking out I start making plans in my head to take Bella out on a proper date.

Sixty-Two | Lie Down Baby

Knocking on her door unannounced makes me feel like a damn intruder.

Yeah, I probably should have called to see if it was a good time and day to take her out for a date, but since Dana put the thought in my head a couple of days ago, taking Bella out is all I've thought about.

Opening the door to me, she's wearing black leggings and a tight tank top that makes her cleavage pop.

Staring for a moment, I force my eyes to look up at her face when she lets out a deep sigh.

"Hey Captain, why are you here?"

"Hey sunshine, I thought you might like to go out for a date tonight."

She shakes her head, stepping back from the door to usher me inside.

I take another look at her outfit, noticing that her hair is a mess, a birds nest of knots pulled off her face in a haphazard ponytail.

She shuts the door behind us, glaring at me.

"I can't go out tonight. I have Nora here and Elyse is out."

"Oh shit, um yeah I probably should've called. I...I just wanted to see you."

What the hell, man? Only a damn pansy would say such rot.

"It's ok. Maybe we could stay in?"

Thoughts run through my mind of what staying in might mean, a night of Netflix and chilling sounding a lot more thrilling than being in a movie theatre and restaurant full of people.

"Sure, sounds great. Should we order a pizza?"

"On it already. I hope Hawaiian is good with you."

I step closer to her, resting my forehead against hers.

"Seriously sunshine, pineapple on pizza?"

"Yeah," she whispers back, our lips almost touching.

"All good, I'll eat any pizza. Pineapple included. But right now I need to taste something else."

Her whimper escapes her mouth, making my cock tent my daks when our lips meet in a soft kiss.

Her hands find my hair, and I grab her ponytail, wrapping it around my hand to pull her closer.

Licking her lips I part them, taking her tongue with mine in a battle fuelled by the desire that rushes through my entire body every damn time she's near.

The taste of fairy floss hits me as I kiss her more, moaning against her lips. She whimpers, pulling back completely breathless.

"Fuck, you can sure kiss, Captain."

My heart hammers at her nickname for me, my body humming with how much I want her.

All of her.

My cock deep inside her, filling her glorious pussy until she falls apart.

"Captain? You thinking about getting dirty on the couch with me, huh?" she teases, looking down at my hard cock that's peaked the front of my daks.

"Oh, you bet I was, sunshine. I want to fuck you, Bella."

"Not tonight Captain, you know, with Nora in the house."
"Fine, pashing on the couch whilst we watch a movie? Your choice."

God, what pansy has possessed me.

Nodding she grabs my hand, leading me to the couch and flicking on the TV before sitting down next to me.
She sits cross-legged, leaning against my shoulder and starts scrolling through Netflix for a movie.
Of course, she chooses something super girly, but a classic nonetheless. 'Clueless' starts playing, Bella reciting every word by heart.
I can't help but smile at how comfortable this feels, but it's scaring me shitless as well.
Tugging on the hair band, I pull it out of the ponytail and start teasing out the knots gently with my fingers, massaging her scalp as well. She looks back at me with a sweet smile.
"That feels good, Captain," she says huskily, smirking at me.
"Really? How'd your hair get like this?"
"I've had a few rough nights with Nora, i've barely slept and Elyse hasn't been home."
"You should've called me," I tell her, feeling my heart thump in my chest.
"It's not your problem, Travis, ok..." she defends, glaring at me.
"Still, you could have called me. What about baby daddy?"
"He's super busy with tax stuff or something as part of his accounting course." She says the words like she doesn't believe them, and I don't know whether to either.

I'm trying to think of a witty comeback, about to reply when there's knocking on the door. She jumps up from the couch to get the door; bringing the pizza back and sitting down again with the box between us.

Opening it she grabs a piece out, giving me an odd look when she leans forward holding it up, near my lips.

"Are you sure you want some, Captain, you know, because of the pineapple?"

"You bet I fucking want some sunshine. Hand it over."

She shakes her head, and I cringe. There's no way she's going to do that, it...feed me.

She's leaning way over and pushes the pizza into my mouth.

"Open up for the pizza, Captain," she taunts.

A sick feeling rises in my stomach and I shrink back, trying to spit the bits of cheese out of my mouth.

"Don't, Bella!" I bellow, "Please don't fucking do that."

She drops the pizza, biting down on her lip.

She looks scared, but fuck, how could she.

She doesn't know you tool. Fucking tell her then.

Standing up from the couch I start pacing the small space, feelings and images racing through me, confirming that this is why I don't do love.

I hear her voice behind me, it's meek, scared, "What the hell? Travis? You're scaring me."

Fuck! Fuck! Fuck!

Stopping the crazy pacing I sit back down the couch, my head in my hands, fisting my hair.

"My ex...she...she um...force fed me..."

Bella gasps audibly, picking up the pizza box and putting it on the coffee table before scooting closer to me.

She doesn't say anything, but I feel her arm grip my back and her thigh pressing against mine.

Looking up at her I continue, "She tried to kill me."

There are tears in her eyes when she speaks softly, "That's horrible. How?"

"She, um...shit...sorry..."

Actually saying these words to her makes me feel like I'm reliving it.

"Don't say sorry, Travis. Please, tell me. I'm here."

Fuck! She's so beautiful, and not running away from me.
I'm so fucked.

"She tried to force me to eat shellfish, lobster."

"And you're allergic?"

"Yeah, severely. Just a touch on my lips and I break out in hives, can't breathe."

"Shit, that's bad."

"I was in the hospital for three days. The bitch force fed me and then left. I could barely speak when I called the ambulance."

She pulls me closer, kissing my neck.

"I'm so sorry, Travis. I didn't know."

"It's not your fault," I reply giving her a soft kiss, before pulling back.

I can hardly believe what I'm doing when I lift my t-shirt over my head, sitting back a bit on the couch.

"And these scars. She inflicted every damn one of them."

"What? Seriously?"

"Yeah, this one," I start, tracing the bird tattoo down my torso, "was when I came home with my first tattoo, she cracked it and told me she'd mark my skin permanently. She sliced straight down with the knife she was holding whilst preparing dinner."

"Shit, that's insane."

"Yeah, that's not even the half of it."

She looks over my body again, touching the one by my belly button, "And this one?"

"She sliced my stomach open with scissors when I found her screaming on the bathroom floor, covered in blood."

"What the hell?"

"She was miscarrying, trying to kill herself, but when I found her, she lashed out at me instead."

"Oh my god, Travis. I...I..."

"Don't, please don't feel sorry for me."

"But...but..." she stammers, her eyes blinking furiously as she fights back tears for me.

It's breaking my heart, and it's why I can't let her fall for me.

"Bella, please," I beg, "I'm not worth crying over."

Brushing the tears from her cheeks with my thumb, I press a soft kiss to her lips and she murmurs against my lips.

"Bella, I...I...lli..."

No, don't, man...don't tell her how you feel. You're no good for her.

I hate my damn conscious for being right, but the look in Bella's eyes is pulling me under.
It's not lust, it's something else like love maybe.

"I know, Travis," she replies, kissing me hard, climbing into my lap.
Straddling me, she deepens the kiss, our lips and tongues clashing together with so many emotions.
I know I should let her go, but I've never felt this all-consuming need.
I need her.
Standing up, still kissing her, she wraps her legs around my back and I stumble towards her bedroom.

Putting her down on the bed, I fall on top of her and break the kiss.
"Bella?"
"Yeah?"
"You're so fucking beautiful. But...we...can't...work...you know that yeah?"
"Um...yeah..I..." she stammers, looking up at me with hooded eyes.

I need her.

Brushing her hair from her cheeks, I press a soft kiss to her forehead, "I need you, Bella."
"I know," she replies kissing me hard, passionately.
Her words and her kiss make my heart hammer in my chest, thoughts tumbling in my head.

Is this what real love feels like? Did I ever love Meaghan?

It sure as hell didn't feel this amazing, like my body is on fire in a good way, like I could never get enough of her.

Breaking the kiss, I crawl under the sheets with Bella, pulling her close and holding her tight, watching her fall asleep.

She's breathtakingly beautiful, but can't be mine, no matter how much I want her to be.

~~

It seems like only minutes have passed when I'm woken up by crying coming from Nora's cot.

Bella stirs in her sleep, and she looks so beautiful and is obviously utterly exhausted. Her soft snoring as she drifted to sleep before me confirmed that.

I contemplate waking Bella, but she looks so peaceful so instead of waking her I climb out of bed and walk quietly over to Nora's cot. She's a spitting image of her mum, her light red hair the only different distinguishable feature.

My heart is pounding, I just want to quiet her crying but I don't know the first thing about what to do when it comes to a kid.

Reaching out into her cot, I touch a hand to her belly and she stops crying for a moment to look up at me.

A smile breaks across her face and it melts my damn heart.

Lifting her up into my arms, I pat her butt, hoping it doesn't feel squishy with shit in her nappy.

Thankfully I'm in the clear on that, but she's starting to let out little wailing cries again.

Cradling her in my arms, somewhat awkwardly I take her out to the lounge room, stopping by the kitchen.

In the fridge I find a row of baby bottles, full of milk, so I grab one out, putting it in the microwave.

She fusses in my arms again and kissing her forehead, I coo, "It's coming sweet girl."

The microwave pings, and getting the bottle out I test a bit on my bare arm. It's the perfect temperature.

Laughing at myself,I can't help but think about how everything comes back to you, the days of helping look after Tessa when she was a baby flooding back.

Taking Nora into the lounge I lie back on the couch, cradling her and giving her the bottle.

She sucks it down quickly whilst I smooth her hair back soothingly. So many emotions are running through my head, a feeling that scares me about how much I want this, a family in my life.

When everything went shit with Meaghan after the miscarriage I blocked out any feelings of ever wanting a kid of my own again as it was the only way to move on and be happy.

But holding Bella's sweet baby girl in my arms is making me feel happier than I have in a long time.

Nora hiccups, gulping down the last droplets of milk from the bottle. Her face contorts in pain, and I lie her down on my chest, patting her back to burp her.

After a moment she lets out a loud burp, and her long eyelashes flutter as she fights sleep. Again I smooth her hair down, watching as she closes her brown eyes, her sweet brown eyes, like her beautiful mothers.

I lay down further on the couch without moving her, letting myself drift to sleep with thoughts of maybe wanting more with Bella.

Sixty-Three | I Care For Her

Jolting awake, I find Bella standing over me by the couch.
Her hands are outstretched to grab a groggy Nora from my bare
chest. There's a throw rug over us, that wasn't there when I came
out to give Nora her bottle the night before.
Picking Nora up and cradling her, Bella rocks her as she stirs from
sleep.

"Morning Captain," she coos at me, smiling.
"Morning, sleep well?" I ask, sitting up on the couch, the throw
rug pooling at my crotch. I see Bella's eyes drift towards it and she
licks her lips
"Yeah, I...um...did. Thanks."
"No worries, you were so exhausted. No biggie."
She sits down on the other end of the couch, unclipping the clasp
on her tank and dropping it down to expose her breast.
Nora shifts in her arms and latches on quickly. I know I shouldn't
stare but Bella looks so fucking beautiful feeding Nora I can't help
but watch on.
Gulping I shift uncomfortably on the couch, hoping that the throw
rug hides the growing of my cock at the sight I really shouldn't be
turned on by.
"Damn, you're beautiful Bella."
"Stop," she protests, her cheeks flushing a deep red.
"Why?"
"Because this," she nods at Nora," is so not a beautiful sight."

I lean closer to her, kissing her forehead.

"You're wrong sunshine. It's turning me on."

She swats my arm playfully, "You're a dirty boy, Travis Banes."

"When it comes to you, yes, sunshine, I am." I laugh, giving her a kiss.

Pulling Nora off her breast, she puts her over her shoulder and pats her back until she burps.

Standing up, she rocks Nora a bit, whilst I watch her, admiring how beautiful she looks holding her daughter in her arms.

"I'm just going to put her down for some tummy time. Want a coffee?"

"Yeah, sure."

"Give me a minute, yeah?"

She laughs, turning away and heading towards the kitchen.

My gaze follows her, trying to not look at her arse jiggling in her tight leggings. They are seriously torture for a man when worn by a woman with a good arse and Bella certainly had the goods in that department.

I want to grab onto her arse cheeks whilst I fuck her from behind. I shouldn't be thinking about fucking her still though, I should be leaving her house and letting her be, but when she returns with a coffee in hand I spit out a stupid offer.

"Why don't you go out for a day of pampering with ya sister? I'll stay and look after Nora."

Her eyes look at me and then at Nora who is lying on her belly on a play mat next to the couch.

"I couldn't do that to you. You've already done enough."

I can't believe the words that come out of my mouth then, literal word vomit, "I want to Bella. I like the kid and you need to do something about that mess of hair."

"Are you sure? Don't you have training or something?"

"Later, yeah. But it's barely ten."

"Ok," she replies, biting down on her lip. I down my coffee in a couple of quick gulps, looking down at her tits again.

She still hasn't done up the clasp and her creamy skin is still exposed.

She notices my staring and laughs, "Whoops."

"Yeah, whoops," I laugh reaching over to caress her cheek with my palm, "I was enjoying the view though."

"I bet you were," she laughs, closing the gap between us on the couch by climbing into my lap again.

My cock strains against the throw rug, pressing into her pussy through the thin fabric.

Whimpering, she fists my hair, kissing me so hard my breath catches in my chest.

"Fuck, Bella, you…take…my…breath away."

She laughs softly, smirking at me with her she-devil grin.

Kissing her again, about to slide a hand into the waistband of her leggings I hear a voice behind us, coming from down the hallway.

"Seriously Bel-bear, there are children in the room."

Bella jumps back off my lap, "Morning Ely-bug. What time did you get in last night?"

Elyse is in the kitchen now, making a coffee. "I don't know, late."

"Cool, so you got any plans today?" Bella asks her sister when she comes into the lounge and sits in the armchair sipping her coffee.

"Nah, should do some uni stuff, but can't be fucked."

"Well, wanna go get our hair done and grab lunch?"

Elyse looks at me, giving me an odd look that I don't really know how to read.

"Yeah, Elyse, I'm going to look after Nora for the day whilst you go out."

"Right, well...I guess you seem capable. You looked kinda cute last night cuddling her." She gives me a wink, but it seems more like a warning, the same warning she gave me previously about breaking her sister's heart.

I don't want to break Bella's heart, but I also know that I'm already in deep, too deep.

~~

It's after eleven am when the girls finally finish getting ready and head out for their day of pampering.

I'd handed Bella a wad of hundy's, not even counting them.

Her eyes boggled at the cash, but after telling her to take it and spend as much as she wanted I gave her a kiss, making sure Elyse wasn't watching when I grabbed Bella's arse, squeezing it.

She'd giggled, called out to Elyse and left, blowing me a kiss as she sauntered out the door.

The minute she leaves, I swear, Nora starts wailing.

Firstly I rock her, cradling her against my shoulder, but still, her cries fill the apartment.

"Shh, sweet girl...shhh," I soothe, rubbing up and down her back.

It doesn't work. And I curse myself for my stupid offer of doing this.

I'm an idiot for even suggesting it, but for some fucked up reason Bella makes me want to actually be a gentleman and makes me want to settle down.

Heading over to the fridge again, thankfully there are some bottles of the expressed milk still.

Still rocking Nora, I heat one up like I did the night before, all the while trying to stop her crying.

Once it's heated I head to Bella's room, sitting in the rocking armchair, cradling Nora in my arms and giving her the bottle.

She suckles on it, her crying subsiding and her sweet brown eyes look up at me.

It melts my fucking heart.

Once she's finished the milk, I put her over my shoulder with a cloth and after a few spit ups that drip almost down my top, she calms for a moment before her crying starts again.

I'm at a loss for what to do.

Think, you idiot. Remember, what you did with Tessa.

Shaking my thoughts aside, I pat her butt to make sure she's not wet, which thankfully she isn't but I get the odour of shit waft up to my nose.

Fuck! I can't do this, I can't do this.

Panicking, I scan the room for nappies and a place where I can change her.

Calm down, you pansy, I tell myself, spotting the changing mat on top of the drawers.

Putting Nora down on it, holding a hand against her belly, I yank her little trackies down to her ankles and pull off the dirty nappy. The stench is horrendous, so taking a deep breath in I fold the nappy up, dumping it in the weird-looking disposer thing.

Pulling out way more baby wipes than probably necessary I wipe her tiny butt, before shoving another nappy underneath her. Once it's secure I pull up the little trackies and lift her into my arms.

"Better, sweet girl?" I coo.

She lets out a little giggle but is still sobbing.

Putting her down in her cot, I kiss her forehead, noticing it's a little warm against my lips.

"Should we get mummy to come back?" I think out loud, looking down at Nora as she cries and kicks her little feet.

It appears she's tiring herself out, as her long eyelashes flutter and her eyes slowly shut.

Not wanting to leave her alone, I sit in the rocking armchair again, finding that my eyes can't stay open either.

My thoughts as I drift to sleep are full of Bella as my everything, with a pregnant belly and pottering around my apartment.

They are scary as fuck thoughts, but exciting.

Yeah, I'm so fucked.

Sixty-Four | Honey I'm Home

Bella

It's just gone two pm when Elyse and I get home. I'm feeling refreshed, my hair trimmed a little and a treatment done that's made it silky smooth and soft.

Elyse had just gone for a treatment, even though I suggested she cut her arse grazing chocolate locks.

She loved her hair, the only really girly thing about her.

My little sister had always been such a tomboy, which sucked growing up as she never was interested in makeup and preferred playing with LEGO over Barbies with me.

Walking in, we're both shocked to find the house super quiet.

For a moment I panic, thinking Travis has skipped out but walking into my bedroom, with Elyse behind me, we find Travis asleep in the chair next to Nora's cot.

"Aww Bella...could he be any more gorgeous?"

"Yeah." I nod, smiling. My stomach does a flip flop at the sight of him, his arms over the sides of the rocking armchair.

He certainly is gorgeous, and after the last few days I've definitely seen a different side to him, which scares and excites me.

I step up to the chair, to him, shaking his shoulders slightly to wake him up.

His eyes flutter open, and he looks at me sleepily.

"Hey you ok?

"Yeah, I'm fine. Sorry, I fell asleep," he mutters rubbing his eyes.

"Was she good?"

"Um yeah...but I ah...think she has a fever," he says worriedly, standing up from the armchair, "she seemed a little warm but I didn't want to bother you unnecessarily."

"That's ok," I tell him, bending down over Nora's cot to check her forehead.

"You're right. I'll give her some Panadol, otherwise it's a doctor visit again."

I'm standing close to Travis now, so close it's making my heart race.

"Is everything ok honey?" he asks suddenly, shocking me not only by speaking, but by the very sweet term of endearment slipping from his lips again.

"Yeah...why are you calling me honey?"

He lets out a soft chuckle, that makes my insides go crazy with butterflies.

"Um...I don't know...I...I'm sorry."

He's looking at me with an odd look in his ocean eyes, so different from the lust that usually shines in them when he looks at me.

Stretching up on my tiptoes I kiss him, softly brushing my lips across his.

"Don't be sorry...I like it."

"Oh really?" He taunts, chuckling again, "Well did you know I like you?"

"Nah I didn't know that," I tease, smirking at him, "show me."

He kisses me this time, a sweet but hard kiss, that I feel from my lips against his, all the way to my feet.

I'm totally melting into him, and moaning I break the kiss, "Mmm...I like you too Travis Banes."

My words scare me a little, but I mean them.

Kissing him again, I revel in the way he pulls me close, one hand on my hips, the other in my hair.

I'm so lost in the moment I gasp against his lips, pulling back when I hear Elyse walking past.

"Eww get a room you two," she teases, standing in the doorway a moment.

Travis and I both laugh at my sisters' cheekiness.

Granted she's caught us pashing twice today.

Travis brushes a stray hair from my cheek, looking down at me with that odd look again. His ocean blue eyes have a new sparkle in them, and it makes my heart race.

"I gotta go anyway, honey...big game tomorrow. Text me if you need anything."

Something has changed between us, for sure. I haven't fucked him, but I just want to be with him, even more in these super sweet moments when he shows me he cares.

"I will," I promise and he hugs me, pulling me close to his muscled chest.

Being in his arms makes me feel safe and stirs up that giddy feeling in my stomach. After a minute or so, he pulls back pressing a soft kiss against my lips before he leaves, taking a part of me with him.

There's no way I'm falling for him.

I can't fall in love with him, but it sure feels like I am.

I know my body loves being with him, as I'm aching for him to come back now, to take all of me, but my heart is still not sure.

Sixty-Five | Tell Her Now

In the change rooms after the game, I'm stripping from my wet Gatorade soaked guernsey when Jairus slaps me on the back.

"Man, that was a good game. Nothing better than whooping Essendon's arse, huh?"

"Yeah," I mutter, sliding my footy shorts down my legs.

"Something up Travis?"

Pulling my daks up, I gaze at my best mate, who's staring at me quizzically. I'm wondering if I should tell him about my feelings or if since he's in a jovial mood, he'll just make me feel like an idiot.

"I um...I'm...I'm..." I stutter confirming my idiot status.

"Your what? Pussy got ya tongue?" He taunts, winking.

It makes me chuckle slightly.

"I um...think...I'm falling for Bella and her little girl." I'm sure a blush creeps up my cheeks.

Jairus laughs, before jeering, "Oh so you're pussy whipped then huh?"

"I told you we haven't fucked...it's different with her. Just kissing her is enough to make me crack a fat...actually looking at her is enough." I laugh, even though my words aren't exactly funny.

Jairus is giving me look now, a serious look, "Tell her how you feel then."

I shake my head at him. "I'm scared to...things are good...what if things fuck up like with Meaghan?"

My eyes drop to the floor. I can't meet Jai's eyes.

He steadies me, stops me from pacing the room with his hands on my shoulders.

"I don't think that will happen Travis ...just tell her how you feel."

I look up at him when he steps back. "Yeah I guess...how's Anni?"

He smiles wide at my mention of his wife.

"Feels like a whale...she can barely move...but still has a month to go."

"Are you excited?"

"Fuck yeah...I can't wait to meet our babies. We've got names picked out already, but since we don't know the genders we're waiting until they're born to share."

It's my turn to smile, my mates happiness is infectious.

"I'm so happy for you bro. You'll be a great dad."

"Thanks," he says, smiling and slinging his bag over his shoulder.

"Anyway I gotta head out. We've got a doctors appointment."

"Ok no worries. Text me bro."

"Will do," he replies, back turned as he leaves me in the change rooms as usual.

I grab my footy from my locker and head out to the training field. My head is so fucking mixed up, that I cant even focus on kicking straight.

It's a wonder we even beat the Bombers, because I played the worst I have in months.

All I can think about is Bella; her kiss on my lips, her curvy body wrapped around mine, how she tastes and sounds when she comes. And I also cant stop thinking about how it would feel to fuck her.

The thought of ever fucking another Sheila other than Bella turns my gut.

I'm cunt struck for sure, but I'm too afraid to tell her how I feel, because telling her means I have to admit to myself that I'm in love with her.

And surely, despite the pounding of my heart I'm not in love.

I don't do love.

Sixty-Six | Time for Twins

I'm contemplating heading to the pub for a Parma when my phone pings with a message.

Jairus: bro, the babies are coming. Anni is in labour!

I quickly reply, grabbing my keys and scooting out the door as I type.

Travis: shit bro. Be there asap. Anni will be fine.

Sliding into the Jag I throw my phone on the passenger seat, practically jumping out of my seat when it rings through the Bluetooth the moment I turn the ignition over.

"Hey honey, you get the text too?" I ask Bella when I press the answer button on the steering wheel.
"Yeah, can you come pick me up? And take me to pick up Nora first?"
"Yeah, of course. Be there in fifteen."
"Thanks, Captain. I'll be waiting out front."
"Sweet as," I reply hanging up and telling my heart to slow the fuck down at her calling me Captain outside the bedroom.
Something has certainly shifted between us since I looked after Nora a few weeks ago.

I haven't seen Bella since, but she's been on my mind constantly. And driving towards her house now, just the thought of seeing her is making me crack a fat in my trackies.

For a Thursday arvo, there's minimal traffic and I'm pulling up outside Bella's in record time, as barely ten minutes have passed since I hung up the phone.

As she said, she's waiting out the front, and fuck me she looks like a walking wet dream in tight leather-look leggings and a skin-tight red v-neck t-shirt that shows of her delectable cleavage.

Her deep chocolate hair is down in waves, swaying from side to side as she saunters over to the Jag to get in.

When she gets in, she smiles at me, blushing as red as her t-shirt when I lean across the console to kiss her.

After breaking the kiss she giggles, "Can I drive?"

"You want to drive the red kitten?"

"Your car is called the red kitten?"

"Yeah, she's red and purrs like a kitten when driven right."

"Right, so can I drive the red kitten, Captain?" she asks, lacing her tone with lust, purring her nickname for me and rolling her r's.

My cock was already hard, but now it's throbbing in my daks, wondering if she purrs like a kitten when she gets fucked.

"Fine, honey. You can drive the red kitten, but only if you show me how well you handle stick first."

I can't even think before her hand is in my daks and she's stroking my cock and squeezing my balls.

"I'm a country girl, Captain," she taunts, locking her eyes to mine, "I can drive a stick hard."

She squeezes my cock like a vice, and I damn near want to explode.

"Fuck Bella!" I bellow grabbing her hair and pulling her lips to mine in a fierce kiss.

Every time she touches me my whole body hums with want, with need, with something I can't explain and that four-letter word I'm too scared to feel pops into my brain.

She's out of the car like a bull, and once we're both back in opposite seats I barely have a moment to think before she's revving the engine giggling as she drives off.

My eyes don't even focus on where we're heading. All I do is stare at her, her taking command of the red kitten, making it purr hard. She definitely knows how to drive stick and I'm super conscious of the fatty in my daks.

Usually, I'm the one who takes command in the bedroom but watching Bella drive my car makes me want her to take the control away next time we're together in the sheets.

She pulls up to a house, sliding into the curb to park effortlessly. Cutting the engine she gets out and I follow her up to the door after stumbling out of the Jag and adjusting myself in my trackies. As soon as she knocks the door opens to her baby daddy holding the capsule with Nora in it. He doesn't even say hello.

"Fucking take her...she's been up wailing all night."
"Don't start Jaxon," Bella warns taking the capsule handle in her grip and walking back towards the Jag.
Nora is still crying, even when I put the top down so Bella can hook the capsule into the backseat.

I admire how quickly she gets it all strapped in, sliding into the passenger seat and putting her seatbelt on.

Glancing at her as I close the top again, I feel a pang of sadness hit me in the chest.

Things are obviously still stressing her out and I notice the bags under her eyes she's tried to hide with makeup.

"Honey, you ok?" I ask wiping my thumb across her cheek where tears have started to fall, streaking the makeup.

"Yeah, Captain. I'm fine. You know how it is."

I nod, caressing her cheek to wipe the tears away before kissing her forehead softly.

"Yeah, " I muse softly, smiling, "let's go meet some twins."

She smiles back at me, and I pull out into the traffic, heading towards the Epworth.

It's crazy to admit, but I'm looking forward to meeting my best mates twins. It makes me wonder again what it would be like to have a family of my own and glancing at Bella as we walk into the maternity ward I can't help but imagine her pregnant again.

I've officially gone crazy. Must be baby fever from being surrounded by the cries of babies.

Yeah that's it; its definitely that, and most certainly not love.

Sixty-Seven | Cuteness Multiplied Twice
Bella

Nora is still crying when we get to the hospital, so I unbuckle her awkwardly from her capsule in the backseat of Travis's Jag and carry her inside, in my arms.

Travis keeps glaring at me, and it not only makes my heart race but my stomach flip flop.

The look in his eyes is caring, and I've got the scary four-letter word tumbling in my head.

Heading into the maternity ward, he saunters up to the nurses' station to ask what room Anni is in and I stand back, rocking Nora. Thankfully her wails aren't out of the ordinary here, but they worry me nonetheless as she's been super restless and out of sorts for months, unwell and not getting better.

Travis comes back, snaking an arm around my back and guiding me towards the elevator. Stepping inside we bump into Austin on his way out with Dana.

"Hey Bel," he says, giving me a smile that dies on his lips when I look up at him. Travis has decided to lean against the railing, seeming a little impatient.

"Hey Aust, hey Dana," I greet them, trying to smile.

"You ok Bel?" Austin asks, touching my arm lightly, "You seem stressed."

"I'm fine Aust. Just Nor hasn't stopped crying since we left Jax's and I..."

Again Austin smiles at me, before cooing at Nora in my arms.

Her sweet little brown eyes look up at him and she instantly calms down. Shock crosses my face and Travis's when he steps up behind me, his hand grazing the small of my back, making my breath hitch.

Nora is still looking at Austin and reaches out her tiny fist to him.

He takes it, shaking it and baby talking to her.

It melts my heart, breaking it as well.

I never knew he was so good with kids.

"How about we take her for the arvo, and tonight too if you want?"

"You don't have to do that Aust. It's fine."

"I want to Bel, and Dan would love to have a baby around for a bit."

He gives Dana a look that says something without words, something that tugs at my heart when Dana looks at me with a wide grin.

"I'd really love to look after her, Bella.

"Ok, I guess that would be good," I reply looking to Travis, and he gives me a wink and sexy smirk that makes my stomach flip flop.

Handing Nora to Austin, she giggles and snuggles into him.

Travis grabs his keys from his pocket, hesitant to hand them over, "Her capsule is in the red Jag, level two."

Dana takes the keys, heading out to get Nora's capsule.

"We will leave the keys at the nurses' station when we leave," Austin says following Dana.

The elevator doors close and Travis presses the button to head up to the maternity ward. He looks at me with the same caring look from earlier, the one that makes me giddy.

"You sure you're ok honey?" he asks, signalling the butterflies in my belly again.

I love when he calls me honey, not sunshine. It amused me that his best mate used to call me sunshine.

"Yeah, yeah, I'm fine...but I um...guess I'm just nervous about Nora being with someone else again."

"She'll be fine, Bella," he says sweetly, before pulling me close and kissing me.

I want to deepen the kiss, a rush of longing coursing through me from the touch of his lips to mine but the doors of the elevator glide open after it has stopped abruptly.

He takes my hand, smirking at me when we walk into the room Anni is in.

Both Anni and Jai look up at us when we enter, both smiling from ear to ear. They both have a baby in their arms.

Letting go of Travis's hand I step closer to the bed, whilst he goes over to Jairus to congratulate him.

I peer down at the sweet, cute as a button baby in Anni's arms.

"Aww, Anni, congrats girl."

"Thanks, Bel. This is Ryder Ayden and Jai is holding Reid Elijah."

"Oh Anni, those names are gorgeous. Twin boys!"

"I know," she giggles, leaning towards me to whisper, "they'll be gorgeous like their dad."

"Yeah, so, your labour must have been the quickest twin birth ever?"

She laughs, looking across at Jairus who nods.

"Yeah, she was practically pushing Ryder out the minute we got here."

"Oh shit really?"

"Yeah, fuck it hurt Bel. Two babies mere minutes apart with no pain relief but I'm just so glad they're here safe."

"Me to girl," I reply heading over to gander at Reid in Jairus's arms. Both boys most definitely do look like their dad, but they're not identical.

"Didn't you bring Nora?"

"I did, but we bumped into Austin on the way in and he's taking her for the night to give me a break."

"Oh, wasn't she supposed to be at Jaxon's this weekend?"

"Yeah, but things aren't good with Jax. He's not stepping up with Nor and it's really frustrating."

I feel Travis step up behind me, his body so close it makes my heart race. His stance behind me is protective and I wonder if Anni and Jai notice the tension between us.

"That's not good, Bel. It will be nice for Austin and Dana to spend some time with her though."

"Yeah," I say softly, shifting uncomfortably when Travis's hands find my waist, "we should probably get going, and leave you two to bond with your gorgeous boys."

"Ok, I'll have you over for a coffee when I'm back home."

"Sounds good," I reply smiling heading to the door and waving back at them.

Travis follows me, taking my hand the moment we close the door. Back at the elevator, he's smirking at me.

"What Captain?" I tease.

"Come back to mine, Bella?" he asks, my name like honey on his lips.

"Why, Captain?"

"I want to make you mine, completely."

My heart skips, and I don't say a word, instead, I kiss him hard and passionately.

When the elevator doors slide open this time, he sprints to the nurses' station to get the Jag keys.

Taking my hand again, his devilish smirk is on his face as he drags me out of the hospital.

My body is tingling in anticipation of what finally having sex with him is going to be like.

Given the last times we've been together, I'm guessing pure ecstasy and even though it scares the shit out of me in some ways, I'm ready for him to have all of me and to tell him the sweetest of confessions.

Sixty-Eight I Sweet Confessions Within

The tension between Bella and me as I gun the jag back to my place has me on edge. My cock is already throbbing in my daks just thinking about tasting her again, and this time I'm not going to hold back from having her completely.

I need to fuck her into tomorrow.

She's smirking at me, a soft flush on her cheeks when she puts a hand into her leather daks and moans.

Thankfully we're pulling up in front of my apartment because I can't take a second longer of the torture of not having all of her.

Cutting the engine, I turn my gaze to her and she pulls her hand out of her daks, bringing them up to her lips, but I don't let her put them in her mouth.

Grabbing her hand I take her fingers into my mouth instead, licking them from her knuckles to her fingertips and tasting her delicious honey on them.

It's my turn to moan, "Mmm, honey, so delicious."

She giggles at me, opening her car door and walking around to sit on the bonnet.

Chuckling I get out, striding around to the front of the Jag and pushing her down over the bonnet with a hot kiss.

When her tongue invades my mouth, my cock throbs pressing against her belly and I pull back from her lips, looking down at her.

"Honey, if we don't get inside now, I'm going to be stripping you naked and fucking you bare right here."

Again she lets out a sweet giggle before sitting up, her body against mine creating the most amazing friction.

I'm gonna explode if I don't get her naked, if I don't slam my cock inside her dripping pussy.

She kisses me again, wrapping her legs around my arse and still with our lips locked I lift her up off the bonnet.

Having her in my arms, our lips locked together makes my whole body heat.

No sheila has ever made me feel completely on fire with need.

Together we stumble towards my apartment, and at the base of the stairs I put her down, groaning when her pussy grazes against my hard cock.

"I can't climb the stairs whilst kissing you honey."

She lets out a delightful giggle, taking my hand as we bound up the stairs together.

I fumble with the keys at my front door, finally getting it open and pushing it closed when we're both inside.

There is nothing to say with words.

She jumps into my arms, wrapping her legs around my back and her arms around my neck, her lips crashing to mine in a kiss that makes my cock throb against her belly, my body heat and my heart race.

God, she makes me feel, makes me need.

Still locked together, I prowl towards the bedroom, putting her down on the bed I'd actually made for once.

Watching her crawl back on her arse towards the headboard has my cock screaming in my daks, and I yank my t-shirt over my head, throwing it on the floor before diving onto the bed, my body over hers, my lips crashing to hers to claim her, as mine.

This night is about her becoming completely mine.

Her whimper escapes her lips, teasing me and groaning I break the kiss to look into her chocolate eyes.

"Strip for me, Bella."

She bites down on her lip, a smirk turning up the corner of her mouth when she pulls her t-shirt over her head, throwing it on the floor.

Underneath, the crop top bra she has on is far from sexy, but the mounds of her cleavage are and I push my face in between her tits, licking them before kissing up her collarbone to the sweet spot on her neck that makes her hips arch against me.

In her ear, I exhale a husky breath, "I want to fuck you, naked and bare, honey."

Again she whimpers, reaching between us to push my trackies and jocks down my legs.

Kicking them off, they fall to the floor and I kneel on the edge of the bed, grabbing her around the waist to sit her up so I can pull the bra off over her head.

"Mmm, Bella, you're fucking perfect," I tell her, leaning over her curvaceous body and kissing her neck.

She arches up to me, as I swirl my tongue over her skin, down again to her collarbone and across her now bare perfect tits.

Taking the bud of one in my teeth, it puckers to attention and I swirl my tongue over the supple flesh.

She starts to let out hushed moans, panting with pleasure and I turn my attention to the other tit, giving it the same sweet torture that is making Bella writhe underneath me.

"Please, captain, please," she pants, my kisses now trailing down her stomach to the hem of her leather leggings.

Grabbing them I yank them down, peeling them off her exquisitely toned legs. She kicks slightly and they drop to the floor.

I take a moment to admire her glorious body.

Just looking at her spread before me is making my cock want to explode.

Lifting her leg up I trail kisses down her creamy thighs and then kiss her pussy through the scrap of lace.

Teasingly through the lace I lick her clit with my tongue and she jerks her hips against my face.

Lifting my head I rest my chin on her belly a moment.

Hooking my fingers in the elastic of the g-string I taunt her, "I hope you don't need these anymore."

She opens her mouth to speak but bites down on her lip instead when I rip the g-string off, throwing it aside without a care.

Her pussy, as usual, is bare and looks utterly edible.

I can smell her arousal, and it's fucking intoxicating.

Chuckling, I smirk before dipping my head between her legs and licking her pussy from the bottom to the top.

A sexy as fuck moan escapes her lips, her whimper of pleasure she knows drives me absolutely wild.

Groaning, I drive my tongue into her pussy, lapping up her sweet honey like it's my last damn meal.

She's squirming in pleasure, whimpering and moaning but I don't want her to come from a tongue lashing.

I want to be buried balls deep inside her and feel her tight pussy grip my cock as we climax together.

Stretching up over her body, I kiss her lips hard, and she licks mine back tasting herself on my tongue.

"Mmm, fuck," she moans huskily against my lips.

My cock is teasing her, at the cusp of entering her, the tip against her clit.

Breaking the kiss, I look into her mesmerising chocolate eyes as I slide my cock slowly into the folds of her pussy.

She whimpers, biting down on her lip, my cock filling her.

Her pussy is like a vice around my cock, but so slick at the same time.

"God, Bella, fuck you feel good," I groan starting to thrust in and out hard.

"Mmm, oh...oh...fuck...fuck...oh," she moans, panting and bucking her hips up against me.

Again I kiss her, slamming my lips to hers and slamming my cock harder, balls deep when I take her tongue with mine.

The taste of fairy floss again hits my tongue and I moan against her lips before breaking the kiss and withdrawing my cock from her pussy completely.

She looks at me like she's disappointed, but I whisper against her lips, "Ride my cock, Bella, please."

She giggles, sitting up against the headboard.

Grabbing her waist I pull her into my lap, locking my eyes on hers as she slides down onto my cock.

Kissing me fiercely she bounces up and down on my length, our bodies smacking against each other.

"Mmm, fuck...so good," I groan, slamming my cock harder into her as our bodies rock together.

I've fucked other sheila's cowgirl, but somehow with Bella it feels like the first time.

I want to stay buried inside her forever because god does it feel like heaven.

Her breath is laboured, whimpers, moans and 'oh's' escaping her lips.

Kissing her zealously I lay her back down on the bed, spearing my cock deep inside her. It feels absolutely fucking divine, and it scares me that this doesn't feel like fucking, but so much more.

She wraps her legs around my arse, embedding my cock so far inside her pussy I feel like we're completely one.

"Fuck, Bella, fuck!" I moan, smashing a kiss to her lips, thrusting slowly in and out against the force of her legs around me.

My heart is hammering so hard in my chest, my breath as I break the kiss mere pants.

I gaze down between our bodies, watching my cock sliding in and out of her slick pussy.

"Touch yourself, honey. Come for me."

Her hand reaches down, flicking her clit and her moans are so loud and so fucking glorious the sound is burned into my memory. I want to hear her make that sound over and over again.

"Fuck Bella! Fuck! I'm gonna fucking come! God...I...I llo...fuck!" I cry out, my cock starting to throb inside her, my climax building.

I can feel her pussy clenching around me, her whole body trembling, climbing towards her peak.

She lets out a carnal moan, her sexy whimper and takes her finger from her clit bringing it up to my lips.

Taking it between my teeth I lick it clean, "Mmm, you taste like heaven, honey," I tease.

She laughs softly, cupping my cheeks in her palms, pulling me down to kiss me. Her kiss is passionate and I thrust into her hard again, my release filling her.

My cock is still throbbing, my release so shattering and prolonged. Bella is trembling, riding the wave of her release and with a final thrust, we come together.

"Oh, fuck, god Bella, I love you! Fuck!"
Still inside her, after my confession, I kiss her softly.
I can't believe the word love just came out of my mouth, but I damn well meant it.
Panting Bella breaks the kiss, locking her eyes on mine when I roll over to lay next to her.
Facing me, she smiles, "I love you too, Captain."
"Mmm," I moan, kissing her again, pouring all my emotions into the kiss.
Pulling her body against mine I hold her close, drifting to sleep and thinking of the future together.
I never want to let her go.
I'm cunt struck, and in love with Bella Mishal.

Sixty-Nine | Freak Out Mode
Bella

Rolling over, I sigh deeply looking at Travis sprawled out next to me in his bed, still completely stark naked. He murmurs in his sleep, reminding me of the murmurs he made against my lips the night before when we fucked until we both came apart.

I can't help but stare at him now, my heart pounding at how gorgeous he is with his unruly ashen locks over his eyes and his lips parting as he breathes.

Scooting closer, I'm about to kiss him good morning when he speaks, "Morning, honey."

The new term of endearment he's started to call me sounds exactly like its namesake when dropping from his lips, sickly sweet and tantalising.

"Morning, Captain," I greet him back, teasingly.

His arm snakes around my bare waist, pulling against his morning wood.

His lips are a whisper from mine. "So, last night, huh?"

"Yeah, what about it?" I taunt him, knowing exactly what he's referring to which isn't the mind-blowing sex but the words we said to each other.

Those three words.

Those three scary as fuck words.

"I meant it, Bella." He smirks at me, and I don't know what to think or feel. I'd meant the words too, they scared the shit out of me, but I meant them.

But the smirk on Travis' face suggests he only said them in the moment, when his cock was inside me and my heart is already shattered.

Playfully slapping his arm, I tease, "You don't have to tell me that to get into my daks, Captain."

"I'm not, honey. I'm so fucking in love with you Bella."

The smirk is gone, but my heart still can't believe his words.

My tongue is stuck to the roof of my mouth, the words 'I love you too Travis' are on repeat in my head, but I can't get my mouth to cooperate again to utter them.

I'd said them back last night, but in the light of day, I can't.

I can't believe he's in love with me. Travis Banes doesn't do love, or so he's told me, so he can't possibly mean the words he's saying, to me of all people.

No other guy I've fallen for has fallen for me. I'm nothing special.

My thoughts are broken with his kiss against my lips, soft but hard, and so full of emotion my heart crashes against my rib cage.

If he doesn't mean his words, I'll be beyond shattered.

Breaking the kiss, he looks at me searchingly with his ocean blue eyes.

They make me feel like I'm drowning.

"What's going through that pretty little head, honey?" he asks, brushing my hair from my cheeks.

"Nothing, I...just...I..."

Fuck Bella, just tell him you love him.

I know my subconscious is right, but it still won't cooperate with my tongue. He speaks again, his tone soft, "Move in with me Bella. You and Nora."

I sit bolt upright in bed, not sure if I heard his words right, his words that are not a question but a statement, a demand.

My heart is hammering in my chest again, this time not in a good way.

'Move in with him'. Not a chance. Things will go to shit Bella.

Grabbing the sheets I stand up, ripping them away from him so his body is bare. My breath hitches seeing him in his naked glory, ready for me, his cock hard and fucking glorious.

"Bella, please, say something."

"I...I...can't...I can't mmm...move in with you."

"Why the hell not?" He bellows at me, making me feel a little fearful.

"Because I can't."

It's a poor excuse, its actually not an excuse but frankly I don't have a reason other than I'm scared shitless to completely let my guard down, to take such a big step with my heart and my life.

Dropping the sheet, I bend over starting to scour the floor for my discarded clothes. Pulling on my leggings, I hear his voice behind me, husky and full of lust.

"Honey, just come back to bed. Forget I said anything. You bending over makes me want to fuck you again."

I scoff but don't say anything. His words 'forget I said anything' and 'fuck you' instead of 'make love to you' are ringing in my head as I quickly slip my bra and t-shirt on.

For a moment I think about kissing him goodbye, but it would feel to final and I can't let go of him.

He's in my heart now, I love him so much it hurts, but I can't play house.

Without another word, without even looking back at him lying still naked on the bed I walk out.

~~

My feet are on autopilot as I run to the tram, my head so mixed up with emotions. Boarding the tram I brush my arm across my tear-stained cheeks and contemplate for a moment before the tram jolts away that I should jump off and go back to Travis's bed, back to his arms to repeat last night, but instead I stay on the tram heading to Austin's to get Nora.

Once at his door I thump my fist hard against the wooden door. The moment he opens it he looks at me like I'm here to tell him someone has died.

"Hey Bel, what's wrong? We were going to drop Nor off later."
I look down at my feet, "I...I...slept with Travis."
Austin gapes at me, but he doesn't speak.
"I'm so in love with him Aust...and I..."
"And he doesn't feel the same way, huh?"
I shake my head, "No he does...I think...but he wants me and Nor to move in with him...I can't."

"Why not Bel?" Austin asks with a caring tone, "It's clear he cares about you and he's good with Nora."

"I know but what if things go shit like they did with Jaxon? I can't bear to lose him, lose someone else I love if things fuck up between us."

"You have to trust your gut, Bel," he tells me, sounding far too wise.

"Hmm yeah," I mumble unconvincingly when Dana comes out holding Nora in her arms.

"Oh hi Bella," she greets me, not waiting for an answer, "she just woke up."

She brings Nora over to the door.

"Hey Dana...thanks for having her."

"No problems...she's such a sweetie and loves this one," she says stepping up next to Austin.

Nora reaches out for him and he grabs her, cradling her in his arms.

"Mummy's here Nor," he says in a baby voice.

She giggles and coos at him, her lips moving and the word 'dada' escaping rather loudly.

Austin shakes his head at my girl in his arms, "No baby girl, I'm not your dada."

There's a lump in my throat, that I swallow down hard.

"Thanks, Aust...we better get going. I'm going to take her to Mums...clear my head," I tell him, still trying to process the first word my baby girl just spoke.

"Ok I'm here for you Bella, anytime," he says handing Nora to me. Even though she's against my shoulder she starts fussing and Austin coos at her when she turns her head to look at him.

"Be good for mummy," he says in a voice that would charm the daks of anyone.

Nora instantly calms, the traitorous devil and I smile, "Thanks again guys...I'll see you soon."

With my words, I turn away from their front door and head back towards the tram. I'm nearly at the gate when Austin comes running down the driveway calling out, "Bella, you might need her capsule."

He has Nora's capsule in his grip. Stopping dead I wait for him to jog towards me.

"Thanks, I'm...um...not thinking straight."

"That's ok. Are you sure you'll be ok?"

"Yeah, I...I just need some space to sort out how I feel."

"Ok," he says hugging me after I strap Nora in the capsule.

His hug feels platonic, friendly and doesn't set my whole body alight like hugging Travis does.

Stepping back, Austin smiles at me, "Travel safe, Bella and call me if you need anything."

"Thanks, Austin. I will."

I head out the gate then, with Nora in her capsule, giggling, completely oblivious and I silently wish I could feel the same happiness.

Seventy | Trust Your Heart
Bella

Getting to Mum's on the bus was nothing short of a nightmare. Nora had practically cried the entire four-hour trip and my nerves were at breaking point.

It's close to seven when I knock on Mum's front door, and she opens it wearing a dressing gown and fluffy sheep slippers on her feet. I've put Nora down in her capsule, thankful she's finally asleep and I fall against Mum's chest.

Her arms wrap around me and I find myself sobbing into the terry towel fabric of her dressing gown.

After a minute or so she pulls back from the hug, brushing my hair off my face.

"What are you doing here Bella beautiful?"

Sniffing back the tears I tell her, "I listened to my body and my heart."

"How so, dear?" she asks bending down to pick up Nora's capsule, carefully to not wake her.

Following her inside, we head straight to the lounge room and I sink into the armchair whilst she puts Nora beside her on the three-seater couch.

"I...um...I slept with him."

"Who dear? That man from Anni's wedding you told me about?"

"Yes, Travis, but I feel like things have moved too fast."

"Why is that?"

"He asked me to move in with him."

Shock crosses Mum's face, but she doesn't say anything this time, so I continue, "And I don't want a repeat of how things went with Jaxon."

"Do you love him? This Travis?"

"Yes...but I loved Austin to and..."

"And what dear?" she prompts, looking across at Nora.

"I think Nora might be his...not Jaxon's."

Admitting the words out loud after this morning makes it seem real, but I still don't want to believe that my baby girl is Austin's. Mum shocks me with her words, even though they are true.

"Well, she does have red hair, Bella."

"It's not just that...she's so calm with him...they had an instant bond and she called him dada today. Her first word was to Austin."

"Oh my goodness, Bella...Maybe you should ask him for a DNA test."

"I can't do that to Jaxon mum...it would break his heart."

"Hmmm yeah, up to you dear. So what about Travis?" she asks, a hint of laughter in her tone like she wants to know more about sleeping with him.

I'm not going to discuss the amazing sex I had with Travis last night with my mother or anyone else for that matter.

It's all I've thought about since leaving his house this morning, but I'm not ready to face how I feel about him until I know he really does feel the same.

"I don't know mum...I don't know what to do."

"Trust your heart, Bella...when you know you know."

"Yeah, my heart is a traitor. I loved Austin, but now I feel nothing for him."

"He wasn't the right man for you, Bella beautiful. How did Travis make your body feel when you were fully together, compared to Austin?"

I can't believe I'm about to say anything about my sex life to Mum, but the words roll off my tongue, "I can't compare them, but with Travis, honestly the sex is on fire."

"Sounds like your heart and body both know the truth, Bella."

"Yeah, maybe. Can I stay a while to sort out how I feel?"

"Stay as long as you need, dear, but don't stay too long or you might lose him."

Standing up from the armchair I mutter a 'hmm,' the thought of losing Travis making my heart feel like it's shattering inside my chest.

But I can't go back to the city now, and be with him, and pretend that he doesn't have my heart completely.

I'm completely, utterly and hopelessly in love with Travis Banes, and even though he's told me he feels the same, I know the words are lies because no man I fall for, falls for me too.

Seventy-One | No Excuses Here

I let her go.

I let her walk out the fucking door.

I didn't even get up off the bed to beg her to stay. And she's gone, not answering my calls, not answering my texts.

It feels like a bad dream, a nightmare.

I finally had her completely, all of her and then I fuck it up, moving too fast for my skittish Bella.

I don't know how much time has passed after I heard the door slam when she left, but the sun is high and is blazing through my open blinds.

I don't want to get up, don't want to face the fact that I fucked up the best thing to happen to me in years.

My whole body aches to be with her again, but the most fucked up thing is my heart fucking aches.

She has it.

The moment she walked out the door, she took my fucking heart with her. And I damn well let her.

I'm such a fucking idiot, a wanker, a complete tosser.

I should have kept my big mouth shut this morning, and just sunk inside her pussy again.

Being inside Bella, fucking her, no scratch that, making love to her was by far the most amazing sex of my fucking life and I can't even comprehend not feeling that bliss again, nor do I want to think about fucking someone else.

It's always been, Bella.

From the first time I saw at Jai's house party a few years back, I've wanted her and when I finally have her, all of her, heart and body, I fuck it up by being a wanker.

Sighing, I sit up to stretch, flipping my legs over the side of the bed. My knees feel weak as I stumble to the bathroom, stepping up to the counter and taking a look at myself in the mirror. Stubble dots my chin, my eyes dilated like I'm high and my cheeks flushed.

My hair is a knotted pile on top of my head, the typical I fucked someone hard last night look.

Raking a hand through my hair, I wince pulling out some knots and my hard cock presses into the cupboard handle which also makes pain whip through me.

For a moment I contemplate having a shower, but don't see the point anymore. I don't have to look good for anyone, so why give a fuck about my appearance.

Quickly and painfully I do a leak, before heading back out to bed. I gather the sheets up from the floor where she left them in a heap, clutching them to my chest and inhaling the sweet smell of Bella's perfume and pussy on them.

Fuck, she smells good.

My cock throbs, memories of being inside her flashing in my mind on constant replay.

Wrapping the sheet around my pelvis, I rock my groin against it, fisting my cock imagining my Bella is still with me.

It's only minutes before I explode, cum wetting the sheets in a burst.

I don't really feel satisfied. Wanking is never going to make me satisfied. Only being inside Bella's pussy will ever make me feel truly satisfied again.

Climbing out of bed for the second time, I pull on my discarded jocks from the night before, balling up the sheets and carrying them to the washing basket.

I partly want to not wash them so I can smell Bella on them, but I'm also trying to not be a dirty fucker most of the time.

After throwing them in the laundry basket, I rub my stomach, realising I've not eaten anything since breakfast yesterday.

In the kitchen, I stand at the open fridge, staring into the abyss like edible food is going to jump out at me. It doesn't, and even the milk right in front of my face is so long expired it's gone all liquidly and lumpy.

I'm fucking hopeless when it comes to cooking, and buying food come to think of it. I should organise one of those meal delivery things, but knowing me even with all the ingredients and a step by step idiot proof recipe I'd fuck it up.

Slamming the fridge shut, I pick up my phone from the bench where it's charging and open the 'Domino's' app.

It's the shittest pizza known to man, but the local one is close by and any food I can have delivered in twenty minutes, no matter how shit it might taste, is good food.

Quickly I order a Hawaiian and a Meatlovers for delivery, thinking of all the grease and how much weight training I'll have to do to work it off.

Pfft, who fucking cares, my life has gone to shit anyway.

Whilst I wait I grab a six-pack of beer out of the fridge, the only 'food' in my fridge that hasn't gone bad and I flop down on the couch, cracking one open and sculling half of it in one gulp.
The cool liquid sliding down my throat feels so good and starts to block out the thoughts.

When the door buzzes twenty minutes later I've already downed three stubbies and I'm feeling a little tipsy.
I buzz the delivery guy in, telling him to leave the pizzas at my front door and once I hear the shuffle of his feet leaving, I crack open the door and grab the pizza boxes and head back to the couch.
Opening each one I put them down on the coffee table and dig in, barely tasting them as I inhale the slices like they are my last meal.
Who knows, maybe they will be. I might not wake up again, and die of a broken heart in the middle of the night.

~~

When I jolt awake after what seems like minutes but is clearly hours by the darkness that's set in outside I hear pounding.
My head feels like I've been hit by a road train.
Looking around the lounge room, I curse myself.

The six stubbie bottles are strewn across the floor, and I've obviously consumed most of the two pizzas I'd ordered as all that is left is a couple of half-eaten slices.

Yeah, I feel like shit.
Hollow.
Empty.
All of those fucking words that signify loss.
This, this empty feeling is exactly why I didn't want to fall in love.

The pounding sound intensifies, and I realise it's coming from the front door, a fist beating against the wooden door when I hear my best mate's booming voice, "Travis! Open the fucking door brother!"
I contemplate telling him to 'fuck off,' so I can wallow in my self-pity a little longer, but he calls out again, "Travis! Open the door, or I'll fucking kick it in!"

Clumsily I stand up from the couch, pressing a hand to my head as a wave of dizziness hits me.
Jairus bellows from behind the door again, "Travis!"
It sounds like he's in my head.
"Fuck, brother! I'm coming! Hold ya fucking horses!" I scream, heading towards the door and nearly tripping over a discarded beer bottle.
It makes a sloshing sound, telling me there is still some rich liquid in the bottle. Picking it up, I stumble to the door, opening it to my best mate.

He saunters in like he owns the place, with a seething look on his face. His fists are clenched and he scoffs at me when I lift the beer bottle to my lips to gulp down the amber liquid.

I don't get to swallow it. He snatches the bottle away from my lips, throwing it on the wooden floor and it shatters from the impact. Dropping to my knees, I'm stupidly about to lick the floor when I feel him grip my hair, yanking it hard and pulling me to my feet.

"Seriously Travis! What the fuck man?"
"What? It's beer, man."
He shakes his head, slamming the door and looking around the open room.
"I'm not talking about that idiocy man."
"Then what? What are you talking about?" I know I'm slurring my words a little, they sound like sloshing beer on my tongue.

"Have you looked around this place? Or in the fucking mirror?"
"Nah, no fucking point anymore."

He starts pacing the room, and looking at him makes me feel like I'm going to chunder. Slipping past him, I head back towards the couch to sit down.
He stops pacing then, standing in his six-foot glory at the foot of the couch, looking down at me. His tone sounds menacing, "You missed training, Travis."
"So fucking what? My life has gone to shit."
"What the hell are you on about? You're the fucking captain of the Tigers. You can't skip out like that."

I glare at him, trying to think of the words and feeling the bile rising in my throat.

Grabbing one of the pizza boxes I empty my guts into it.

It feels a little better, but the real pain still plagues me and the reality that Bella walked out on me after I confessed my being in love with her hurts like fucking daggers in my heart.

Jai shakes his head, coughing at the putrid stench of my chunder. "How much did you drink?"

"Six stubbies. But not near enough to block it out."

"Block what out?" He looks at me concerned.

"That she left."

"Who left?" he asks the question as though he has no clue.

"Bella. Who else would I be fucking talking about?"

He sits down on the edge of the couch, raking a hand through his hair, and muttering something incoherent.

"She left me."

Jairus looks at me, his face constricting. "What happened?"

I sigh deeply, telling my brain to let it all out.

"We came back here after meeting the twins yesterday, and I fucked her."

He doesn't reply, just nods, telling me silently to continue.

"And I told her how I felt whilst my cock was buried inside her pussy."

"Seriously? You told her you loved her during sex?"

"Yeah, and again this morning."

"Did she say it back?"

"Last night yeah, but this morning she shut me out like I was fucking kidding."

"You're not kidding though?"

I sit up, punching his arm. "Would I tell you I was in love with her if I was fucking kidding?"

"No, but...shit...fuck..."

I laugh, "My thoughts exactly, but it's my fault she left."

"How so?" he asks, raising an eyebrow at me.

"I asked her to move in with me. Her and Nora of course."

"Oh shit, right."

"I fucked up. I should have just...."

"Yeah, you fucked up...but do you honestly really love her?"

"Yeah, I'm so fucking in love with her. I've never felt this all-consuming need shit before."

"Then man up Travis. Go and find her and tell her you love her until she listens."

"I don't know where she is. She won't answer my texts or calls."

"I'll ask Anni, but I have a feeling she'll have gone to her Mum's."

I stand up, shakily stumbling against my best mate's side when he stands up. Wrapping an arm around his torso, I taunt him, "When did you get so damn wise?"

He laughs, "When I fell in love."

"Yeah, it has a funny effect on people."

"You said it, brother."

He pushes me aside towards my bedroom.

"Go get in the shower, clean ya self up and I'll text you deets to go get ya woman."

"Thanks, brother. I owe you."

"No, you don't Travis. I just want you to be happy."

"I hope I will be. When I get her back."

He nods, heading towards the front door.

"Might want to clean up ya digs before you head off."

"Yeah, ok Dad. Fuck off!" I jeer at him.

He gives me the finger, opening the door and calling out, "Catch ya, bro. Speak soon."

I head to the shower, dakking myself and getting under the warm spray of water to wash the wallow away.

I think about what I'm going to say to Bella, and what I'm going to do with her when she's back in my arms, starting with fucking her in this exact spot.

Seventy-Two | Man Up Confession

Getting out of the shower I shove some clothes into my training bag and pull on some Adidas trackies with a Mossimo t-shirt.

I check my appearance in the mirror, content that I'm feeling a little more myself.

I've even shaved, so I can kiss Bella senseless when I see her and not give her pash rash. Giving her pash rash though would feel like marking her as mine, but I can always give her a hickey and not just one in a visible area.

Just thinking about her, as I grab my bag, keys, wallet and phone has my cock throbbing in my trackies.

Yeah, all day I (do) dream about sex. Especially sex with Bella.

If I don't calm the thoughts in my mind, I'll have blue balls from hell when I get to her. And as much as I want to just fuck her again, I also want to convince her that I'm not lying about my feelings for her.

It's fucking crazy, that I've fallen in love, but I've gone and done it. Locking the door behind me, I glance at my phone to read the text from Jai.

Jairus: her mum's addy is 25 Stawell-Ararat Rd, Ararat
Go get ya woman. I'm rooting for ya, bro

Sliding into the Jag I throw my bag on the passenger seat and start the engine before I type a message back.

Travis: thanks, bro. I owe ya.

I don't wait for a reply, but tap the address into the GPS before heading out into traffic.

I have one stop to make before I head off to find her and just the thought of setting foot in such a place has nervousness rising in my chest.

If I don't get Bella back, don't have the chance to have Nora in my life as well I'll be flushing hundy's down the proverbial drain, but it's a small price to pay to convince my Bella that I love her with my whole fucking heart.

~~

After a good hour in the baby shop, I'd spent close to a grand on everything a near one-year-old could want or need.

The most important item was a brand new car seat that looked odd in the back of the Jag, so much so that I can't help but stare at it in the rearview as I drive towards Ararat.

It's strange driving out of the city, watching trees and paddocks pass by the car in a blur. Memories flash in my mind of when I went on a holiday with Mum, Dad and Tessa, a road trip to Sydney from Melbourne. It was before Mum's cancer diagnosis, before our lives as a family changed forever. Tessa was barely a year old herself, and it still breaks my heart thinking about that last family holiday that she'll never remember.

Mum just went downhill after that, and Dad even though he tried his best was always working or looking after Mum when she wasn't in the hospital. Even though I was only five, the responsibility to look after my kid sister fell on my shoulders, but I never resented Tessa. It just made me love her more and when Mum passed when I was seven I helped Tessa remember the good times through looking at pictures and telling her bedtime stories about Mum.

Realising the GPS is screaming at me to do a u-turn, I sniff back tears from remembering Mum and glance around doing a head check for traffic before I turn hard, back in the opposite direction. Less than five minutes later, I'm pulling up in front of a quaint cottage-style house, the traditional white picket fence in the country house.

It dawns on me, as I cut the engine and get out, checking the address in my phone again that I actually don't much about Bella's life.

I'd shared so much with her, but she hadn't completely opened up to me other than briefly mentioning something about finding out more about her Dad.

Making a mental note to talk to her more about her past, I open the gate and try to calm my breathing and pounding heart as I head to the porch.

I try pressing the doorbell, but nothing happens, not a sound, so wrap my knuckles hard against the door. I'm feeling anxious, trepidatious as I know Bella isn't going to answer the door, but her Mum.

When the door opens, I'm looking down at my feet, feeling like a complete idiot for how nervous I am. I'd never met any sheilas parents before, having only spoken to Meaghan's grandparents overseas on the phone due to her parents passing when she was only a baby.

The woman at the door is looking me up and down, and licks her lips before she says, "Can I help you?"

I take a deep breath and swallow the lump in my throat when I look up at her. I'm sure recognition flashes in her eyes.

"Hello, Mrs Mishal. I'm Travis, and I was wondering if Bella was here." I blurt the words out rather quickly.

"Oh, hello Travis," she says, her tone husky. A blush rises up her cheeks and she ushers me inside. "Please do come in, I'll let Bella know you're here."

Following her inside, I close the door behind me and glance around the small house. Just inside the front door is a tiny lounge room, and sitting in an armchair rocking her daughter in arms is Bella.

She looks heart shatteringly beautiful, her dark chocolate hair down and wavy. She's wearing purple polka dot pyjama pants and a tank and just looking at her makes my heart skip.

Before her mum can say anything, Bella stands and says sweetly, "No need to let me know." She smiles at her mum, handing her Nora before grabbing my hand without a word and leading me down a narrow hallway, past a country kitchen, and a bathroom to a very simply decorated bedroom.

Bella is staring at me like she's waiting for me to speak, but seeing her again even though it's only been a day feels like forever and I'm completely mesmerised by her.

Striding into the room, I push her back to the edge of the desk along the wall.

Her breath hitches when I step between her legs, my forehead to hers.

Her lips part, and the sweet as fuck whimper escapes them.

I'm about to close the gap between us and kiss her, tell her how I feel without words, but her hands push against my chest and I stumble back.

Her voice comes out low, a touch louder than a whisper, "Please Travis, don't."

I'm shattered, heartbroken at her rejection again, and anger rises in my chest.

"Why the hell not Bella?"

"Because...you...you...don't..." she cuts her words short, stepping aside and sitting down on the single bed across from the desk.

"I don't what Bella?" I ask sitting next to her, but not to close just in case she freaks out again.

Her pretty brown eyes meet mine when she looks up at me.

"You don't feel the same way about me that I do about you."

I try not to scoff, but I can't help it. I scoot closer to her on the bed, our thighs brushing and thankfully she doesn't move away.

"You're fucking kidding? Did you not hear me tell you I've fallen for you?"

She whimpers, "I heard you, but then you told me to forget you said anything, so you obviously don't love me like you say you do."

Again I scoff at the words coming from her mouth.

"Would I be here? Chasing after you? Meeting your mum, if I hadn't fallen for you, Bella?"

"I don't know. Maybe you just want to fuck me again," she says meekly, sounding naive.

"Of course I want to have you back in my bed Bella, but I won't be fucking you."

She looks at me oddly, her eyes wide, but she doesn't reply.

"Exactly, Bella, when you're back in my bed and you will be, I'll be making love to you."

"I...I...still don't know whether to believe you. Guys I fall for never fall for me."

"Well, I guess they were fucking wankers because Bella Mishal I'm so in love with you."

She leans closer to me, her lips just a mere centimetre from mine.

"I love you too, Travis Banes."

"Mmm, music to my ears honey. Kiss me, please."

Her whimper escapes her lips before her mouth meets mine in a kiss that is passionate but desperate. A kiss that conveys how much love is coursing through our veins.

Breaking it I'm breathless, panting out my words, "Come... back...to...the city with me."

"And move in with you?"

"Yeah, honey. I want to go to sleep with you in my arms, wake up to your beautiful face every morning and make love to you over and over again."

She opens her mouth to speak, but then closes it and presses her lips back to mine.

Against her lips, I mutter softly, "Is that a yes, Bella?"

"Yes, I'll move in with you."

I pull back from the kiss, laughing. "Thank fuck, cause I bought a shitload of stuff for Nora that's being delivered tomorrow."

Her eyes light up, a smile on her lips. "You did what?"

"Spent a grand on spoiling your little girl to convince you that I love you, and want you both in my life."

"You didn't have to do that, captain."

My heart pounds at her use of my nickname again. "I didn't have to, no, but I wanted to. Makes me feel like I'm spending my dough on something worthwhile."

"Well, I'll pay you back, I promise."

"No, you won't. Don't ever entertain a worried thought about money again. I want to take care of you, honey."

She laughs, a sweet laugh that makes me feel oddly giddy.

"Since when did you get so damn sappy?" she asks with a laugh.

Chuckling I reply, "When I fell in love with you."

"Hmm, well I love it, captain, and I love you."

"Too sappy Bella," I laugh standing up from the bed and taking her hands to pull her up for a quick kiss.

We exchange unspoken words, our eyes taking each other in slowly. She laces her fingers with mine, leading me back out to the kitchen to find her Mum trying to make it seem like she's busy with something.

Over coffee, we chat to her about our plans for heading back to the city and help make a roast beef dinner, that tastes utterly delicious, reminding me of times I'd spent with family.

The night passes by quickly, with easy conversation about Bella's childhood. Her mum shows me pictures of her growing up, making Bella blush but smile so wide when her dad is in a picture and her mum talks about him.

Again I make a mental note to talk to her about her past more and we head to bed, close to midnight.

I fall asleep in minutes with Bella wrapped in my arms, dreaming of a new life together back in the city.

Seventy-Three | Goodbyes Suck Hard

Elyse

Standing in the doorway of Bella's room, I'm trying to hold back my tears watching her pack up her clothes into suitcases. I can't help but feel a little bit pissed with her, moving out when I've only just moved in. But at the same time when she came home, with Travis by her side a month ago I'd never seen her so happy.

Now as she packs up her things, I don't know how to react.
"Bel-bear, are you sure about this?" I ask softly.
She stops throwing clothes in the suitcase, giving me an odd look.
"Why wouldn't I be?"
"I don't know. How do you know you really love him?"
"I just do. I've never felt like this before Ely-bug."
I mutter a 'hmm' in response, my mind drifting to thoughts of Kaden. I've not told Bella a thing about whats happened between us, and the guilt is eating me alive.
But at the same time, I don't want to tell her a damn thing as she'll just warn me away, telling me I'm only going to get my heart smashed to smithereens.
I damn well know this, but just looking at Kaden makes my damn knickers wet and his kisses make me melt, my whole body on fire, and when he touches me or his dick is inside me I see stars.

I'm broken from my thoughts by Bella waving her arms in front of my face.

"Ely-bug? Earth to Ely-bug!"

"Oh...um...yep...what?"

"You ok? You're blushing."

"Yeah, I'm fine. Just thinking about um...when we talked about the time Travis went down on you."

She glares at me like she knows I'm lying, but she doesn't say anything more about the topic.

"Right. Well, um...could you help me take this out ready for when Travis gets here?"

"Sure, what time is he coming over?"

"He said around eleven. When's Lillie officially moving in?"

"Tomorrow. I'm scared to be here by myself, Bel-bear."

She reaches out to hug me, "Aww Ely-bug. You'll be fine. Put ya big girl knickers on, it's time for my baby sis to grow up."

"Yeah, I suppose so," I mutter, thinking again about Kaden and how much I've grown up in other ways since meeting him earlier in the year.

"Um, Bel-bear...can I..." I start to tell her, wanting to share with her that I slept with Kaden, more than once.

"What Ely-bug?"

"Um...nothing...I...I'm just going to miss you, that's all."

"I'm only moving a few suburbs over, and you know you can always text me Ely-bug. I'll always be here for you little sis."

"I know Bel-bear," I reply, hearing knocking on the front door.

I follow her out, dragging the suitcases behind us. She opens it to Travis, smiling wide at him, and stretching up on her tiptoes to kiss him quickly.

Turning to me, when Travis takes the suitcase from me, she says softly, "Well Ely-bug I guess this is it. Don't do anything I wouldn't do."

"Never, Bel-bear," I reply, feeling the blush rise up my cheeks, and the thump of my heart increase. I can't tell my big sister that Kaden is coming over tonight, as she would catch me out in my lie of being alone for the night. I also can't tell her that when Lil moves in I've planned a big housewarming party.

Bella thinks I'm little miss innocent but she really has no idea that her little sister is far from innocent.

"Of course, Bel-bear. I'll be good. Now get going!"

She laughs, taking Travis' hand as she follows him out to his red Jaguar convertible.

My big sister is so lucky to have caught herself not only a gorgeous guy but a rich as fuck one. I'm a little jealous.

Before closing the door though, I gulp down the lump of guilt in my throat, waving and blowing a kiss to my big sister as she gets into the Jaguar to drive away.

I miss her already, and the only thing that stops me from breaking into tears is the vibration of my phone in my pocket.

Grabbing it out there's a text from Kaden.

Kaden: cant wait to see you tonight Lys

I smile, feeling my knickers dampen as I type a text back.

Elyse:cant wait to touch you and maybe taste you x
Kaden: tasting sounds fun...

I don't reply then, instead head to Bella's now old bedroom, and lie back on the bed to relieve the ache in my knickers, thinking about later when Kaden is going to be the one both fuelling and extinguishing the fire in my knickers.

Seventy-Four | Honey Sweet Home

Pulling up to the Prahran townhouse, I sneak a glance at Bella beside me. Her eyes are wide, her mouth falling open.

"Captain, this isn't your place."

"No, it's our place, honey. Brand new, and all ours."

"You bought a house?"

"You betcha. Had to do it sometime and what better time than now."

"Oh my god, Travis. I can't believe it. I don't deserve you."

I chuckle, turning her gaze to mine with a finger under her chin.

"Yes, you do, Bella. It's me that doesn't deserve you."

She doesn't reply, instead leans over the console and kisses me softly.

"Thank you, for this," she muses gesturing towards the house, "and everything you bought for Nora, and just being you." Her tone is soft and she sniffs back tears as she opens the door to get out.

I follow, flipping my seat forward to get Nora out of her new car seat in the back. She's fast asleep and cradling her in my arms I follow Bella inside.

At the front door, I reach into my pocket handing her a shiny set of keys. Her smile nearly breaks her face as she unlocks the door and steps inside.

As soon as we cross the threshold, she looks around the open-plan space, full of brand new modern furniture, a far cry from the shitty furniture I had in my old apartment.

"Travis, it's amazing. This place must have cost a packet."

"Just a few hundred grand," I reply laughing.

"Yeah sure, and then some Captain."

Again I laugh, heading down towards the stairs to the bedrooms.

"Ok, fine, add a mil to that and you might be on to something."

"Travis, come on. That's insane, but fuck."

"I've got the money, honey."

She gives me an odd look following me up the stairs. "I get that, but why stay in that shitty old apartment for so long if you could have afforded something so much better?"

"Old habits die hard. And I had no reason to move before."

"True, I..." she cuts her words off, stopping dead in the doorway of the room on the right side of the stairs. Her eyes boggle at the mini nursery I'd set up for Nora. It's a Lion King theme, with baby Simba bedding in the new white cot. The walls were painted a pale yellow and I'd filled the whole room with everything a little girl could need, including a dollhouse and a mountain of stuffed animals.

Bella turns to look at me, as I walk over to put Nora down in the cot. She stirs a little but doesn't wake up.

"Travis this is amazing," Bella says shocked.

"Anything for you honey...I love you and Nora."

"Mmm...say it again, I never get tired of hearing you say that."

"Say what?" I chuckle, grabbing her around the waist and pulling her close to me. "That I'm head over my footy boots in love with you...and I want to spend the rest of my life with you, proving to you how much I love you."

She lets out a lighthearted laugh and her hot as whimper. "Yeah... you're not proposing are you?" she asks teasingly.

I laugh squeezing her arse, "No...unless you want me to be?"

"Not yet...but I love you too Travis. I thought I loved Austin, but what I felt for him is nothing like I feel for you. You set me on fire and you have my heart, soul and body."

Her words are sweet, perfect and full of promise. They make my heart swell with love for her and my body ache to be with her, in her, as one again. "Oh really....your body to, huh?"

"Yep...and that bed across the hall looks like it needs to be messed up."

I don't reply instead let out a moan taking her mouth with mine in a fierce kiss. When she whimpers against my lips, I break the kiss, effortlessly picking her up and throwing her over my shoulder to take her to the master bedroom.

Throwing her down on the bed, she taunts me by starting to strip off her clothes. I just watch her, my cock growing painfully hard in my daks.

When she's naked I crawl onto the bed, kissing her hard, "maybe we can give Nora a brother or sister," I say against her lips.

"Sounds like a plan," she replies, breaking the kiss, "But you need to be naked for that plan to happen, Captain."

"Mmm, Bella, I love when you call me Captain."

She laughs, biting down on her lip and watching me as I strip. Desire is flashing in her eyes and once I'm free of my clothes she grabs my cock, stroking it as she crashes her lips to mine.

"Honey, please, that feels so good, but I...ah...fuck...I..."

"What Captain?"

"Need to fuck you, now." I reach between her legs, locking my eyes to hers as I slide a finger inside her pussy, finding her so incredibly wet.

"Seems like someone is turned on?" I laugh bringing my fingers up to my lips and licking them. "I'm wet for you, Captain," she teases, whimpering and pulling me down for a kiss. Her hands find my hair, grabbing it and slipping it through her fingers, her tongue dancing with mine in a kiss so heated I'm panting when I pull back.

"Fuck, Bella, you're insatiable," I groan, "roll over, honey so I can fuck you from behind."

Without a word, she rolls over until she's on all fours, her arse in the air.

Grabbing it, I pull her to the edge of the bed and stand up at the foot of the bed. She turns to look back at me, my cock teasing her, just the tip at the entrance of her pussy.

"Please, please fuck me, Captain," she begs huskily. I obey her request pushing my whole cock into her dripping pussy. Whimpers and moans escape her lips as I dive into harder, my cock slipping in and out of her wet hole.

"God, Bella, fuck you feel good and the view, honey, fuck it's glorious."

"Mmm, yes, captain," she moans, "fuck me harder."

I groan, pushing my cock balls deep into her pussy.

Her moans and whimpers turn me on, my cock throbbing inside her.

Spearing my cock in harder, I rub my thumb over her other tight hole and the moan that escapes her lips is bordering on a scream of pleasure, "Fuck! Captain! Fuck!"

I lean over her back, kissing her, and whispering against her lips, "Can I touch your tight arse hole, Bella?"

"Yes, yes, yes," she whimpers, pushing her arse against me.

Without warning, I push my thumb inside her tight arse hole, massaging it as I plunge my cock into her harder. Her moans increase, her whole body trembling as waves of pleasure rock through her.

"Oh yeah, honey. Come for me...squirt all over the bed."

A scream of pleasure escapes her lips, my hot cum filling her pussy as we both tip over the edge of release, her screaming out, "Fuck! Travis, fuck, I'm coming, oh fuck!"

Her whole body trembles and her release is violent shudders, wave after wave of pleasure. Pulling my cock out I lay down on the bed and pull her against me, kissing her softly. "Bella, that was incredible. I love when you squirt for me."

Her dark eyes look at me lovingly, "I've never come so hard before."

"I can tell, honey. You're still trembling."

"Yeah, so amazing. I love you, Travis."

"I love you too, Bella. I never thought I'd fall in love again."

"I know exactly what you mean, now shut up and kiss me."

I comply, crashing my lips to hers in a heart-pounding kiss.

Kissing Bella, I know I'll never feel this way again. I'm so in love, and glad its all worked out. Jairus was most certainly right when he told me feelings don't play fair, but in the end, hearts don't steer us wrong.

Epilogue | Poorly Little Girl

A few months later
November 2019

Watching Nora being loaded into the ambulance on a stretcher is making my heart shatter. Bella's scream when finding her baby daughter unresponsive with a fever and cold sweat is a sound I'll never forget.

The ambulance is driving away and I'm holding Bella in my arms, stroking her hair as she sobs into my chest. My heart is pounding from the stress, but it's breaking for my Bella.

We'd been in our blissful love bubble in the new place for a few months, but Nora had been getting worse, with constant trips to the doctors for tonsillitis that just wouldn't shift. And now the worst has happened.

I can't bear to think about losing another child.

Bella pulls back from my embrace and I kiss her forehead softly.

"I'm ready to go, now. Please."

Her eyes are red, bloodshot and puffy from crying as I lead her towards the Jag to head to the Royal Children's hospital.

Once in and on our way I touch her thigh comfortingly.

"I should have gone with her. She's probably scared."

"You would have made things worse, honey. Let the ambos do their job and we'll be there soon."

"I know, but I'm so scared. I can't lose my girl."

"We won't lose her, honey. I promise. It's going to be ok."

She tries to smile, and I take her hand, lifting it and kissing it. "I love you, Travis. I'm so glad you're with me and not Jax right now."

"I love you too, honey. Let's just get to the hospital, huh."

She nods, turning the radio up and trying to sing along to Make me cry by Noah Cyrus.

It seems like the longest drive ever when we arrive at the hospital and park the Jag in the underground carpark. Holding hands, with our fingers locked together we head straight to the emergency department.

We ask for details at the desk and they let us in straight away.

Bella rushes to the tiny bed Nora is in, kissing her forehead.

"Oh, baby girl. It's ok, mummy's here," she coos to Nora who is thankfully now awake, but clearly distressed.

I slide two chairs up to the bedside and help Bella sit in one whilst I sit next to her in the other chair.

A doctor comes in, taking the chart from the end of the bed.

"Good morning, I take it you're the parents of this little one?"

"Yes, I'm her mum, but this is my partner. He's not her dad biologically."

"Right, so the father written here, a Mr Jaxon McMasters is correct?"

Bella blushes, "I'm not sure. Has he been contacted?"

"Yes, Ms Mishal. He's on his way now."

"Great, so can you give me any insight into what's wrong with my baby?"

"Not at this stage, we've run some routine blood tests and given her some painkiller medication but at this stage, we can't tell you anymore."

"Ok, thanks, doctor. Is it ok if we stay with her?"

"Of course, I'll send Mr McMasters in when he arrives and let you both know when the blood results come back."

"Ok, thanks."

The doctor turns to leave, but stops a moment, "Ms Mishal, you don't happen to know your blood type do you?"

"Yes, I'm A negative."

"Great, thank you," he replies leaving.

I kiss Bella's forehead. "You doing ok, honey?" I ask taking her hand.

"Yeah, I just want to know what's wrong. That's all."

"Yeah, I know. Hopefully, the results will come back quickly."

Nora closes her eyes, drifting to sleep and we watch her, hoping that everything is going to be ok.

Jaxon arrives about twenty minutes after the doctor had left and seems visibly distraught even though he hasn't been around much lately. Bella slides her chair back, rushing to hug him and it pisses me off a little considering her words to me in the car, but I swallow the lump in my throat and let them be a moment.

When she steps back from the hug in tears, I stand up, crossing the room and pulling her against my side. "Shh, honey. It's ok," I whisper kissing her hair.

Jaxon shakes my outstretched hand, "Hey, man. Any word yet?"

"Nah, the doctor should hopefully be back any minute." And speaking of, he enters the room greeting Jaxon.

"Mr McMasters yes?"

"Yes, sir, any info on my daughter yet?"

"Yes, and not good news I'm afraid. Could I speak to you and Ms Mishal in my office a moment?"

"Um, yeah sure," he mutters, "Bella?"

Bella breaks free from my arms, sniffing back her tears and looking at me pleadingly. "I'll stay with her honey."

Bella

I follow Jaxon and the doctor down the hallway to an office that is far from clinical. My heart is pounding in my chest, so scared to hear the news the doctor is about to tell us.

"Please, take a seat."

We both sit in the tub chairs in front of his mahogany desk, whilst he sits in his swivel chair.

"So, unfortunately, tests have come back with an indication that Nora has a very low white blood cell count and we believe she has Acute myeloid leukaemia."

I gape, "What? No way! My daughter can't have cancer."

"I'm sorry Ms Mishal, but that isn't all."

"What else could there be?" I ask, completely aghast.

He turns his attention to Jaxon whose mouth is open in shock as well.

"Mr McMasters, are you aware of your blood type? Is it O negative?"

"Um, yes, why?" Jaxon asks the doctor, before looking at me with fear in his eyes.

"I'm afraid that based on that there is no way that Nora is your daughter. We will, of course, have to do a DNA test, but blood test results are pretty inconclusive."

Jaxon stands up angrily storming out of the room, and I contemplate following him, but there's no point.

The truth, the words coming out of the doctor's mouth mean there's only one explanation.

The one thing I'd been denying for months is the truth.

And now his heart is going to break, as he's going to find out he's a father when his daughter is dying.

The End (for now)

Australian Slang Glossary

Ute-Truck

Ripper- something really good/great

Ridgy-Didge- Cool

Bonzer-Great, awesome

Pash/ing/ed- to kiss/make out

Arvo- afternoon

Chunder- Vomit, throw up

Gobby- Blowjob

Aussie Kiss- going down on a girl

Daks- pants/trousers/underwear

Undies/Knickers/Jocks-underwear (female knickers, male Jocks, undies both)

Dakking- to pull someone daks down (see above)

Thongs- Footwear, otherwise known as flip flops

Esky- Cooler-you keep drinks cool in it

Dunny- toilet

Bogan-white trash/trailer trash

Old Fella- Your father/Dad

Franger- Condom, Trojan etc

Macca's-MacDonalds

Fair Dinkum- used to emphasise or seek confirmation of the genuineness or truth of something

Stuffed if I know- *a nicer way to say fucked if I know*

AFL- Australian Rules Football

If there was any other slang in the story that left you wondering what in the hell I was talking about, please feel free to message me on Instagram or Facebook. I love chatting to readers about my stories!

Playlists

Travis

https://open.spotify.com/playlist/

7r1u5N4icYWOmVFy2YG5jR?

si=_kbZOPgASK2fFiTi4pQXcA

Bella

https://open.spotify.com/playlist/

5Ffl9myrVXqq0V1Q0aKRnc?
si=_MKo_UrhQBqvQpuQB9RdcA

Jairus

https://open.spotify.com/playlist/

3dGY59GcVTnLtEH0flni6O?
si=6EyqqhmkQpePp9MQUUcPbw

About the Author

Caz May is a librarian/teacher by trade, but was always destined to be an author from a young age. In her spare time, she can be found devouring books or writing her own stories with characters that may not be the typical romance heroes but are loveable just as much.

Caz is married to her own real-life bearded hero and has two fur babies.

She lives for Iced coffee, especially from Gloria Jeans or a Farmers Union but pretty much just loves food in general.

When she's not writing, or reading a book most likely she can probably be found asleep or binge-watching shows on Netflix.

Check out her Instagram or other socials to get in touch.

Instagram- @cazmay25

Facebook- @CazMayAuthor

Wattpad- @Caz-May

Spotify- cazcat25

Website- https://cazcat25.wixsite.com/cazmay-author

Acknowledgments

Well, here we are! Acknowledgements for Book Three!

Firstly, I need to thank all of you have supported me on this journey and have read all three books. Your support means the world!

But for this book, I need to give some special shoutouts to some of the people who have made the writing of this book a much more enjoyable journey. These are in no particular order.

Amanda (@amandalovesbooks Instagram) Being able to share parts of this story and your enthusiasm to read everything I write is so motivating. You're the best girl!

Ashlee Rose (@ashleeroseauthor Instagram) Again being able to share parts of this story with you, especially as a fellow writer means the world. I love our convo's and your support with my writing and other things happening outside of it even though we're on the other side of the world. Love ya girl!

J. S. Andersson (@j.s.andersson_author Instagram) Your kind words as an early reader always helps keep me motivated and I love that you don't think I'm crazy with all the ideas I bounce off you. I'm so glad to have found you lovely! And to whoever is reading this go support her books as well.

Lena Moore (@iamchaoticprincess Instagram) So glad we started chatting hun! Meeting fellow Aussie authors gives me encouragement and I'm glad we can share in this indie author journey together. Your support means the world!

And also my new in real life friend Shantelle (@thedeadlyseriesinsta Instagram) Meeting you hun has been such a blessing in my life! Being able to talk writing with someone in person over a coffee is beyond amazing. I'm incredibly grateful to call you my friend!

My bestie of course needs mentioning. She has always supported my writing and loved Travis's story from the start. Having her read my books as an early reader will forever be motivation to share my books with the world. Her love and support for over twenty years is a constant I don't ever want to lose in my life!

As always I need to thank my ever supportive and amazing husband, Cam. He is my rock and we have a new running joke now I've finished this book. He laughs, whilst telling me to stop writing 'porn'. He never fails to make me laugh, and his support on this journey even

with the costs along the way as I find myself in the indie writing world never ceases to amaze me.
He's the best!

Anyway, that's all from me! For now!

Caz May

xx

Look out for Book Four
(Kaden's Story)

Coming 2020

Teaser chapter below

Prologue | Wild Boys

March 2020

Having Austin back in my life has been super grouse. Yeah, seeing him so in love with a chick hurt like some cunt had grabbed my balls and cock and was ripping them off my body. But all I want is to see my mate happy, which he clearly seems to be.
After all the shit that went down with us, when we fucked the first times whilst he worked out his sexuality and then again this past year I feel beyond honoured that he still wants me in his life and that I'm going to be best man at his wedding.

Firstly though I organised the bachelor shindig we are now enjoying. It's a simple affair, Having drinks at mine, but Austin is clearly enjoying himself, beer in hand and chatting to some of our boxing mates.
I'm anxiously waiting for the knock on the door, for the naughty entertainment, I'd ordered to arrive. I'd decided on a Male and female strippers show, to appeal to not only my own fantasies but Austin's lack of male attention since we had a dirty afternoon with his fiancé together.

I quickly grab a beer, and head over to Austin to chat.

"Hey, man, enjoying yourself?"

"Of course, Kad...but there's a bit too much testosterone in here at the moment."

"Yeah, got something special organised. Should be happening in a few. Wanna another drink?"

"Yeah, might as well. Dana isn't expecting me home tonight."

"You gonna crash here?"

"If it's cool, yeah?"

"Why would it not be cool with me?" I ask, winking at him.

"We can't Kad, not unless Dana knows we're hooking up. That was the deal."

"I know," I reply, running into the kitchen to grab some more beers when I get distracted by the doorbell ringing.

Racing to open it, the strippers barge in, a chick dressed in a naughty maid outfit and a guy dressed in a cop uniform. They're both gorgeous as fuck and I beckon them towards the lounge room where they instantly start performing, stripping their clothes off in time to the music playing in the room. I watch Austin out of the corner of my eye, he's definitely enjoying himself and I reach down to cup his cock in my palm.

He shifts back and pulls me aside.

"Seriously Kad? Don't tempt me."

"Sorry, Aust. I just miss being with you sometimes. And seeing you getting turned on by the strippers, I just couldn't help myself."

"I know. I miss you in that way too Kad, but you know the deal I have with Dan."

"Yeah, you really love her, huh?"

"More than anything. And um...thanks for this mate. I appreciate it."

"No worries. How did you know you wanted her?"

"What do you mean?" He asks with an odd tone in his voice like my question makes no damn sense.

"That you just wanted to be with a girl after realising you were bi and we hooked up?"

"I don't man. I'm worried sick every damn day I'm going to fuck up, but I can't imagine my life without Dana in it."

"Yeah, I get you," I muse, thoughts of Elyse popping into my head. I want her more than anything, but she doesn't deserve someone who can't love her back.

"Why you ask? Are things not good with you and Elyse?"

Shaking my head, I reply, "they're better than good in the bedroom, but I..."

"What Kad?"

"I don't know if I can just be with a chick all the time."

"You'll work it out, mate. Just trust ya heart and ya gut, not ya cock."

"Easier said than done," I mutter, heading back into the lounge room where our mates are getting lap dances from the strippers.

I laugh, watching our straight mate Ethan grimacing as the male stripper grinds on him.

"Kaden," he screams out, "get this fucker off me. I'm gonna chunder!"

Stepping up behind the stripper I grind my crotch into his arse, and he steps back from Ethan's lap. The stripper eyes me, and Ethan sighs in relief.

"You down?" The stripper asks in a super husky voice.

"Nah, mate. Not this time," I reply, walking away to go deal with my hard-on in the bathroom, whilst thinking about Elyse.

Caz May